UPON
THIS
ROCK

Alexander Tait

Published by Olida Publishing
www.olidapublishing.com

First printing: November 2011

Printed in the United Kingdom and the U.S.A.

ISBN: 978-1-907354-43-4

Acknowledgements

Publisher: Allan Sneddon

Editor: Ian Baillie

Encouragement, counselling, formatting and cover design:
Paul Murdoch

Cover photograph: Joe Porter

Other Titles by Alexander Tait...

Whiskey in the Jar
ISBN: 978-0-9558789-4-7

The Cup
ISBN: 978-1-907354-00-7

This book is dedicated with love to my daughter,

Margaret Catherine Scobie

This is not a history book. It is a historical novel. I am not a trained or professional historian, but I have taken great care to set the story firmly within historical reality. The major events described in the narrative are true to recorded fact. I have taken the liberty of romanticising minor elements of the tale. If I have made any mistakes, I hope the reader will forgive me. Details of the raid on Dumbarton Castle were taken from a first-hand account. I have tried to give fair representations of the major historical characters involved.

Alexander Tait

II

Prologue

She was Irish, she was beautiful, and when Margaret Lafferty eased her hands into the rich, dark soil of Dumbarton Rock, she could never in her wildest dreams have imagined that she was setting in motion a chain of events which would profoundly affect the course of world history.

There had been roses here since the time of the Romans. There were roses in the heraldry of the Earls of Lennox, whose fortress this great rock had once been. But this one would have to go. It had been a joy to behold in all its crimson glory, but now it was diseased, its petals blackened and decayed beyond all healing. Pruning had been in vain, so it would have to be uprooted before it spread its malady.

Though used to hard work, the hands of the raven-haired young woman were fair, with slender, sensitive fingers. They probed deep into the unyielding roots of the condemned flower and, in their digging, they encountered a shining hardness which was not stone. Gently she unearthed what turned out to be a slender silver cross. It was about half the length of her index finger. The arms were of equal length, one having a small loop for a chain or thong. Margaret's dark eyes shone brightly when she saw, in the centre of the pendant, an engraved trefoil, for all the world like the three leaves of a shamrock, which she knew to represent the Father, Son and Holy Spirit. She held the little treasure to her breast. Raising her head to the blue, morning sky, she gazed over the water of the River Clyde, in the direction of her homeland, and silently offered a prayer of thanks.

*   *   *

A shrill, terrible scream echoed off the walls of basalt and rang out over the wide river as the leather thongs lashed into flesh, lacerating and drawing blood on the third stroke. The girl, bent over the wooden trestle, had gritted her teeth and been determined not to give them the satisfaction of that cry, and for the first two lashes she had borne the searing agony in an almost superhuman silence, but for the remaining eight hellish strokes she shrieked like an animal, agitating the multitude of seagulls which were swooping and wheeling high above.

The punishment was being carried out on the castle-green, so that it could be witnessed not only by the garrison but also by such townsfolk as were nearby. A reminder – not that such were needed – of the power of the Keeper of Dumbarton Castle.

A ring of twenty soldiers stood around the trestle to resist any possible interference with the proceedings, not that any opposition was likely. The victim, bound to the instrument of torture, was naked only from the waist upward. Decencies required to be observed. The chaplain prayed loudly as the sentence was carried out. There was a big turn-out. Many of the soldiers and some of the townsmen were frankly glad of the opportunity to leer at the semi-exposed body of a beautiful young girl, and most of the women present were there out of sheer morbid fascination. There was little sympathy for the victim.

The Keeper, Lord Fleming, had a daughter. In her early teens this daughter was plump and plain. She was also petty and vindictive. She had seen and she resented the attention given to this Irish bitch by the men of the place, low and high. This daughter had happened to observe Margaret's discovery of the silver cross and she discerned an opportunity to bring the dark-haired beauty down a peg or two.

She cunningly let matters rest until Maggie was seen around the fortress wearing the cross conspicuously, nestled in her cleavage. The spiteful daughter then approached her father explaining that the Irish girl had stolen the silver cross. Her logic, and there was an element of law in it, was that anything found within the castle was the property of the Keeper. The wearing of this pendant was a blatant affront to her father's authority.

Lord Fleming was a man with a great deal more on his mind than this scullion and her trinket. He was, however, an indulgent parent who had neither the time nor the energy to argue with his wheedling offspring. What matter a few swipes on the back of some menial anyway ? Corporal punishment in one form or another was a more or less daily occurrence in his world...

*   *   *

John Hamilton, Archbishop of St. Andrews, wished to appear aloof. It would never do to give the impression that such a spectacle would be of any interest to him. Nevertheless, from a narrow window of his luxuriously furnished accommodation, high in one of the castle's towers, he kept a discreet eye on the proceedings. The flesh being weak.

One might have expected that the wielder of the whip would have been some huge, muscle-bound thug. Oddly enough, however, the man who ripped open that naked back with such strength and purpose, was a slight, meek looking, but admittedly wiry individual; a sergeant who maintained his authority by sheer malevolence of spirit. His name was Carpenter.

*   *   *

If he'd gone down to the castle-green he'd have had to be held back. Knocked senseless. He'd have choked the life out of the little weasel. He'd do that yet. Best, though, for the time being, not to let his feelings be known. From a lonely and unobserved point on the battlements, Duncan Robertson, archer of the castle guard, looked down, fists clenched in impotent fury. Tears of pity, rage and frustration ran down the cheeks of the rugged young Highlander. Listening to those heart-breaking screams, he swore terrible vengeance on the creature Carpenter... and on Lord Fleming.

When the final lash had been delivered, the crowd slowly began to disperse, faces flushed. As the sobbing, bleeding lass was untied and dragged away, Lord Fleming turned from his own lofty vantage point. He was not a vicious man, not a sadist... there had been rather more severe punishments he could have ordered in the circumstances, but, in sentencing Margaret Lafferty to a public whipping, John, Fifth Lord Fleming and Great Chamberlain of Scotland, had made the biggest mistake of his life.

VIII

Chapter One
Arthur and Merlin

Perhaps it had all happened before. One thousand years before.
With the same people, in the same places, and in a similar cause.

There were three great fortress rocks studded across the narrow
waist of Scotland. In the west at Dumbarton: in the centre,
Stirling; in the east, Edinburgh. Three mighty sources of power
which held the nation together.

From a small window in the Prince's Tower of Stirling Castle, a
little boy looked westward over long, hazy miles of flat, wooded,
sunlit countryside. From behind the boy an old man spoke.

"Tempus circumit... Aye, time goes round, lad."

The speaker was a man in his mid-sixties. He looked older, weary
of the world. In spite of the heat which came from a small log-
fire, he wore a black robe and a cowl. Bright, beady eyes and a
large, beaky nose gave the distinct impression of a bird of prey.
This man was renowned throughout all of Christendom for his
learning and the power of his words.

A grubby white ruff framed the little boy's round face. He had big, brown, nervous eyes. He was highly precocious and, although he was only four years old, the sage spoke to him entirely as though he were an adult. This was a rare day in which the boy's usual class-mates, Jocky o' the Slates, Willie Murray and Wattie Stewart, were absent on account of childhood maladies, thus giving the Master freedom to speak privily of confidential matters.

"Wid thon no' break yir hert ?"

He pointed through the window towards the wide tournament field far below. There, on the southern stretch of the greensward, was a huge, circular grassy mound of earthwork.

"Lang forgotten. The Round Table o' Arthur and his knights… Barbour, him that was Archdeacon o' Aberdeen, speaks o' it in his poem aboot the Bruce… and William o' Worcester makes it clear enough in his writing."

The large brown eyes glowed.

"Aye… yon was ane heroic struggle. A richt valiant contribution. But incomplete, mind. Imperfect, like all human endeavour."

The sage turned from the window and applied his gaze to the interior of the schoolroom in the tower. Dust danced in the shafts of golden sunlight which illuminated rows of shelves stacked with books and parchments.
There were books in Latin, Greek, French, Scots and English. There was, of course, a Bible. There were maps and charts and illustrations and instruments of learning relative to the scientific

knowledge of the day. The old man drew a parchment from its place and spread it ostentatiously on a table.

"This here is the Genethliacon, which, as ye weel ken, the dullards o' this generation tak tae be nae mair nor poetry – an expression o' joy ower yir ain royal birth, yir Grace. But you an' I ken better. This is nae less than prophesy... soothsaying... a clear and true seeing into the future."

The boy smirked as though in the satisfaction of a secret shared with his revered elder.

An old finger ran along the script as the teacher recited and expanded on his meaning.
"See here – '...a golden age and the end of warfare... Henceforth the Saxons will leave the Scots alone, nor will the Scot harry the Saxon... his kingdom more extensive than it would be if it stretched from the Indies to the shores of Hesperia.' – ye must understand your task, your destiny."

The beady eye flashed and the old finger poked at a map of the known world.

"There are two great purposes which you must serve, towards which you must strive with all diligence and wisdom. You must above all else defend Christ's Gospel and bring about the peaceful Union o' the peoples o' these British Isles. As it should have been then, so it will be in the future. I can see it. I know it. Yet... and here's the bit yi willna grasp – although it is achieved, it remains for you to make it so. We canna change the future, but we must make it in the here and now. Aye, a richt paradox yon."

He ground old teeth and sought clearer expression.

"It's akin to the clash between predestination an' free will. D'ye see ?"

Exasperated in the awareness that such concepts, which baffled most adults, were unlikely to get through to even the most precocious of four-year-olds, the old master seemed to run out of steam for a moment.

The lad made no pretence of understanding, but tremulously posed a question that had been much troubling him.

"Maister Geordie, ye speak o' knowing the future... o' seeing it, but how can that be ? What mean ye by it ?"

His elder tugged a ragged, grey beard.
"Well, lad... yir Grace. Aye... see I'm a poet. An' fae ancient times poets, seers, hae been the visionaries among men. Poets hae subtle senses that ither folk lack. They reach depths o' feeling and heights o' discernment, glimpses o' revelation that are denied to their fellow creatures. It's a richt dangerous faculty. Aye, a double-edged sword, ye may say..."

Perhaps he would have offered a keener elucidation, but the mention of a sword prompted another fearful question.

"Maister, ye speak o' Arthur, his knights and his battles, ye speak o' then, but this time... must there be mair battles... mair o' blood and killing ?"

The boy was on the verge of tears.

"Arthur was a great war-leader, yir young Grace. Commander o' the Britons, but there will be nae swording for Jamie Saxt. It's yir wits that we must sharpen for the battles that you will win, young Sire. Wits! Education! That's the thing."

The black-robed figure paced the floor of the schoolroom like some strutting crow.

"Ye must aye mind that today's enemies oft times turn out to be tomorrow's friends. Consider this realm of yours. It was a union of four peoples – our ain Britons, the Picts, the Scots... aye, and even some Angles o' the Lothian. Those who had been our deadly foes in due season became our compatriots. Aye... in due season."

The boy fingered his ruff with grubby hands and, pursing his lips like some aged don, nodded approvingly as his tutor gained momentum.

"Union. That is the thing. Union – the principle behind all. Anither great mystery. A' things hae the appearance o' being different, separate and apart, but the great truth is that a' things are in ane grand universal unity. St. Paul has a stab at it when he writes o' the parts o' the body being in disagreement rather than serving the heid... or when he says – '...ye are all one in Christ Jesus.' But the Union canna be just at any cost, mark ye. No' in the spirit o' surrender or being swallowed up. Yet it is better that peoples can live in unity than die in enmity. War is the great evil. You, your Grace, like the King of Kings, whose humble servants we are, will be known as a Prince of Peace. Aye... Unity – seek it... strive for it. Such is God's work."

The child's great brown eyes widened in an expression which was close to horror.

"But, the English, Maister Geordie... of a' folk.. whit will the Lords, the common folk, even... they'll no' hae it, man... they'll no' staun fir it."

"Never you bother a wheen aboot the Lords, lad... I mean yir young Grace. There'll be lands and position, gold and siller for the taking. Wir proud, patriotic Scots Lords will no' be lang in seein' whaur thir ain interests lie. There'll be nae bother fae that airt."

The lad waved has hand around, gesturing down towards the town of Stirling cluttered around the castle-rock.

"The common folk then... what o' them ?"

"The common folk will plough their fields and sell their wares and struggle after their next bite as ever. They'll serve whatever master they must. It was aye so. Och, they'll girn, but mind ye this, it'll be you, the King o' Scots, that will sit on the English throne, no' an English king sitting on the Scots throne, an' that will mak a' the difference as faur as folk's thinkin' ll go."

He peered down on his royal charge with a predatory glare which defied contradiction.

"I'll gie ye, the English have tried tae crush the Scots by force o' airms fir ower five hunner years. An' I'll grant they are ane richt arrogant, overbearing race. But take it fae me, yir Grace... the English are a great people, and God will do great things through them... through this o' Union."

To the background sounds of shouting men-at-arms from the Lower Square of Stirling Castle, George Buchanan, tutor to the young James the Sixth of Scots, in this Year of Our Lord 1571, began to recite (yet again) the nature and extent of the empire of which his royal pupil would effectively be the founder.

"Greater than that of Alexander... more extensive than the rule of the Romans... from the furthest reaches of the New World to beyond the Indies... taking in lands and races that are as yet unknown. Its people will be as the sands of the seas. A civilizing influence the like o' which the world hasnae seen. All of this mighty empire will proceed from the wag of your ain royal sceptre."

The sage turned his head and the beady eyes, bright with emotion, looked down, out of the schoolroom window. His mood gradually mellowed.

"It's a right fine morn. What say ye, yir Grace, tae a bit daunder doon by the Table ?"

The boy felt a rush of exhilaration at the prospect of release from that chamber of dust and books and discipline. That little room in which the prodigy would become proficient in French, Greek,

Latin, Scots and English, competent in Arithmetic, Geography, History, Astronomy and much else.

In due course, and accompanied by a dozen men-at-arms of the Royal Guard (for the safety of this prince was ever a grave consideration), the odd pair progressed through the castle buildings and downhill onto the old tournament ground.

On the long field which stretched beneath the mighty rock on which Stirling Castle perched, man and boy ambled toward the great mound which was all that was left of the legendary Round Table. Acting on the authority, not so much of the young king but of the Earl of Mar, Hereditary Guardian of the young King of Scots, the old pedagogue instructed the soldiers to take themselves off to a distance where they would remain effective protection and yet be out of earshot.

Listening to the birdsong and watching the play of sunlight on the trees of the nearby King's Park, for the boy it was a glorious day in which to be alive. It was one of those rare February days which, after long, slow months of winter's heavy, depressing weight, opens out a clear blue sky through which sheer joy may lighten the heart.

"Aye... they were the finest men of that Age. Brave and bonnie. They gave their very all to save Christ's Truth for this land... protect it from the pagan Angles and Saxons who would have dragged us back into the darkness. It was the blood of yon knights – martyrs if the truth were told – which saved Britain for Christendom. Now they lie forgotten, except in the silly distortions of fable and courtly play-acting. You know, lad... yir young Grace, when I was a penniless student in France... this was monie a year ago ye'll understand... I used to watch the lads wae siller playing thirsels at the tourney. Ye wouldna credit the nonsense spoken about Arthur and his doings."

Becoming agitated again, his beak sniffing angrily at the air, George Buchanan flung his arm in a southward gesture.

"Lyoness... Lyoness they call it in their romances, and have nae clue whereof they speak. A land of legend and mystery. A land submerged beneath the sea. It might have been here. It could have been there..."

The grey beard fairly bristled with contempt, and the boy tried desperately to conceal a smile on hearing yet again this oft-told tale.

"They lack the basic wits tae calculate that the so-called 'Lyoness' of their blethers was none other than oor ain Lennox... Lennox, where Merlin was born, where I was born, and of which your grandsire, Regent o' this realm, is Earl. Nae mair under the watter than yon castle rock."

With a final splutter and a shrewd glance around to make sure that his outburst had not been overheard by royal guards or common folk, the speaker adjusted his cowl, made efforts to compose himself, and turned to the subject which was uppermost in his mind.

A trembling finger pointed uphill towards the Church of the Holy Rude, Stirling's town kirk, situated on the hill alongside the ancient fortress.

"Cam alang, yir Grace. I must speak with you o' delicate matters."

So boy and sage, flanked by two files of heavily-armed royal guardsmen, retraced their steps from the tourney-field round by the south side of the great rock into the Royal Burgh of Stirling itself. The town crouched beside the River Forth, where the Scottish Highlands met the Lowlands. It was steeped in a thousand years of that ancient nation's history. In the busy Broad Street they walked in the shadow of merchants' houses, of the Tolbooth and Mercat Cross. Here was the bustling heart of the community. Conducted noisily this morn was the usual workaday bustle of the butcher, baker and candlestick maker, so to speak.

In accordance with the Scots character, most of those who witnessed the procession of men-at-arms, poet and monarch, showed more interest in the famous Geordie Buchanan than in their child-king.

*　　　*　　　*

In that ancient town, only the castle itself was older than the parish church. It had been founded in 1129, during the reign of David I and, since the 14th century been known as the Church of the Holy Rude – "Rude" or Rood meaning the Cross of Christ. Destroyed by fire in 1405, it had been rebuilt in 1414. Under the impressive roof of oaken beams Buchanan swept imperiously through the nave to the south-east aisle. The boy tottered after him as best he could.

At this time of the day the sacred building was conveniently empty and although the large, timid, brown eyes and the small ears above the ruff gave full attention to the sage, Buchanan was more or less aware that he was effectively speaking his thoughts aloud to himself.

"Ye belang tae a line o' kings which gaes back a thousand years, and we are standing, yer Grace, on the very spot where ye were crowned nae sae lang since. In yon very pulpit John Knox preached that day. Your Coronation was in accordance with Scotland's reformed, Protestant faith, unlike the Roman ritual o' yir baptism…"

The old man seemed suddenly to feel the cold within these ancient stone walls and he pulled his thin robe tightly around stooping shoulders.

"Yon was a sorry affair. Ye see, yir mither, the queen, as she wis then, being Catholic, had ye baptised according tae hir ain religion. But Scotland was by then a Protestant realm… and mair tae the point Elizabeth's England is Protestant, and unless you are known to be the Protestant king o' a Protestant nation, then ye'll ne'er sit on the English throne, lad."

Head bowed, brow furrowed, Buchanan paced between the stout pillars of the old church. Young James trailed at his back, hanging on his every, incomprehensible word.

"Ye have the right, boy! Ye are descended fae thae Tudors through Margaret, who married yir great-grandfaither, James the Fourth o' Scots, an' sic is the sorry state o' the Tudor line ye have the strongest claim to the English throne, unless Elizabeth produces an heir."

A shaft of wintry sunlight fell on that lined old face, exposing all the frustration and concern etched on the features. He made no mention of the claim of James's mother to the English Crown.

"Unless ye join these two kingdoms in your royal person there will be nae Union and nae Empire… and the world will be the worse for it, believe me."

With a hopeless shrug at the kirk door, Buchanan accepted the futility of imparting dynastic and political hopes and fears to a bemused infant. The soldiers, who had again maintained a discreet and not too distant presence, escorted the pair back within the castle walls.

*　　　*　　　*

From the small window of the schoolroom in the Prince's Tower, he peered over the vast, marshy expanse of Flanders Moss, remembering his childhood home on the shores of Menteith Loch. Turning back, he bent over a table on which was unrolled a map of the Kingdom of Scotland. There was just one place which worried him… Dumbarton.

Chapter Two
Piety and Policy

In silken thread of emerald, crimson and gold, stitch by patient stitch, nimble fingers created the image of a luscious garden. A veritable Eden.

Embroidery was one of the few pleasures left to her. It had been a winter of bitter cold, which had taken its toll on her health. The young woman, once celebrated by courtiers, painters and poets as one of the greatest beauties of the Age, at twenty-eight years old felt like a repulsive, ancient hag.

She laid aside the needle and lifted a hand to her temple where a violent, stabbing pain was bringing on waves of nausea. She only toyed with her meals and barely slept now, tormented by recurring pains under her ribs. Occasional, restricted outings on horseback had seemed to bring her slight and temporary relief from these tortures, but the reality of her imprisonment was confirmed by daily indignities. The horse-riding had ceased and her personal staff, for example, had been cut from sixty to around forty.

Held securely in this ugly, square tower of Sheffield Manor Lodge, the Queen of Scots was the "guest" of George Talbot, Sixth Earl of Shrewsbury (a kindly gaoler), and his wife, Bess of Hardwicke.

Mary maintained a little court, of course. She read a lot – books in the various languages in which she was fluent. In the evenings she was permitted to play cards and listen to music (thank God for music, which could lighten her soul as nothing else seemed to). Through the short, yet endless, winter days there was the embroidery that she shared with Livingston, Seton and her gaoler's wife.

The queen's sense of ugliness and self-loathing had not arisen solely from the physical. There were moral causes. She was finding it increasingly difficult to reconcile the Christian piety, which she sought and professed, with the deceptions and hypocrisies which had become her daily stock-in-trade.

After losing the Battle of Langside and fleeing from Scotland, Mary had sought protection and sympathy from Elizabeth of England – Elizabeth whose throne she was determined to seize. Indeed, she had even quartered her heraldry with that of England as an assertion that she, Mary Stuart, was the true successor to Mary Tudor.

Bitterly she recalled her humiliation on being forced to sign a deed of abdication from her own Scottish throne, an abdication which, of course, was null and void, having been extracted under duress. When she had escaped from that other prison, the tiny island on Lochleven, she had wanted to head straight for

Dumbarton Castle. Her wisest advisors had agreed with this. Sit tight and secure in the tower of Dumbarton Rock and draw support to herself. They had, in fact, been on their way to that fortress when the Hamiltons had insisted that they could defeat her enemies in open battle. Now here she was... with her embroidery.

Another wave of nausea engulfed her being and it was all she could do to resist the urge to retch. All of the medical charlatans had failed her. She now sought medicines from far and wide which might be effective in releasing her from these endless miseries. It was the smell of cinnamon in one of these tinctures which had unconsciously brought Dumbarton to her mind. When four years old, she had been taken from the monks of Inchmahome Abbey to Dumbarton Castle, where she had contracted measles. Some potion she'd been given then had precisely the same fragrance of cinnamon. Of that illness she remembered almost nothing, but there were memories from the episode which followed which remained vividly in her mind.

She remembered the crowd of courtiers and nobles gathered on the castle green, beneath the towering rock, the colours of the flags, the heraldry, the waving handkerchiefs. How, as she was led to the water's edge, the men had stood back and bowed, and the women curtsied. With extraordinary clarity, she could see the broken, purple veins on the cheek, above the whiskers of Lord Erskine, and she could hear the gentle, reassuring voice of her nurse, Janet Sinclair. She recalled being fascinated by the way in which a certain little tree grew out of the rock-face. As a child it had seemed to her, looking back upward, that those towers were so high against that blue sky that theirs must be the very windows of heaven.

*   *   *

Briefly, Mary took in her present surroundings. In the light of the chandeliers, at the other end of the long, polished table, she rested her eyes on Mary Seton. One of her "Four Marys". Seton, then just an infant also, had been with her on that day... nearly a quarter of a century past. The queen considered for a moment bringing her companion into her thoughts with some vocal recollection, but decided that she preferred private nostalgia for the moment. Seton, head bowed, stitched on, unaware.

*   *   *

As the royal procession had boarded the personal galley of the King of France – the "Reale", where the River Leven flowed into the Clyde, the little princess had taken a last, tearful farewell of her dear mother... and so, on to France.

*   *   *

She picked up the needle and, furrowing her brow in concentration, continued with the stitching of a large letter "V". A scroll wound around two trees and a huge hand which descended supernaturally from a cloud. The hand held a pruning tool, and the motto written on the scroll would read – "Virescit Vulnere Virtus" – Virtue flourishes by wounding.

Her left hand reached up to her breast. In her cleavage, through rich, heavy clothing, she could feel the presence of the diamond ring which had been a secret gift from the Duke of Norfolk. This man whom she had never met was, all going well, to be her fourth husband. Through such a marriage she might gain her release and perhaps Elizabeth's throne. Secret plotting to this end was ongoing, in spite of the fact that Norfolk had secured his release from the Tower of London on the basis of a promise to his sovereign that he would abandon any intention of marrying the Queen of Scots. Of course, Elizabeth, as an illegitimate, should never have been made Queen of England in the first place. All Catholic Christendom accepted that Mary was the rightful monarch of England. In the meantime, she was seeking Elizabeth's help in regaining her own Scottish kingdom.

The English queen had laid down certain conditions upon which that help depended. Among these conditions were an insistence that Scotland must remain a Protestant land, that Mary's son, King James, would be brought up in England, and that Mary would on no account challenge Elizabeth's right to the English throne… God help her, she was being sorely tempted to agree to all of it. After all, in order to become Queen of France, she had easily enough signed a secret agreement to make Scotland a French possession in the event that she should die childless. Queen of France… Queen of England… what was Scotland compared with these, but a stepping-stone?

Suppressing another potential wave of self-disgust, Mary reassured herself that such manoeuvrings were not, properly interpreted, deceitful or treacherous in the normal way of things. They were policy. Policy set out by her advisors. Anyway, Elizabeth was now an excommunicate.

Mary thought of her little son, James. He had been less than a year old when she had last seen him. She had been attempting to send him small gifts, to remind the bairn that his mother loved him, but she had reason to believe that, in accordance with a policy of monstrous cruelty, Elizabeth had prevented these tokens from reaching the boy.

*   *   *

Another stipulation which had been made by the Queen of England was that Dumbarton Castle must be placed under English control. It was presently being held by a beleaguered garrison under Lord Fleming for the Scots Queen, and Elizabeth well knew that Dumbarton was the one place where a Catholic French or Spanish army could land and set about the business of retaking Scotland for Mary and the Pope. Elizabeth did not know, however, that Mary, in spite of her assurances to the contrary, had secretly instructed Archbishop Beaton to propose a French invasion of Scotland.

This reminded Mary of her second visit to the Rock. It had been two years after her return to Scotland, after the tragic death of her first husband, Francois. She had been undertaking a royal progress through the western lands of her little realm. When she had spent a couple of days at Dumbarton, a great, strapping Highlandman called James McConnell – how was it he had styled himself ? – yes, "Lord of the Outer Isles", had been there with his wife, a daughter, as Mary recalled, of the Duke of Argyll. It had been a beautiful summer's evening and Mary and some of her court were high on the battlements looking northwards towards the Highland mountains and speaking of the next day's visit to Colquhoun's Loch Lomondside castle at Rossdhu. They had been discussing whether to travel on horseback, or to take small boats up the River Leven and into the loch, and it was then that McConnell's wife had appeared with servants heavily laden and presented them all with beautiful outfits of Highland clothing in splendid tartans of scarlet, green, purple and white. They had all laughed to see Tom Randolph, Elizabeth's English diplomat, clad as a Highland laird.

*   *   *

Mary looked up from her sewing to catch Bess of Hardwicke hurriedly averting her gaze. Lady Shrewsbury had a suspicious eye on her royal prisoner. It was known that the Scots queen was plotting and somehow smuggling messages out of Sheffield to her supporters. Many of these communications had been apprehended, but others were getting through. Lately Queen Elizabeth had made it clear that she expected the Earl to maintain tighter security, or she might well consider removing this responsibility from him – he had even received a royal reprimand for having left the Manor Lodge to seek treatment for his gout. This was the reason that a stop had been put to Mary's horse-riding. An atmosphere hung heavily in the grand chamber where the three women stitched busily and in brittle silence.

*   *   *

There was a certain Italian banker, a Florentine called Roberto Ridolfi, who was conducting business in England, and who was an agent of the Pope. It was intended that this Ridolfi would take messages from Mary to the Duke of Alva, the King of Spain and the Pope.

The silence was broken by the sound of Mary's lapdogs yapping in an adjoining hall. At the far end of the Great Chamber a door opened and young Willie Douglas, sweeping off his feathered bonnet, bowed himself into the royal presence.

" It's gie snell again the day, Your Grace. Might I suggest a wee tot o' the aquavytae afore ye tak yer turn aroon' the yaird ?"

Not yet twenty years of age, small in stature, but with a most pleasingly innocent countenance and manner, this was the hero of Mary's escape from Lochleven. He was utterly devoted to her.

Mary's illicit and coded missives were smuggled out of the manor in a variety of ways: in the heels of shoes, left under certain stones... even stitched into her embroideries. Douglas's use of the Scots word "snell", meaning bitter cold, was the predetermined acknowledgement that the Queen's letters for His Holiness and the King of Spain were safely out and on their way to Ridolfi. Included in these communications was Mary's pledge to hand over Dumbarton Castle to Spanish invasion forces.

In a voice accented with a delightful blend of Scots and French, Mary thanked her messenger. She bowed her head and looked down at the rich Turkish carpeting so that Bess of Hardwicke would not detect the light of hope in her eyes.

Chapter Three
The Robin and the Hoodie-Craw

To the north, way beyond the ferry and the hills of the Vale of
Leven, stood mighty Ben Lomond and the Highlands. Across the
river, to the east, there was the quay, with its fleet of small craft.
Beyond the town, on the far horizon, were the cliffs of the
Langcraigs. About half a mile to the south-east, at the confluence
of Leven and Clyde, loomed the two hundred and forty feet twin-
peaks of Dumbarton Rock.

Duncan Robertson sat beside the holy well of St. Shear and
reflected on the ancient tradition which was associated with it.
King Arthur (so ran the legend) had granted certain lands to Loth.
These lands subsequently became known as Lothian. Loth had a
daughter who became pregnant outwith the sanctity of marriage.
Her father, being mortified at this perceived stain on the honour
of his house, had the poor young woman, Thenew, thrown from a
cliff. Miraculously Thenew had survived this dramatic exaction of
rough justice, so it was decided to set her adrift on the Firth of
Forth in an open boat. The boat came safely to land on the shores
of Fife, at Culross. There, the resident Celtic holy man, Saint Serf,

had taken in the beautiful young refugee, caring for her and her baby boy.

The boy grew up, under Serf's tutelage, to be Saint Kentigern, better known as Saint Mungo, who effectively founded the city of Glasgow. Serf, known also by the Latin "Servanus", allegedly had cause, at some time in his evangelical wanderings, to visit Dumbarton. On encountering an ancient pagan well which had long been resorted to by the local populace for miracle cures, Serf, in keeping with the usual practice of the Celtic missionaries, sanctified the spring, thus converting it to a Christian place of healing.

Duncan found himself wondering when and why the good folk of Dumbarton had taken to calling Serf "Shear", because it had been as "Shear's Well" that this place had been known to them for some hundreds of years.

With the coming of the Reformation, the new Protestant ministers had made zealous and repeated efforts to stamp out what they saw as the ignorant and superstitious practice of seeking cures and other favours from holy wells. They had, however, been notably unsuccessful in these endeavours, with people of all classes continuing to believe in, and to seek miraculous healing from, sacred springs.

*　　　*　　　*

Duncan Robertson, a twenty-three year old Highlander of the Parish of Luss on Loch Lomondside, was dark-haired, of medium height and muscular build. Although some of the soldiers of the castle garrison wore uniform in the Fleming colours of scarlet and white, the archers wore their own hunting garb. Duncan was clad in leather boots and wide breeches. On his calf-hide belt there was a sharp dirk. His leather jerkin was covered with a shoulder-plaid of a simple green and blue check. His four-foot bow was slung over his back and a quiver of arrows hung by his waist. On this occasion he was bare-headed, but when on duty in the castle, or in any combat situation, he wore a morrion, a steel helmet with brim and plume.

Also at St. Shear's Well that morning were two sniffy-looking, middle-aged women who eyed the archer somewhat askance, relations between townsfolk and soldiers of the castle garrison having been somewhat mixed in recent times. The Reformation, which had officially taken place some ten years previously, had been in reality a lengthy process rather than a single event. It had been a kind of revolution, and all revolutions bring out, to a greater or lesser extent, the worst excesses of human behaviour. On a small scale, Duncan had witnessed something of this in his home parish of Luss. As in communities, large and small, throughout the land, there had been division. There were those who, for varying reasons, embraced the new Kirk, and those who, also with diverse motives, adhered to the old Faith. In Luss a crowd of villagers who had been persuaded that statues of saints were idolatrous had taken it upon themselves, among other acts of spiritual vandalism, to behead a stone effigy of Saint Kessog, patron saint of the Lennox. Duncan had been among those who'd rescued the head of the statue and concealed it, with other sacred objects, in a cairn at Bandry Bay on the loch-side, where Kessog was said to have been martyred.

In the Royal Burgh of Dumbarton the divisions and destruction had been of a more extensive and dramatic nature. Even civilians carried arms for protection when about their daily affairs, and the disturbed state of the country provided sufficient excuse for many to settle old grievances. Since the deposition of Mary, the queen, the realm had been, to all intents and purposes, in a state of civil war. On the one side there was the Queen's Party, those who in theory sought to return Mary to her Scottish throne. On the other hand there was the King's Party, those who claimed to support the child-king, James. In fact the country was being ruled by a Regent, in the name of the royal four-year-old.

In 1568 some of Mary's supporters had gathered in Dumbarton Castle and come to an agreement – thereafter known as the "Dumbarton Bond" – to defend the cause of the imprisoned queen. In that year Lord Fleming, a step-cousin of Mary, had, with a hundred hagbutters (musketeers) surrounded the burgh with trenches, fortified the parish church, and held the town for the queen. In the following year, however, the Earl of Moray, Mary's illegitimate half-brother and Regent of the realm, chased Fleming's soldiers back into the castle and occupied the town, laying siege to the fortress. Before long Moray had had to concede that Dumbarton Castle was effectively impregnable and he entered into negotiations with the castle's Keeper. In January of 1570, the Regent was, however, assassinated by one of the Hamiltons in Linlithgow (the assassin subsequently being rewarded for the murder of her half-brother with a pension from Mary). On receiving word of this, and fearing an attempt to kill or abduct the young king, the soldiers of the late Regent abandoned Dumbarton and made at once for Stirling. This opened up an opportunity for Lord Fleming's force to recapture the town of Dumbarton. As matters stood there was presently a fairly well observed truce in effect, but that was due to expire in a matter of weeks.

The point of all this was that although the fortress on the Rock had been consistently and securely held for Queen Mary by Lord Fleming for some six years, the burgh (which was predominantly on the side of the King's Party) had changed hands several times with much destruction of property, both secular and spiritual, by the military. Building materials had been taken from private houses, from the parish churches of Cardross and Dumbarton, and from the Collegiate Church of St. Mary, to be used in improving fortifications. Even gravestones had been employed in this way. Punitive taxation had been imposed to pay the wages of men-at-arms. As well as these affronts there had, of course, been the usual abuses endured by an occupied community at the hands of swaggering soldiery. The big-chested, handsome, though sour-looking, woman at the well was the wife of a prosperous burgh merchant. The outbuildings of her house in the High Street had been demolished by Lord Fleming's men. Her companion, a scraggy, long-nosed seamstress had a daughter who had been sexually assaulted by an officer of the Regent's army. These experiences might go far to explain a certain coolness toward a member of the castle's garrison.

*   *   *

In the few days immediately following the public flogging of Margaret Lafferty, Duncan had learned that she had been coming to the well to take holy water with which to bathe the cruel weals on her back. Duncan was unmarried. He was a fine-looking man, but he lacked confidence and experience with women. On this particular morning he was there solely with the hope of striking up some sort of acquaintance with the beautiful Irish girl who had so attracted and fascinated him since he'd first set eyes on her. He was brooding over a couple of practical problems – how would he explain his presence at the well, and how would he engage her in conversation ? When he saw the ferry, some few hundred yards upstream, push out from the town's Boat Vennel, his hunter's eye picked out the long, dark hair of his quarry in the ferry-boat and his heart began to race.

As Margaret slowly approached St. Shear's Well, Duncan could see that she looked tired and drawn. Her features bore the signs of pain, but when her eyes met his there was a certain glint of lively challenge. She wore a glowing saffron mantle which fell almost to her buckled shoes. Her hair was tied back with an emerald ribbon. For his part, Duncan, when he met those dark eyes, felt his face flushing in an agony of self-consciousness. He had hoped that he would be alone with this beautiful young woman and this hope was fulfilled when the two townswomen, with further sniffings and airs of superiority, walked quickly away from the spring.

Duncan had still failed to come up with any plan of conversation, but this was of no matter, because, as is so often the case, an apparently random factor of circumstance took over the proceedings. Margaret was carrying a wooden bucket, and just as she drew up to the well, a tiny robin alighted on the rim of the bucket.

"Oh, my wee darling. You'll not be getting a drink out o' this till I've drawn a drop o' water. Are you the thirsty wee burdie ? Look at you now, with your wee beating breast just as red as the face o' yon brave soldier."

Responding to this mockery, delivered in such a delightful lilt, Duncan blurted out the first absurdity which entered his head.

"You're Irish, aren't you ?"

The dark eyes flashed.

"Indeed I am, and proud to be so! You'll be a Scotsman, but never mind, we can none of us help what God made us."

Duncan could not prevent a smile from creeping into his flustered features. For a moment he hesitated then found a rush of courage from he knew not where.

"Well… God made you right bonnie, lass. He surely did."

Her chin raised, she gave him a defiant look.

"And did he make me a thief ?"

Duncan rose to the challenge and spoke quietly but with emotion.

"If you are a thief, then thon wee robin is a hoodie-craw."

Secretly in her glory, Margaret betrayed not the least sign of pleasure. She thrust the bucket into the archer's hands.

"Take this and fill it for me. I'm sure you can bend a sight more easily than I can."

A frown came over Duncan's features at this coded reference to her flayed back. He took the bucket more than willingly and stooped to the holy spring. She spoke in the Irish Gaelic and he in the Scots Gaelic and together they found understanding.

*　　　*　　　*

It transpired that nineteen-year-old Margaret Lafferty had been born and raised in the Tyrconnell village of Creeslough. On a visit to an aunt on the Irish coast she had been, to all intents and purposes, kidnapped by the first mate of a small trading vessel. She had managed to keep her abductor at bay with her feet and fingernails until the ship's captain heard her screeching below decks. By good fortune there had been some important Frenchman on board, and the captain was determined there would be no rape aboard his ship under such circumstances. Accordingly he had threatened to have his second in command gelded if he laid another lustful finger on Margaret. The vessel's cargo, the French notable... and the lass from Creeslough, had all been discharged at Dumbarton Quay. Without anything but the torn clothing she stood in she'd had no choice but to seek employment in the town or in the castle itself. For these past several months, therefore, she had been a general skivvy in the fortress, simply to get food for her belly and a roof over her head. Given her state of penury and the restrictions which the civil war had placed on shipping on the Clyde, she'd had neither the means nor the opportunity to return to Ireland. She said nothing to her listener about the many times she'd looked out homeward, beyond the hills of Renfrewshire, and wept bitter tears at the thought of her family in an agony of anxiety about where she was and what had become of her.

*   *   *

Duncan needn't have bothered fretting about how he was going to explain his presence at the holy spring. Margaret, with a woman's unfailing instinct, knew perfectly well.

The Irish girl had a natural affinity with Scots Highlanders simply because the so-called galloglass and redshank clansmen of Argyll and the Western Isles – MacDonalds, MacDougalls, MacSweeneys and their like – had for centuries been fighting alongside the O'Donnels of Tyrconnell against the English invaders of her homeland. Yet in truth, and in spite of her flashing eye and boldness of speech, she too was naturally shy and struggled to keep the conversation from faltering. Again she received inspiration from one of God's creatures. She caught sight of a horse grazing in the glebeland of the nearby Kirk of Saint Serf.

"Yon horse there – he minds me o' my Uncle Johnny's Thomas. I was just a wee tot. One bleezin' hot summer's day it was. I was at my Uncle Johnny's land at Derryherriff. Well, Thomas – his horse – was pullin' a cart o' hay down from the high field. Uncle Johnny, he lifted me right up onto Thomas's back, and he held me up there. Well, I squealed. I thought I was on the top of the world. I looked up into that blue sky and I thought I could reach up and touch it. I did…"

Her speech trailed to an embarrassed halt as she became conscious of the irrelevancy of the reminiscence. They both laughed and she ended the tale.

"Anyway… I got awful burnt with the sun that day."

For his part Duncan was able to suggest that the French dignitary on the Irish vessel had possibly been a Monsieur Verac, an agent of King Charles IX, who had come to Scotland, through Dumbarton, to encourage the nobility to support Mary and the Auld Alliance.

Margaret learned that Duncan's home was in Glen Finlas, not ten miles away, and well visible from the Rock. He was the youngest son of a large family, having been born in the year that Mary had sailed for France. As a boy he had learned to hunt with bow and arrow on the mountains and in the forests around Loch Lomond, not for sport but through sheer economic necessity. Genuine modesty had prevented him from saying it in so many words, but she gathered that he had become an archer of exceptional skill. Duncan had been fifteen years old when Mary, now a young widow and the Queen of Scots once again in her realm, had visited the Colquhoun castle at Rossdhu, but an hour's walk from the Robertson holding.

"I mind it well. Will – my elder brother – and I were up on the slope o' Creachan. We had our bows. Doing a bit hunting. The game was poor and we'd grown tired of it. Will had this thing he used to do. He knew it maddened me and it fair entertained him. He'd fire an arrow straight up into the sky. Right above us. We'd have no way of knowing where it would fall. It was crazy. It could have come down into the skull of either of us. He was roaring with laughter as I bolted for the cover of some trees. It was as we were tearing down the hillside we saw the bright colours of the fine clothes of the folk down at Rossdhu, by the lochside. Then the sound of their music drifted up to us."

Margaret's eyes were wide.

"Did you see her ? Did you see the queen ?"

"We knew she was there, among them. We'd heard she was coming. But I'd be a liar to say that we could make her out at that distance. I wish I'd seen her close. They say she's right bonnie, but…"

Duncan looked at Margaret and flushed again.

*   *   *

The Robertsons' feudal superior was Sir John Colquhoun of Luss. Perhaps because, like most men, he had been much affected by his queen's personal charm, Sir John became a staunch supporter of Mary, who in turn had shown him favour. After her escape from Lochleven, however, Colquhoun had been summoned by Regent Moray (who was by then governing the kingdom in the name of young James) to join his army. The Laird of Luss had failed to appear and so placed himself in a situation which had been regarded by the King's Party as treasonable. Colquhoun had been left with little choice but to submit to the Regent, who had consequently pardoned him.

Arising from these pressures, the Colquhoun levies, which included Duncan's two brothers, had fought against Mary's army at Langside. Duncan had shamefully insinuated to Margaret that he had chosen to join the other side on point of principle. In fact he had no particular political bias and the truth of the matter had been decidedly cynical. Duncan's father was a wily old fox and worldly-wise. He saw no good reason why the common man should not employ a tactic which the gentry had been up to for centuries. Before the older Robertson brothers had been marched off with Colquhoun's contingent for the Regent, William Robertson had "advised" Duncan to slip quietly off and offer his services to Lord Fleming. That way at least one of the Robertsons would end up on the winning side. As it had turned out, of course, Duncan found himself joining those of the Queen's soldiers who'd made a swift retreat from the field of Langside to the safety of Dumbarton Castle.

*   *   *

As they walked back along the riverside, taking in the sights, the sounds and smells of that morning – the swooping of the ever-present gulls, the creaking of ropes on the little ships, the general cackle and bustle of burgh trade carried over the water – Duncan expressed his concern regarding how Margaret was faring since she'd been dismissed from service in the castle. It transpired that, while working in the fortress, she'd made a friend – another Margaret, as it happened – Margaret Kennedy, who'd taken her into her lodging in the Kirk Vennel, and was looking after her until such times as her back had healed and she could look for other work. Duncan was keenly aware of the fact that here was a young woman who had suffered badly at the hands of men. He knew that he would be wise to handle her with gentleness and patience. Fortunately these were qualities which he possessed.

On the way back over to the town on the little ferry-boat, they were both aware (or did they imagine it ?) that certain other passengers were making note of the fact that the castle archer was in the company of the "Irish thief". Around midstream Duncan became conscious of a change in Margaret's demeanour. Her colour, which had returned a little as they'd exchanged life stories, was now a deathly pale. The pain had returned to her features and, when they stepped onto the riverbank at the Boat Vennel, he had to support her when she almost fainted. When she returned to a more or less normal awareness of her surroundings, she confessed that the wounds in her back had become infected. There was some poison in them. His features set in a grim mask of cold anger, Duncan resolved all the more determinedly to deal out justice to Lord Fleming and the creature, Carpenter. He delivered Margaret, and the bucket of holy water, into the caring hands of the Kennedy lass, and strode off in the direction of the Parish Kirk, his thoughts in turmoil.

Chapter Four
The Darkness and the Light

Formal lessons were over for the day. The sun had begun to set over distant Ben Lomond as master and pupil left the Prince's Tower and walked around the Royal Palace on their way to their respective quarters. The palace had been built by the little king's grandfather, James V, and had been, in its day, one of the most advanced architectural undertakings in the British Isles. At a time when France was considered vastly more civilized than little Scotland, French masons had, apparently, influenced the creation of the classical facades which bore niches in which statues had been carved representing the planetary gods, James V himself, and the devil. The evening light gave these features a particularly sinister aspect on this occasion and, as they were passing the stone form of the devil, the boy looked fearfully upward and, tugging the hand of his mentor, drew them to a halt.

"Maister Geordie... ye hae spoken o' the Auld Kirk and the New – the Auld Faith o' ma mither, and the New Faith o' yirsel' and Maister Knox an' a'. But what means a' this o' Catholic and Protestant ? What makes ane sae bad and the ither guid ?"

Buchanan bent his head and clawed at his cowled brow with ink-stained fingers. He was a man of words, seldom at a loss for them, but he was painfully aware that, though it was an essential part of his duty to bring this boy up secure in the principles of the Protestant Faith, it would be no easy matter to answer such a question in a way which would impart any kind of understanding to even an exceptionally bright four-year-old.

He stood for long moments staring sightlessly at the graven image of the personification of evil, silently seeking inspiration from the source of all that was good and true. At length he decided to begin by telling something of his own personal experience. He took the boy by the hand and led him away from that diabolical symbol.

"When I was a young man I wrote a poem... a satire, about the monks o' the Franciscan Order. They were corrupt, ignorant men who were bringing religion into disrepute. I wisnae alone in yon sort o' thing. Davie Lyndsay o' the Mount that was Lyon tae yir grandfaither, he had a rare swipe at them wae his Satire o' the Three Estates."

They walked slowly over the Lower Square in the direction of the Great Hall.

"Anyway, the long and the short o' it was I got arrested on the orders o' Cardinal Beaton and flung in gaol."

Young James halted in his tracks, eyes wide, trying to cope with the concepts of his aged tutor having once been young and having once been wicked.

"Thank God I managed to escape and I got tae England where some good friends looked after me till I got away tae France... tae Paris where I'd been a student. Well... Beaton never forgot nor forgave, and years later, when I was teaching in a University in Portugal, he got the Jesuits on tae me – let me think... aye, I'd hae been in my forties by then. Well, they accused me o' eatin' meat durin' Lent an' sayin' that Augustine favoured the reformed thinkin' on the Eucharist. So the Inquisition made me a prisoner for eighteen months in a monastery... for my 'instruction' as they ca'd it."

Absently he turned back toward the palace, young James following closely as the light faded.

"Ye see, yir Grace... men hae tae be allowed tae think, and speak thir minds in discussion, and be free tae come tae thir ain conclusions. God gave folk minds. He gave us the gift o' thinkin' that we might contemplate oorsels an' the world around us. Men need that freedom tae learn and grow..."

Buchanan glanced down to see how his young listener was taking this. Was there any sign of comprehension ? The boy's features seemed to reflect a certain understanding, so the master continued.

"The Auld Kirk had become a tyranny. The men at the heid o' it, popes an' cardinals an' the like, they lived like kings in palaces that wid make this here look like a tinker's tent. They were worldly and greedy and given over tae a' manner o' vice, but worse than that, they were cruel, lad... monstrous cruel."

It was cold now in the castle courtyard.

"Here, in this yir ain realm o'Scotland, the Auld Kirk had twenty-one folk put tae death for what they ca'd 'heresy' – no' thinkin' what they were telt tae think… speakin oot o' turn. Burned mostly… or hung, or drowned, for readin' the Bible an' discussin' its meaning and coming tae thir ain opinions o' it. In England it was hundreds, and throughout Europe, thousands. There was a wummin in Saint John's Toun o'Perth was drowned because she prayed tae God an' the Lord Jesus tae ease the pains o' childbirth, rather than the Virgin Mary…"

The old man stopped, realising that he was going too far. This was not suitable talk for the lad.

"But see… ye may ask, does it make the Protestants right just because they wir burnt for it ? Is their teachin' any mair true fir them bein' martyrs ? Well, yon wid be a right guid question."

The old beak raised and sniffed the evening air.

"Christ is the Light o' the World – never doubt it. Christ's Gospel – his Good News – is the only way to human salvation. But in the hands o' the Auld Kirk, the Church o' Rome, that light was burnin' right low. There was mair black smoke an' noxious fumes by the hinner end than the pure light o' God's Truth. Ye know, there wir parish priests that couldna read nor write. They had barely a word o' Latin in thir mouths… well, it cam tae a heid when the Pope started chargin' money tae hae deid folk taken oot o' Purgatory an' let intae Heaven. They say that's what set Luther off."

They stood in the deep shadow of the palace building. What Buchanan had to say was best finished out of doors and in a low voice.

"Even when I was in the hands o' yon Inquisition I held to the Auld Kirk. It wasna till some years after that I began tae study the Scriptures wae a view tae decide for my ainsel' whither the Protestants were right in their teaching an' interpretation. By the end o' it I was rightly persuaded that the Reformers were nearer to the spirit o' Christ's Gospel. But mair than that, I became assured that wae the New Kirk, folk wid hae a wee bit mair freedom tae read thir ain Bibles, in thir ain tongues, an' think thir ain thoughts."

The old man glanced keenly around making sure he would not be overheard, for he knew that his next words were injudicious.

"Make no mistake, though. The New Kirk is far frae perfect. I've served as Moderator o' the General Assembly o' oor Reformed Kirk o' Scotland mysel', an' I can tell ye, nae human institution can ever be free o' the sins o' men. Maist o' the great lords only cam ower tae the Protestant cause tae get thir hauns on the wealth and the lands o' the Auld Kirk. There will be mair persecution in the years tae come, for there is a wicked streak in the hearts o' men that must aye be seekin' victims o' some sort an' fir whatever reason. If it's no' religion it must be something else."

Far below, candle-light and tallow lamps could be seen in the widows of the Burgh of Stirling. In the night sky stars were becoming visible.

"But believe me, yir young Grace, the New Kirk liberates folk tae commune directly wae thir Maker, wae nae dependency on the intercession o' any priest or saint. Aye, it is my honest conviction that, wae a' its many faults, the Protestant Faith is a better light to travel by –

post tenebras lux – after the shadows, light."

They entered the palace together.

Chapter Five
Father and Son

Matthew Stuart wanted to die.

And he believed this longing might be fulfilled. He wondered if a man could die of nausea. He felt as though rusty blades were sawing through his skull and through his mind. The concussion had been delayed. He'd fallen from his horse. He remembered the cobbles striking the back of his head, the blinding light. There had been a moment of unconsciousness. He'd been lifted to his feet though, and after a short time he'd seemed to recover, but...

He lay in a bed, in a darkened room. There was something wrong with his sense of the passing of time, and he felt a very strange, very disturbing dislocation from his identity, his personality. He wasn't sure that he was himself. Something terrible had happened to him. Something very profound. Events of his past replayed themselves in his consciousness with an unnatural immediacy. But they belonged to a stranger. He had lost himself.

*　　　*　　　*

The Earldom of Lennox extended from Loch Long in the west, beyond the top of Loch Lomond in the north, to around Kilsyth in the east. It was bounded by the rivers Clyde and Kelvin in the south. It included most of Dunbartonshire, a part of Stirlingshire, and parts of Perthshire and Renfrewshire. The lords of this territory would originally have been "mormaers" (from the Gaelic, meaning "great steward"). Although there was a tradition that the Lennox earls descended from a Northumbrian family, the earliest recorded names indicated a Celtic rather than Anglo-Saxon pedigree. The first Earl of Lennox of whom there was dependable evidence was Alwyn, who died in 1155. In 1238 Maldowen was confirmed as the third Earl of Lennox by a royal charter from King Alexander II. Dumbarton Castle, which had been a stronghold of the Earls of Lennox, was excluded from this charter, the fortress becoming a possession of the Scottish Crown. In 1321, Robert the Bruce rewarded Malcolm, Earl of Lennox, for his steadfast support during the Wars of Independence, with the hereditary sheriffship of Dumbarton and the keepership of the castle.

When James I returned to Scotland in 1424, having been a prisoner of the English for nineteen years, he established himself on the throne and set about the destruction of the House of Albany, which had abused its power in the rule of the nation during the king's absence. The House of Lennox was connected by marriage to that of Albany, Duke Murdoch of Albany being married to Isabella, daughter of Duncan, Earl of Lennox. Considered guilty by association, the seventy-nine year old earl was beheaded with Duke Murdoch and his two sons at Stirling Castle. As a result of these executions, the Earldom changed hands. A "partition" was put into effect, whereby the lands were divided between the Stewarts of Darnley, the Napiers of Merchiston, and the Haldanes of Gleneagles, with the actual title going to the Darnley Stewarts.

Matthew, the tenth Earl, married Elizabeth Hamilton, who was the niece of James III. The twelfth Earl of Lennox (fourth earl of the new creation) also a Matthew, was born on September the 21st, 1516, in Dumbarton Castle. He was a great-great-grandson of James II, and his lifelong obsession was to be the right of his family to the Scottish throne.

*   *   *

Like Duncan Robertson, Matthew Stewart became an archer. At the age of sixteen he sailed for France and served as a bowman in the Scots Guard of the French king. After eleven years of soldiering Matthew returned to Scotland. He was now calling himself "Stuart", in the French fashion.

James V having died the previous year, Scotland was left with an infant queen. Back in his homeland, Lennox was cultivated by Marie de Guise, Queen Dowager, and Cardinal Beaton, Archbishop of St. Andrews. Between them, these two had been running Scotland very much in the Catholic French interest, Beaton having claimed the Regency on the basis of a forged document which he had passed off as the will of the late king. On this deception being exposed, James Hamilton, Earl of Arran, was made Regent, and Lennox was useful to dowager and cardinal in opposing Hamilton's claim to the throne, there having arisen bitter dispute as to whether Arran or Lennox had the more legitimate claim – this at a time when a relatively small and weakened Scotland was effectively being forced to choose between the domination (or "protection") of Catholic France or Protestant England.

*　　*　　*

The sound of a tolling bell awoke Matthew to a different reality. There were people in the darkness. Standing around him. He felt stirrings of dread. They were his interrogators. He was back in the Tower of London...

*　　*　　*

He had courted Marie de Guise. It would have been a most advantageous marriage, from Matthew Stuart's point of view. The Earl of Lennox had been a fine looking young man. Tall and strong, handsome and pleasing. But the dowager queen had rejected him. To make matters intolerably worse, Cardinal Beaton brought Arran back into his favour. Lennox had turned in disgust from the French Catholic party, to which he had naturally been allied, and sought advantage elsewhere.

Eight French ships had sailed into the Forth of Clyde and berthed at Dumbarton Castle – a stronghold described by Henry VIII as "the Key to the Realm". Marco Grimani, Legate of Pope Paul III, had been sent to Scotland with ten thousand gold crowns which were to be used in a campaign of resistance against the English king and his Protestant expansion. Matthew Stuart, to whom this money was entrusted, was soon, however, to make an offer of his support to the Tudor monarch. By 1544 Henry VIII, though only in his early fifties, did not have long to live. He was in notoriously bad health. The Earl of Lennox calculated that he could extend certain promises to the obese and ailing monarch that he, Lennox, would not, in all probability, need to fulfil. Accordingly he had pledged to recognise Henry as "Protector of Scotland", to use his influence toward the marriage of Mary Queen of Scots to Henry's son, Prince Edward, and to hand over Dumbarton Castle to the English... all in return for the hand in marriage of Margaret Douglas, daughter of Margaret Tudor and Henry's niece. Lennox would be appointed "Governor of Scotland". Accordingly, in July of that year, Matthew Stuart had married Margaret Douglas, a union which seemed to guarantee dynastic success for the House of Lennox, and which, perhaps surprisingly, had blossomed into true, lifelong love.

*   *   *

The little king and the wise old man had been to church. In the Kirk of the Holy Rude they had listened to the black-gowned minister of Stirling Parish preach a sermon on the Parable of the Sower. George Buchanan had, of course, paid heed with rather more concentration than young James, who had tended to let architectural features and the idiosyncrasies of individual members of the congregation divert his youthful attention. His tutor, however, had come away from the service with certain ideas germinating in his mind, ideas relating to the planting of seeds. These thoughts, it should be noted, were not spiritual, but dynastic.

Back within the greater security of the castle walls, infant and sage strolled alone in the little garden which lay adjacent to the Prince's Tower. In truth James did not stroll. His young legs were weak – because of the poor quality of the milk of his wet-nurse, it was alleged – so he tottered. For this reason Buchanan took every available opportunity to exercise the lad, albeit within the close restrictions of the castle and its immediate vicinity.

"Yon business o' the guid seed bearing forth a grand crop has set me thinkin', yir young Grace. We hae the man Killigrew – Queen Elizabeth's envoy – comin' tae see yi this week…"

Sir Henry Killigrew had visited Scotland on several occasions, assessing the health and development of the boy-king and reporting to his royal mistress.

"…and as ever we must make a guid impression on thae English."

The nostril were flared and the old eyes had a faraway look.

"The Tudors, yir Grace, being Welsh, as yi ken, have aye felt a sair need tae justify thir rule o' England. Or, as they aspire, to rule Britain."

James gave every appearance of attending to his master, while inwardly brooding about the seeds which had fallen by the wayside and been snatched by the devil.

"So they hae made much o' their descent fae Brute o' the Trojans, wha they say was the first king o' Britain, and fae Arthur… The Henrys were sair distracted wae it, and so, I hae heard, is Elizabeth. They hae a' this fae the likes o' Nennius an' Geoffrey o' Monmouth."
The tutor's mouth turned down in an expression of private doubt, but he continued.

"You and I, yir Grace, are right fully conversant wae the realities o' Arthur's place in things, yi mind ? When the Roman legions left Britain, the British tribes wha dwelt between the Walls – the Antonine and Hadrian's – they were sair pressed on a' sides. Wae Irish fae the west, Picts fae the north, but – worst o' a' – thae Angles and Saxons fae the south – they needed a right capable general tae unite the tribes and lead them against a' yon invaders…"

He gave a downward glance and ascertained that the boy was following all of this.

"Arthur was just that man. He led the Gododdin, the Rheged and the Strathclyde Britons in a great war o' resistance. A' this we hae in history written in the Welsh language. But in thae days Welsh was the tongue o' the Britons a' the way up tae Edinburgh and the Highland Line by Loch Lomond…"

Buchanan gestured with a bony claw along the line of the grey-green Ochil Hills.

"Clackmannan – thon was the land o' the Gododdin. Arthur scored great victories, and his effort surely saved these islands for Christ's Gospel – Britannia Christiana – but in time, ower the centuries, the Welsh culture an' language was driven southward intae the land we now ken as Wales an' folk began tae entertain the mistaken notion that a' Arthur's great deeds had taken place there and in Cornwall."

Little James fingered his sticky doublet and looked down over the fields which stretched on the banks of the meandering River

Forth... thinking of soil and seeds and poor souls snatched from salvation. Far to the west, beyond the distant mountains, there was an ominous build up of dark, heavy cloud which threatened thunder. James was afraid of thunder. He thought of the statue of the devil on the palace wall... and he resolved to be good.

George Buchanan interlaced his fingers in front of his chest as though in prayer, wagging his cowled head.

"Aye... but we must present a' this tae Killigrew right circumspectly. Play our tune to suit the Tudor ear. We are going to sow seeds, yir Grace – if I may so mix my metaphors – just that... sow seeds."

*   *   *

In the month following his marriage, the Earl of Lennox had attempted to take Dumbarton Castle – his place of birth and the central stronghold of his earldom. With a fleet of ten ships which carried a taskforce of pikemen, archers and hagbutters, Lennox sailed from Bristol and first seized the Isles of Arran and Bute. Proceeding up the Firth of Clyde he arrived at Dumbarton on the 10th of August. The Deputy-Keeper of the castle, Stirling of Glorat, was offered a pension of one hundred merks per annum from Henry if he would hand over the fortress. He rejected the bribe and sent Lennox packing. With a Douglas-led Scots army of some four thousand men nearby, Lennox considered withdrawal the better part of valour and set sail southward.

At the Cross of Dumbarton, Matthew Stuart was summoned to answer charges of treason. Naturally he did not appear. A Scots parliament promptly passed a sentence of forfeiture against him. He had lost all of his Scottish possessions at a stroke.

In the summer of the following year, a French expedition consisting of two thousand gunners, two hundred cavalry and two hundred archers, had entered Scotland through Dumbarton. With characteristic lack of subtlety, Henry VIII had been attempting to persuade the Scots to accept his policy of marriage between Mary and his son by having an English army lay waste to Southern Scotland; it became known as the "Rough Wooing". The French contingent joined the Scots army and their combined force drove the English invaders back over the border. Lennox made one more attempt to capture Dumbarton Rock that winter. Sailing on this occasion from Dublin, with a force which included English, Irish and Scots warriors, he failed yet again to gain entry to the ancient capital of the Strathclyde Britons. On the 7th of December, however, there occurred the most wonderful event in Matthew Stuart's life. In their Yorkshire home of Temple Newsham, his wife, Margaret, bore him a beautiful baby boy, whom they called Henry.

*   *   *

It was two bells. Gavin Dunbar had given them to the cathedral when he had been Archbishop of Glasgow. The bells were chiming and broad daylight was streaming into the room. Lennox remembered who he was and that he was in the Bishop's Castle in Glasgow. But he also remembered the shattering thing which had made his life almost unbearable. Henry, his beloved son, was dead.

*   *   *

Henry Stuart had a most interesting childhood. His parents were highly placed in the dynastic reckoning of the Tudor court, young Henry's grandmother having been a sister of Henry VIII. Their position, so close to the English throne, gave them great hopes and privileges, but it was also very dangerous. Henry Stuart's proper Scots title was the Master of Lennox. "Lord Darnley" was but an English affectation.

Henry's tutor was John Elder, who had been a canon of the Collegiate Church of St. Mary in Dumbarton, and a great believer in the union of the Scots and English thrones. In 1559, when Mary and Francois had been made King and Queen of France, it was John Elder who had accompanied the thirteen year-old Master of Lennox to their coronation. In the following year, when Francois died so tragically, young Henry travelled to Orleans to extend the condolences of the House of Lennox. On his return to England, however, he was placed under arrest, along with his parents, and detained in the Palace of Westminster. Spies had informed Queen Elizabeth that the Lennox family had been scheming against her and slandering her. The Master of Lennox, nevertheless, at just fifteen years of age, with considerable courage and resourcefulness managed to escape and return to France. His father, Matthew, was placed in solitary confinement in the Tower of London.

By 1563 Elizabeth had had a change of heart and the Lennox family were released and reinstated at court. It was safe for Henry to come back from France. Indeed, Lennox prospects had improved so much that around this time the Spanish ambassador in England observed in a letter to Philip II that it was widely believed that Elizabeth might, in certain circumstances, name young Henry Stuart her successor. So the family lived in dread of Elizabeth marrying and giving birth to an heir. They looked forward with a morbid anticipation to the English monarch's death. But in the meantime there was always the Scottish throne.

In 1564 Elizabeth had granted permission to the Earl of Lennox to return to Scotland so that he could attempt to have the forfeiture of his lands reversed by Mary Queen of Scots. In this he had been successful and the following year he was joined by the Master of Lennox.

When Mary had returned to Scotland she was an eighteen year-old widow. Apart from the very genuine grief she had felt at the loss of her husband, Francois, it would have been unnatural if, after having been Queen of France, that major power with all its sophistication and splendour, she had not experienced a depressing sense of being diminished on finding herself relegated to poor, little, ragged-arsed Scotland. Accordingly she focussed her desires and set her policies all the more obsessively on the English throne, which she had been brought up to regard as hers by God-given right. A major factor in the pursuit of this object was an advantageous marriage.

Suggested husbands had included the Earl of Arran, the Archduke Charles, son of the Emperor Ferdinand, Eric of Sweden, Don Carlos of Spain and Charles IX of France. Elizabeth understood fully that Mary hoped to wed a Catholic prince who would use force of arms to place the Scottish queen on the English throne, so she made her own insulting offer of Robert Dudley, her Master of Horse and presumed lover. However, Henry Stuart, Master of Lennox, being so close to the thrones of both England and Scotland, had also to be given serious consideration.

He had grown into a most impressive young man. His most striking physical feature was his exceptional height. He had the strength and build of an athlete. His blond hair was cut short and his complexion was fresh. He was proficient in all the manly and martial sports. A first class horseman, he was an outdoor man, skilled in hunting and hawking. He possessed the courtly accomplishments, being a graceful dancer, a talented lute player and singer. He penned eloquent poetry. Those who encountered the Master of Lennox were generally greatly impressed. In the palace of Stirling Castle, Mary and Henry fell in love.

Early in the morning of the twenty-ninth of July, 1565, they were married in the chapel of the Palace of Holyrood. The queen was escorted to the altar by Matthew Stuart, father of the groom. Finally a Lennox had become a king.

* * *

Sir Henry Killigrew was a spry little man. In his forties, neatly bearded, richly dressed without being ostentatious. There was an unmistakable firmness of purpose beneath the shallow sugar-coating of diplomatic etiquette. As was to be expected of an emissary of the Queen of England, he bore himself with a pride which fell just short of condescension. An interesting man, he had been, in his day, both soldier and sailor, and was now an accomplished painter.

The audience was being held in a spacious chamber of the King's Old Building. Present were King James, seated uncomfortably in a small, especially crafted throne, George Buchanan, in his finest attire, Sir David Lindsay of Rathillet, the Lord Lyon, and, of course, Killigrew. Lady Mar had left them after the initial civilities. It was evening, and the sun setting in the west shone through two large windows, the gentle light setting off magnificently the gold and scarlet of the Lyon's heraldic tabard. A small group of four musicians were playing carefully chosen traditional Welsh and Cornish airs to, as it were, set the tone. Killigrew was a Cornishman. As the last plaintive note faded, Buchanan took up the conversation.

"Your Excellency will have observed that His Grace has grown greatly since last you saw him…"

The broad Scots dialect had been dropped effortlessly, as was Buchanan's policy when dealing with English courtiers.

"…and that he is in robust good health."

In fact little James was not the strongest of children. He had not long recovered from a bout of measles and he was pale and underweight. Killigrew, however, quite naturally affected not to notice these indications and took the opportunity to praise the kingly appearance.

"His Grace looks to have the strength of a veritable Lion."
The envoy smirked agreeably and gestured in the direction of Rathillet, whose office and garb expressed the royal personification of the king of beasts. All present beamed approval.

It was an important part of Killigrew's remit to assess the extent of the young king's educational development. This was of great interest to Elizabeth. Buchanan, needless to say, was fully aware of this and had, over the previous few days, and with the assistance of Lord Lyon – an essential part of whose office was the knowledge of royal genealogy – schooled James in a certain exercise.

"Indeed so, Your Excellency. Not only does King James prosper in bodily matters, however, but greatly beyond our hopes in matters cerebral, it is my joy and satisfaction to report."

Stirring restlessly on the cushioned throne, James was intimidated by the presence of this English stranger. He had no memory of the man's previous visits, when he had been but a babe-in-arms, and his child's instinct saw right through the smirking insincerities of Killigrew's polished performance. His tutor took a few measured paces and struck one of the poses with which James was so familiar.

"Already His Grace reads and writes passing well. He has made a good beginning with Latin and can speak French remarkably for his years. Her Majesty need have no fears in matters spiritual, for His Grace is greatly fond of Holy Scripture, in which he is carefully mentored by myself and the most learned ministers of our Reformed Scots Kirk…" That was allowed to hang in the air for fullest effect.

As though at some secret signal, Lord Lyon advanced to stand behind his infant sovereign. Buchanan continued silkily.

"His Grace's powers of memory have quite astonished us all, Your Excellency. Perhaps you would care to hear for yourself an example of the royal precocity in this regard ?"

The Englishman was, needless to say, most keen.

James turned in his throne, looking anxiously over his shoulder and up at the eagerly encouraging features of Sir David. James faced forward again, turned large brown eyes determinedly in the direction of Killigrew, raised his little chin and gave voice.

"I am James, by Grace of God King of Scots, sixth of that name. Son of Henry... son of Margaret... daughter of Margaret... daughter of Henry..." And so he went on through an almost endless line which included the likes of Owen Tudor, King Arthur (of course), Cadwaladr, and on – embracing the fantasies of Geoffrey of Monmouth and others – till he reached Brutus of Troy, the alleged first King of Britain. Although James was descended from the Tudors through both his mother and father, Buchanan had shrewdly elected to trace the royal pedigree, not through the imprisoned and disgraced Mary Queen of Scots, but through the little king's father, Henry Stuart. Back through Henry's mother, Margaret Douglas, through his grandmother, Margaret Tudor, to Henry VII, then right through the Welsh Tudor line into the glorious myths of and legends which were of such importance to Elizabeth Tudor. It was a masterstroke.

Killigrew could not fail to be impressed. It was perhaps the first honest expression which had graced his features that day. He marvelled at the word-perfect performance of this boy, not yet five years old, and he took to heart most profoundly the dynastic message which had been Buchanan's essential purpose.

As evening light faded, the distinguished company sauntered in the castle garden. Favouring James with his most approving countenance – little realising the value of this to the boy – the old tutor sniffed appreciatively at the smells of soil and the flowers of the season. With a certain satisfaction he thought of seeds sown.

*   *   *

At the time of the royal marriage Henry Stuart had been given absolute assurances, by public proclamation and private promise, that he would be king in the fullest sense of the term. Mary promised to defer to his authority as husband and as sovereign. Her promises were, however, quickly broken. Henry was not granted the Crown Matrimonial, which was essential if he was to continue to rule in the event of Mary's death. She did not, in reality, accept his authority. In military matters she sought to replace Henry's leadership with that of the Earl of Bothwell. In matters of rule she denied her husband the right to independent decision making and the authority to sign official documents lacking her approval. This was an age in which no self-respecting man – never mind a king – could allow himself to be so publicly humiliated by his wife. The new king was a spirited nineteen year-old. Finding himself betrayed in this way and effectively excluded from the proper role of kingship, he not unnaturally turned his back on the court and, with a company of young supporters, went hunting and hawking by day, and roistering by night.

Henry had been almost universally admired until he reached the throne. Perhaps in the minds of some Protestants it was bad enough having a Catholic queen, never mind a Popish king. In fact, although Henry had been brought up as a Catholic, he was personally open-minded in matters of religion. Nevertheless, for whatever reasons, he became the target of envy and spite.

*　　　　*　　　　*

The young king had been far from alone in distancing himself from affairs of state. As a result of Mary's tactless and inept rule a majority of the nobles who should have been helping to govern her realm had removed themselves from the court. A typical example of the queen's lack of consideration was her elevation of an Italian singer, David Riccio, from his role as a court musician to that of her French Secretary, and increasingly influential advisor. Mary incredibly permitted this resented foreign commoner to become the real power behind the throne, and Riccio, for his part, increased his unpopularity by strutting like a peacock and treating members of the nation's natural leadership with an insufferable arrogance.

In spite of the cooling of relations between king and queen, Mary became pregnant. She had taken to staying up until the early hours of the morning, listening to music and playing cards. She was often alone with Riccio and she extended intimacies to him which encouraged wide speculation of a sexual relationship. Indeed, the queen spent so little time with her husband, and so much with her secretary, that it was quite inevitable that there would be suspicion that Riccio, not the king, was the father of the child she was carrying – all of which was more than a husband could be expected to tolerate.

*   *   *

On Saturday evening of the ninth of March 1566, Mary Queen of Scots was entertaining a small group of relatives and servants. In a tiny room just off the Queen's Bedchamber in the Palace of Holyrood, a cosy company of six sat around a candle-lit supper table. To everyone's surprise the king entered from his private stairway. He was at the head of a small group of armed men. As Henry held his six months pregnant wife securely, Riccio was dragged screaming from the queen's presence. In a room nearby the hated Italian was butchered with fifty-six dagger wounds.

The removal of Riccio was an element of a plot by which alleged supporters of the king were pledged to gain for him the Crown Matrimonial. In the event, however, it became clear to Henry that he was as much a prisoner of the conspirators as was Mary. The royal pair managed to escape from the Palace of Holyrood, riding through the night to Dunbar, soon to return to Edinburgh at the head of a loyal army.

*   *   *

It was essential to Mary that her child would be accepted as legitimate. Accordingly she feigned a reconciliation with the young king. On the nineteenth of June 1566, Charles James Stuart was born in Edinburgh Castle. Sadly Mary felt the need to assure Henry that the child was his own, but as soon as he had publicly acknowledged his son, the queen began to treat him again with open contempt, denying him her company and access to the marital bed. In response to this humiliating rejection the king once more took to a life of hawking, hunting, swimming and drinking. At length he even threatened to leave the country. Meanwhile Mary's infatuation with the Earl of Bothwell – a married man and notorious womaniser – had become a public embarrassment. She began to show an interest in divorce, but realised that such would jeopardize the perceived legitimacy of Prince James (as the boy would be called). Accordingly, in November, the queen had informed her clique of advisors that she wanted to be rid of her husband. Dealing with such men in such an age it is almost inconceivable that Mary would not have understood that the murder of Henry would be the inevitable consequence of her instruction. She had asked only that she be left in ignorance of the specific arrangement.

Henry badly needed the advice and support of his father. On the journey between Stirling and Glasgow the king had taken suddenly unwell. The exact nature of his illness was not conclusively diagnosed, but poison was the first and obvious suspicion. Later smallpox, or even syphilis were suggested. While Henry lay in a sickbed in the Bishop's Castle in Glasgow, Mary spent Yuletide in the company of Bothwell, whose divorce she had arranged.

Henry Stuart loved Mary Queen of Scots until the last breath of his short life – a fact which she heartlessly exploited. Pretending yet another reconciliation, and promising the sick man a resumption of full marital relations, she lured him back to Edinburgh. He was given accommodation in the Old Provost's Lodging at Kirk o' Field on the edge of the capital. In the early hours of the tenth of February 1567, while Mary laughed and danced in the Palace of Holyrood, the Old Provost's Lodging was blown to pieces by a massive, secret store of gunpowder. The king was found strangled in the garden. He was twenty-one years old.

*   *   *

Almost universally regarded as the prime suspect for the regicide was James Hepburn, Earl of Bothwell. Three months after the murder, Mary, in a Protestant ceremony, married James Hepburn, Earl of Bothwell.

*   *   *

Matthew Stuart remained silent until the bells of Glasgow Cathedral finally ceased to chime. He looked around the room, which was crowded with servants and advisors. At fifty-four years of age and still recovering from the concussion, and though not looking his best, he bore the all appearance of natural authority. The high brow gave him the look of a thinking man. The large, dark eyes and long nose left one in no doubt about his royal Stewart lineage. The fierce throbbing in his head had been largely replaced by the more familiar searing agonies of gout. He would have preferred to stand to address this body of men but the swollen and inflamed joint of his right knee dictated that he speak from a sitting position. As he had got older and the attacks had become more frequent he began to fear that they would worsen to the point of being a permanent, crippling affliction. Not that it mattered anymore. The Earl of Lennox, Regent and ruler of Scotland in the name of his grandson, King James VI, went through the motions of existence for one thing only. As he had once been obsessed with the quest for a crown, he now burned with a longing for revenge. Vengeance on the French whore who had murdered his dear, beloved Henry.

The dark eyes smouldered as he glared around the company he had called to order in the Bishop's Castle.

"This last while our hands have been tied. We have had no choice but to observe the truce which was forced on us by Elizabeth of England. We dare not offend her if we are to see our policies succeed."

The accent was English.

"But in just two weeks, on the first of April, the truce ends and we may act. Our priority has to be Dumbarton Castle. For as long as Fleming holds the Rock for that adulteress bitch there is a constant danger of a French or Spanish landing which could be the spearhead of a full invasion. I don't have to tell you what that would mean..."

The bearded chin jutted defiantly as he let the significance of these words sink in.

"We do not know the moment it might suit Elizabeth to release yon trollop, and I will drain the last drop of blood from my body before I'll see his grace, King James, lose his throne to her."

The Earl bitterly recalled the humiliation of his own various unsuccessful attempts to recapture Dumbarton Castle. He was painfully aware of the generally accepted conclusion, after long and earnest efforts by the late Moray to reduce it by siege, that it was impregnable. All of the military minds in the King's Party had failed to come up with a solution to this problem. The Regent knew that some higher intellect was called for. Thinking of his young grandson he received a sudden inspiration.

"Bring me George Buchanan."

Chapter Six
Love and Hatred

Duncan Robertson was not the best archer in the company of a dozen. That distinction went to a MacGregor from Strathcashell on the eastern shore of Loch Lomond. The man from Glen Finlas, however, was good and had a natural, competitive urge to be the best.

The bow had been a Highland weapon for centuries. It was used in warfare and for hunting. By the command of Robert the Bruce, hero-king of the Scottish Wars of Independence, yew trees had been planted on the island of Inchlonaig in Loch Lomond, around a dozen miles from Dumbarton Castle, for the bows of his archers. Curiously, Saint Kessog, Patron Saint of the Earldom of Lennox, was remembered as having been an archer himself, and the men of the Lennox had a considerable reputation as bowmen in warfare. Although the bow and arrow were gradually being replaced by the hagbut, archers continued to make a decisive military contribution, as had been the case in the recent Battle of Langside. Unfortunately, from Duncan's point of view, it had been the archers of the enemy.

Prior to the Reformation, the Parish Church of Dumbarton had possessed six altars, each dedicated to a particular saint, and each endowed with certain lands, the revenues from which maintained the upkeep of the altar. There were altars to the Virgin Mary, Saint Peter, the Holy Rood, Saint Ninian (who was Scotland's first Christian evangelist), Saint James (the Patron Saint of the Stewarts) and Saint Sebastian. The lands which had been dedicated to Saint Sebastian lay about a mile upstream from the burgh on the western bank of the River Leven. Although the Reformation had done away with the various altars, Saint Sebastian having been the Patron Saint of Archers, the tradition survived that bowmen from the castle's garrison conducted their practice on that stretch of meadow. This had not been possible during the lengthy periods when the castle had been under siege, but during this spell of truce the twelve bowmen from the Rock regularly rowed up-river in three little boats to hone their shooting skills.

The sun had risen a few hours earlier above the cliffs of the Lang Craigs to the south-east. It was another fine Spring morning. There were only the sounds of wildfowl, distant cattle and the gentle murmur of the river. They had the long stretch of meadow to themselves and the light was good for shooting, but Duncan was not giving of his best.

"Man, Duncan, you're not worrying me this morning at all. I am thinking your mind must be on other things."

The dark, stocky MacGregor strode through the long grass at Duncan's side as they went to retrieve their arrows from the packed straw target. Out of courtesy to their Lowland comrades-in-arms they spoke in Scots rather than in their native Gaelic.

"Ach, Malcolm, you have the rights of it as ever. But you'll forgive me, I'm sure, if I say that it's not something I'm free to be discussing."

The MacGregor furrowed his brows, pursed his lips in a show of polite discretion.

"Indeed, no, man. Your business is quite your own. Malcolm MacGregor would be the last man to intrude."

When a good archer takes aim he does so, not in a mechanical way such as might be expected by the layperson, but rather there is an inexpressible correspondence between the aimer and the target, something which is mental or even, in a sense, spiritual. That morning, it was true, Duncan Robertson's mind and spirit were not attuned to that mode of detachment which was necessary for keen shooting. The session ended just before noon and the twelve archers piled into their little boats at the point where a small burn entered the Leven at Pillanflat, Duncan being on the receiving end of some barbed banter about his unusually ineffectual performance. On such a golden morning as this it was not easy to feel the reality of it, but each man had an unspoken awareness that this was not a game – that an ounce of skill, gained or lost, could make the difference in action of life or death. As the small craft travelled easily downstream with the swift current, Duncan allowed the rhythm of the splashing oars to bring some order to his thoughts.

He was being torn between extreme and opposite emotions. On the one hand, he felt the joy of a heightened interest in, and gratitude for, life, simply because he had fallen in love with Margaret Lafferty. On the other hand, he was consumed with hatred for Lord Fleming and the man Carpenter because of the brutality and humiliation they had inflicted on the object of his love and desire. The conflict between these passions had engendered an inner tension that prevented him from fulfilling either. He could not soften his heart to allow his love for Margaret to flower and grow until he had cleansed the detestation of these two men out of his system by acts of effective retribution. Yet because he was constantly being distracted by images of the Irish girl's beauty, because he found himself struggling to plan a strategy of courtship, he could not focus his mind on the tactics and detail of specific deeds of vengeance.

Carpenter he had determined to kill, but naturally this must be done in such a way that Duncan would not be caught and brought to justice. Lord Fleming was another matter altogether. This was the man whom the queen had appointed Great Chamberlain of Scotland. It would be no easy thing to get close enough to the likes of him to murder him and get away with it. In the meantime... Robertson couldn't shoot straight.

The Highlander's strong hands gripped the oars tightly, his muscles tense and the green-blue plaid flapping in the morning breeze, as the massive presence of Dumbarton Rock loomed closer.

*   *   *

Margaret Lafferty loved music. It was because music spoke to her soul that she had been drawn to Saint Mary's in the first place.

*   *   *

Shortly after King Alexander II had made Dumbarton a Royal Burgh, in 1222, a chapel dedicated to the Blessed Virgin Mary had been built in the town. Over two hundred years later, in 1453, Isabella, Countess of Lennox, was granted by the bailies, council and burgesses, permission to convert the chapel into a collegiate church. Saint Mary's was like a small cathedral, it was a considerable physical and spiritual presence. Its central purpose was the saying of perpetual prayers and masses for the souls of the father, husband and sons of the Countess after they had been beheaded at Stirling. Attached to the collegiate church were a mansion house and manses for its Provost and six priests. Surrounded by gardens and an orchard, Saint Mary's had a hospital and a "sang schule" which provided young students with an education in spiritual music.

The first Provost of Dumbarton's collegiate church had been George Abernethy, who just happened to be the nephew of its founder, the Countess Isabella. He had lived in relative luxury off the revenues of various parishes, while poorly paid and semi-literate vicars struggled to minister to their equally impoverished congregations. Abernethy, who as a priest should of course have been celibate, was actually succeeded as Provost by his son, Walter. These were examples, albeit at the low end of the scale, of the type of abuses which had in part brought on the Reformation.

The Protestant majority of Dumbarton Burgh had inflicted some structural damage and general vandalism on the town's collegiate church. Over a period of time some of the masonry from the ecclesiastic buildings had been taken and used in the construction of town houses, and of course for strengthening the defences of the castle. By and large, however, although most of the townsfolk turned their backs on the Romish activities therein, and the merchant class ceased to do business with the Catholic clergy, those priests who remained at Saint Mary's were left unmolested to live a leaner and less prestigious existence without the benefit of their revenues (these having been granted by Lennox to Cuthbert, son of the Laird of Drumquhassil). A small and courageous Catholic minority still unobtrusively attended Saint Mary's during these difficult times of transition.

The mediaeval music which had been performed at Saint Mary's was, like the architecture of Stirling Castle, much influenced by the French. The choristers, priests and burgh students, had chanted the liturgy of Canonical Hours, masses, prayers and hymns. There was an English influence also, from the time that Margaret Tudor had come to be queen of James IV. Even so, the Scots themselves had some fine composers of sacred music – there were the likes of Carver at Stirling, Scott at Inchmahome and Richardinus at Cambuskenneth…

At home in Tyrconnell, Margaret had loved the music of her people – the pipes and the harps and the fiddles which she'd heard in the little rural communities and in the towns. But when she'd heard the Franciscan Chant of the monks in their Abbey at Donegal Bay, she had been transported to another world. So when Margaret Kennedy had told her about Saint Mary's surviving choir she had wasted no time in hearing it for herself. The saying – and singing – of Mass, as such, was now against the law, but just as they had failed to stop folk going to holy wells, the Reformed Kirk authorities had so far failed to silence church music. In fact, many of the reformers loved spiritual music – particularly in accompaniment to the psalms – but they abhorred the Latin of the Catholic arrangements. When Margaret heard the exalting melodies and wonderfully complex harmonies sung and chanted to a seemingly supernatural perfection, she could not believe that such was the work of mere men, but rather that the voices of angels had come down from Heaven.

*　　　*　　　*

The bracing Spring morning had turned to a heavily overcast afternoon, bringing with it that irrational sense of impending danger which is often experienced with a change of light. As Duncan left the Quay and walked down the High Street in the direction of the Kirk Vennel, the first cold splashes of rain began to splatter on the cobbles. Such was West of Scotland weather. Avoiding human and animal ordure underfoot, scowls and inquisitive glances from the citizenry, he reached the lodging of Margaret Kennedy just as the shower gained force. On the doorstep that young woman recognised him at once and, with an expression of some anxiety, invited him in. Duncan looked around for his Irish sweetheart, but saw no sign of her in the single, small room. He looked questioningly at the other Margaret.

"I fear she's ta'en a right turn for the worse. A' through the night she moaned and raved, burnin' up and in the grip o' a fever.

Shiverin' wan minute an' throwin' the claes aff hirsel' the next. By this morn' she dinna even know me."
The girl clutched at the edge of her shawl, on the verge of tears.

"But… where is she now ?"

Duncan felt a sick sensation in the pit of his stomach.
"I managed to get her intae Saint Mary's. Canon Carmichael gied her a draught. I left her sleepin'. He says he'll dae whit he can fir her, but he says she's right bad."

Although the Protestant Kirk Session now impressively undertook responsibility for the burgh's social welfare, the hospital which was attached to the collegiate church, like its choir, still functioned after a fashion for those who had need of it and were prepared to risk the social consequences of consorting with the priests.

"Will you take me to her, lass ? I must see her."

*   *   *

The hospital was a long, low, single-storey building which had been left more or less intact, there having been an unspoken respect for its humanitarian function. There were half-a-dozen patients lying silently in simple wooden cots. The room was dimly lit by such daylight as filtered through the heavy clouds and narrow windows. Margaret lay face-down and unconscious.

"She will sleep for a few hours and I've given her something to cool her blood, but there is bad poison in these wounds…"

The priest was a young man, tall, broad of shoulder, with curly dark hair, a strong aquiline nose and a gentle manner.

"Her friend tells me she has been washing these weals with water taken from Saint Shear's Well. It may sound strange to hear a Catholic priest speak against the water of a holy spring, but I fear that this is where the infection may have originated."

He glanced up from the mess of Margaret's lacerated and festering back to meet Duncan's eye.

"Are you a relative… a friend?"

A sense of embarrassment was added to Duncan's anxiety.

"I am a friend… yes, a friend."

Canon Carmichael gave him a knowing, wary look.

The archer turned around to Margaret Kennedy, who was now weeping openly.

"There, lass, compose yourself. Sure Margaret will be just fine. Is that not so, Canon?"

The priest's hands disappeared into the deep sleeves of his monkish habit and he eyed Duncan grimly.

"If I cannot by some means cleanse her blood of this poison, she may have but a short time left in this world."

Duncan could not keep the horror from his features. Margaret Kennedy ran from the room, hands pressed to her stomach. With eyes like those of a frightened child the Highland warrior spoke.

"What is there can be done for her ?"

The young priest bowed his head in thought or prayer, was silent for a few moments then look up with an air of decision. He waved his hand vaguely in the direction of Saint Mary's garden.

"Bring me some dandelions."

*   *   *

Over and above his habitual and natural desire to heal and to save life, Canon Carmichael had an especially desperate and compelling motive to bring about the recovery of this particular patient. He had feelings for Margaret Lafferty which were entirely inappropriate to his priestly calling.

Chapter Seven
Books and Battles

Since his visit to the Regent at Glasgow, military matters had loomed large in the mind of George Buchanan. Indeed, they had somewhat spilled over into his educational curriculum for the boys here in Stirling Castle. He became uncomfortably aware that he had allowed himself to digress from what should have been the lesson in hand, and determined to steer his lecture around to a proper subject. He and his young pupils had been discussing the tactics which had been employed by the victorious Scots army on the occasion when it had been led by William Wallace at the Battle of Stirling Brig, the site of which was clearly visible to them from the castle walls.

"Och aye… well thir's mair tae conflict than swords and lances."

It was an observation which met with the silent approval of little King James, who found bloodshed and any form of violence quite horrifying.

"Ye see, words can be made warriors, and books can win battles."

Secretly pleased with this turn of phrase, the tutor allowed himself to meander away from his intended subject yet again.

"Aye… and books can cause battles just as well, mind ye."

He turned his keen, beady eyes on the row of little students.

"Can any o' ye bring tae mind an example o' a book causin' a battle ?"

Young James knew fine well where this was leading, but decided to hold his tongue. Willie Murray and Wattie Stewart looked blank. Jocky o' the Slates picked his nose. Buchanan affected disappointment and carried on.

"We need look nae further than oor ain Saint Columba."

The predatory beak tilted upward, drawing in a mighty sniff, and the great mind travelled back a thousand years.

"It is written that as a young man Columba borrowed a book o' psalms fae Saint Finnian o' Moville. Columba made a copy o' this book which he intended to keep. Now, Saint Finnian was indignant at Columba's presumption. A quarrel arose between the two men about whether Columba really had the right to make an' keep a copy of the psalter."

Another keen glance to make sure he held the full attention of his young, and easily distracted, charges.

"Now, we hae to remember that Columba was a prince before ever he was a saint. So, strange though it may seem to us, there were political consequences arising fae the dispute between Finnian an' Columba. The long an' the short o' it was that it a' ended up wae a terrible conflict o' arms – the Battle o' Cul Drebene – in which thousands o' men were killed."

He had a quick look to see how the little king was taking this return to carnage.

"The loss o' these lives was something which affected the conscience o' Columba maist profoundly. Aye... he wis sair tormented – to the point that he chose to be exiled fae his native Ireland, an' that was just how he came to oor ain Iona."

The fur-lined robe was pulled tightly around the stooping shoulders and purposeful pacing around the little schoolroom commenced as the master continued.

"Noo, Columba wis much mair than just a missionary, an evangelist... he, being o' the blood royal, had a diplomatic role in the auld kingdom o' Dalriada. It was Columba's statesmanship which led to the union... "

He directed a sharp and telling glance at James.

"...Aye... Union... o' the Scots an' Picts that led to the founding o' our great nation."

A bony index finger tapped, as though to express emphasis, on the leather binding of a Latin Bible.

"Columba is considered by many as the true faither o' Scotland. So ye see, there is a sense in which that book o' psalms may be said tae have led tae the creation o' this realm…"

The right hand performed rhythmic chopping motions, as though indicating the links in a chain.

"The psalter led tae the copy… the copy led tae the quarrel… the quarrel led tae the battle… the battle led tae the remorse… the remorse led tae the exile… an' so on tae the mission on Iona and a' the diplomacy that followed… an' tae the founding o' the Scottish nation."

The three pairs of young eyes were bright with interest. Buchanan rubbed his grey beard with the back of his hand, looked wistful and almost unconsciously glanced through the small window downward toward the site of the Round Table.

"Aye… now ye know, it's a strange thing, but there have been those who have thought that Columba an' Merlin were one an' the same. Och, it's nae sae far fetched as it might sound. See you, Columba was right friendly wae Riderch the Bountiful, who was ane o' the kings o' the Strathclyde Britons. He had his fortress at Petra Cloithe – which is tae say the Rock o' the Clyde – Dumbarton. Now, think on this… Riderch had his palace wae his court up the river a wee at Partick. Of course we know that Merlin was a Strathclyde man. We know also that he is written o' as being resident at the court of Riderch. D'ye see whaur a' this is drivin' ?"

James did.

"There are amazin' concurrences between Columba an' Merlin. Baith wir prophets an' poets. Columba was credited wae miracles and Merlin wae magic. Baith wir men o' exceptional learning wha had great political influence. Each was a kingmaker. Each was nicknamed after a bird – Columba the dove and Merlin the hawk. Each o' thir lives was radically changed by a battle for which they felt personally responsible. Och aye… I could gae further, but what think ye ? Columba as Merlin ?"

It was a rhetorical question, of course, and, with what passed for a twinkle in those formidable eyes, Buchanan exchanged knowing looks with King James.

It dawned on the old master, giving rise to some irritation, that the particular example he had chosen did not fittingly illustrate the point which he had intended. The battle had been brought about by the copying of the psalter, not by its content. He engaged more directly with the subject.

"Aye… the ideas expressed in a book, or a poem maybe, can open men's minds to great truths. Men can be changed by ideas. They can be inspired. But… an' this is maist important – there are ways o' using words to give ideas power. It can be done well or done badly. When done with skill… with a certain talent… the poet, who is himself inspired, may light a fire in men's hearts and minds. The readin' o' a guid poem can make a man see himsel' and ither men, aye, and the world around him, in a right different light."

The man regarded as the finest Latin poet in Christendom spoke, as so often, to little King James rather than to his classmates.

"This is what I mean when I tell you that words can wage war and books can conquer nations."

The pedagogue found himself drawn back to military comparisons.

"Ye see, the skills o' the author are nane sae different fae those o' the general. It's a' a question o' marshallin' the forces at yir disposal. Wae the soldier it's infantry, cavalry, pikemen, archers… and sae on. Wae the writer it's imagery, pace, the sound and the placing o' particular words and phrases. Och, ye'll get ma drift…"

Jocky o' the Slates had stopped picking his nose, but was now howking wax from his ear.

Buchanan's mind drifted back to the occasion of his recent interview with the Regent Lennox. There had been an unusually ill-informed English diplomat present who had had the effrontery to remark that though Master Buchanan was a man of undoubted literary genius, perhaps he might be lacking in the specific military knowledge that was required for this matter in hand. The old mouth twisted defiantly as he recalled his reply.
"Sir, I will have you know…" (speaking a very proper English)
"… that from an early age I have made it my business to study the art of war. At the age of seventeen years I left my home in Menteith to join the Scots army of the Duke of Albany in its expedition into your own country. That was but the beginning of my military education."

The Englishman listened in polite silence, but with raised eyebrows.

"I later spent a number of years tutoring the son of Charles du Cosse, Comte de Brissac, an eminent soldier and, indeed, Marshall of France, of whom you may have heard. Such was the Marshall's opinion of my understanding of military matters that he saw fit to include me in his councils of war. Do you doubt the wisdom of the Regent of Scotland in doing the same ?"

This had the effect of wiping the superior smirk off that English face.

When the lesson was over and the young pupils had scampered off, noisily boisterous with the release from discipline, George Buchanan retired to the castle's Chapel Royal. Yet again he confronted the inescapable fact that in every apparent sense Dumbarton Castle was impregnable. He and the Regent were in total agreement about the absolute necessity of capturing the Rock. That door must be locked. The Regent was motivated by his hatred of Mary Queen of Scots, and Buchanan by his prophetic vision of a United Kingdom and a British Empire.

Alone in the sanctity of the chapel, the tutor bared his head and prayed sincerely and profoundly. Having prayed, as he was walking over the Upper Square in the direction of the King's Old Building, he recalled certain words he had spoken not an hour beforehand to his little class.

"Columba was credited wae miracles an' Merlin wae magic."
George Buchanan was very much a Renaissance Man. His learning and his interests took in a wide range of subjects. In France and in Portugal he had learned more than Latin and Greek. There were many kinds of wisdom, and this was, after all,

an exceptional case. In his chamber high on the ancient rock of Stirling, the sage first securely locked the door, for what he was about to do would have gotten him burned at the stake. He then closed the shutters of the single, west-facing window. He sat at a table and lit a candle. In front of him there was a goblet filled with pure, clear water. He drank deeply of that water. Sitting in a state of perfect relaxation he began to breathe deeply and rhythmically as he looked into the steady flame of the candle. When he felt ready he began to visualise that other rock at Dumbarton with incredible clarity and detail...

Chapter Eight
Loyalty and Betrayal

Standing on precisely the same spot as that from which, some eight years earlier, Mary Queen of Scots and her entourage had contemplated their visit to Colquhoun of Luss, Duncan Robertson was on sentry duty. It was the tenth of March – Saint Kessog's feast day – causing him to remember the old celebrations in his home parish. He peered northward, under the brim of his steel morrion, towards Glen Finlas, thinking of his parents – and of his brothers in the army of the Regent. Often, over these last few months, he had seriously considered simply deserting the garrison here at the castle, turning his back on the queen's cause and walking the few miles to his Loch Lomondside home. During the truce nothing would have been easier but, like all the soldiers in the castle, he believed that at any time a French or Spanish fleet would sail into the Firth of Clyde and an invasion force would recover Scotland for Mary. Then he would be a hero and, as his father had intended, one of the Robertsons would be in favour with the winning side. Yes, he had thought these things, but in truth he had latterly just wanted to be close to Margaret Lafferty… and now her life was hanging in the balance.

He would be relieved of his duty at noon. Then he must go immediately to the College hospital to find out how she was.

It was impossible in such a confined fortress to avoid seeing Carpenter, the sergeant, with an unwanted regularity. The sight of him made Duncan's blood boil. It took almost superhuman restraint on the Highlander's part not to just cut the man's throat on the spot, and to the devil with the consequences. Absently he noticed that there was still a little snow on the slopes of Ben Lomond. Oddly he found himself thinking of the melting wax of a burning candle and in that instant he experienced a "eureka" moment. Suddenly it became clear to him how he could bring about the ruin of Lord Fleming and the death of the detested Carpenter with no danger of personal repercussions. That is to say, what to do, but not yet just how to do it. He need not have been concerned, however. All of that was about to fall into place in an almost uncanny manner.

*   *   *

In a chapel, and at an altar which bore the profound scars of Reformation hammers, Canon Carmichael knelt in prayer. He was unaware of the silent presence of Duncan Robertson. Desperate to rush to the cleric, to grasp him by the shoulder and ask him what was the news of Margaret, the Highlander set his jaw, clenched and unclenched his fists, as he stood in an agony of self-control at the back of the chapel. The praying seemed to go on forever. Duncan himself offered up a sort of hopeless, wordless and inarticulate plea to the Almighty.

At length the young priest got to his feet and when he turned to face Duncan it was all too clear from the bleak expression on those handsome features that there had been no improvement in the patient.

"Come with me, Duncan."

The pair walked grimly through the garden towards the hospital building. At the entrance Canon Carmichael stopped, placed a hand on Robertson's shoulder, and warned.

"I took the juice of the crushed dandelions and applied it to her wounds. I have known such to overcome this poison in certain cases... I fear, though, that she is now quite fevered, raving at times... burning."

In spite of himself, Duncan swept the priest aside with his left arm and strode wild-eyed to Margaret's side. He could feel the heat rising from her body as though it were a blazing fire. She'd had to be tied face-down on the cot lest in her delirium she rolled over onto her suppurating wounds. The place stank... Hardly knowing what he was doing he grabbed a handful of the damp raven hair and bent to kiss it. Canon Carmichael's face was a stone mask.

Outside, in the cool air again, the two men found no use for words. At length the awful tension was broken by the intrusion of clattering hoof-beats. A dozen horses were galloping two-abreast up the Cross Vennel, the riders showing the arrogant disregard for the safety of lowly pedestrians, which was common in bands of mounted men. In spite of his preoccupation with the fate of Margaret Lafferty, Duncan found himself looking questioningly toward Canon Carmichael. The young priest's mouth twisted in an expression of distaste.

"John Cunninghame of Drumquhassil."

He indicated the leader of the troop.

"He bears the rather curious title of 'Half-Treasurer of Scotland' – which is to say he is a tax collector."

He looked questioningly at the Highlander to see if he had registered the biblical allusion.

At the great oaken door of Saint Mary's, the spiritual leader of that depleted community, Brother Andrew, stood with sad dignity to greet these apparently unwelcome visitors. Canon Carmichael continued his explanation.

"The Protestant lords greatly affected to deplore the lands and wealth of Mother Church, but they are by no means backward in grabbing as much of it as they can get hold of for themselves."
The riders drew up to a disciplined halt in the shadow of Saint Mary's great tower.

"Last year the Earl of Lennox, who is now acting Regent for his grandson, granted - by what right I'd like to know - the Provostship and revenues of Saint Mary's supposedly to Cuthbert, the son of this Cunninghame."

The leader had by now dismounted. He was tall, broad-shouldered and lean. He had a long, thin face, of which both nose and chin were large and pointed. The mouth was wide and slack, and an insolent smile revealed long, white teeth. The eyes were sleepy, yet had a roguish twinkle. The overall appearance was wolfish. Strangely, Duncan felt that he might be able to like this man. The canon carried on.

"The boy – for he is little more than a child – seems to have some genuine piety, but the whole thing is a blatant device to reward Cunninghame himself for his loyalty to the earl and the so-called King James. It is said that the queen caused Cunninghame some offence at the castle of Stirling and he has never forgiven her for it."

Knowing that Duncan was a soldier of the Queen's Party, the canon knew he could voice his own partiality in this way. On learning of Cunninghame's prominence among the opposition, as it were, Robertson's interest sharpened.

"Cuthbert has granted – with effect from this very month – various lands in the parishes of Luss, Cardross and Bonhill, which are the property of the Provostry, to his illustrious father. Cunninghame is here to gloat."

The tall beneficiary of this gift was now in what appeared to be perfectly civil and respectful conversation with the chaplain, Andrew. At a word from their leader the company began to dismount. As his men led their horses to stabling, the Laird of Drumquhassil was ushered indoors by Brother Andrew. Neither Cunninghame nor any of his men appeared to have so much as glanced in the direction of the two figures who stood by the door of the hospital.

Duncan Robertson's mind was in a turmoil. This was his moment of decision. Instinctively he looked over his shoulder toward the Rock, some half a mile distant.

*   *   *

Wisely the archer from Glen Finlas resisted the urge to act on impulse. He gave pause and considered. There were certain matters of simple common sense which had to be acknowledged. It would be folly for a known member of the Marian garrison of Dumbarton Castle to be seen in conference with any significant figure of the King's Party. How could Duncan be sure that Canon Carmichael, for example, clearly loyal to Mary Queen of Scots, would not send a report of any such approach to Lord Fleming ? The Highlander's desertion would be apparent by that evening, but there was a world of difference between absence without leave, so to speak, and – the word was surely unavoidable – betrayal. But then his original allegiance to Fleming and the queen's cause had been entirely cynical. Would this be any worse ? The moral conclusion, to one brought up in the Highlanders' code of honour, was inescapable. He would become a traitor. Not just to his rightful sovereign, but more importantly to the comrades-in-arms with whom he had stood at the Battle of Langside, with whom he had lived and shared a rough fellowship these past few months on the Rock. Again he was torn between conflicting emotional demands. Again the lust for vengeance triumphed. Yet could he, at this very time, when Margaret's life appeared to be running out, leave her side ? Although he recoiled from the awful, cold, dark emptiness of acceptance, he knew in one part of his heart that Margaret's fate was sealed and that if he did not embark on the business of avenging her that very day he would probably never do so.

*　　　*　　　*

Under the cover of darkness, through the rural parishes of Bonhill, Kilmaronock and Drymen, Duncan made his way on foot towards the estate of Drumquhassil. To someone so used to his native mountains and glens, these dozen or so flat, Lowland miles were easy going. Turning eastward out of the Vale of Leven, he kept up a steady pace through Auchincarroch to the Gallangad Burn. Following the course of the little stream until it became the Catter Burn, he discerned the distinctive shape of Duncryne Hill to the north, and was aware of the vast presence of Loch Lomond beyond. These Lennox lands were notoriously prone to nocturnal cattle-raiding by the Highland clansmen, such as MacFarlanes and MacGregors, who dwelt around the great loch. It was as well, therefore, that Duncan was skilled in the business of covering terrain with stealth. In fact he derived a special pleasure from being in the countryside at night. He had always felt that it was like another dreamlike world of mystery and strange romance. Around midnight, having passed the tower-houses of Finnery and Catter, he finally reached the meandering River Endrick. Fortunately he had a reasonable knowledge of these parts, living as he did not so many miles away on the western side of the loch, so it was without too much difficulty that he found the ford by which he crossed the river. Luckily the water here was unusually low for the time of year.

In a stretch of woodland a mile or so south of the village of Drymen,　　Duncan　at　last　stood　before　the　imposing

Cunninghame stronghold of Drumquhassil. Fifteen minutes later he found himself alone in the pitch-darkness of that laird's dungeon.

Chapter Nine
Cannon-fire and Conspiracy

Like those of Matthew Stuart, the roots of John, Fifth Lord Fleming, went deep into the soil of Dumbarton Rock. Originally the family had come from Flanders, but the first Fleming to settle in the Lennox was Hugh, who had held land in Kilpatrick, within sight of the Rock. Sir Robert Fleming was a strong supporter of Robert the Bruce during the Scottish Wars of Independence, and the king rewarded him with the barony of Lenzie. Robert's son, Malcolm, built a castle at Cumbernauld, which remained the seat of Lord Fleming. Sir Malcolm, who possessed lands on both sides of Loch Lomond, had been Governor of Dumbarton Castle and Sheriff of Dumbarton. John's father, the third Lord Fleming, was killed at the Battle of Pinkie. His mother, the Lady Janet Stewart, was close to royalty. She was, in fact, an illegitimate daughter of King James IV. As governess of the infant Queen Mary, Lady Janet had accompanied her to France. There the governess caught the eye of the French king, Henri II and they became lovers.

Lord Fleming's sister – "La Flamina" – was generally considered to have been the most beautiful of the queen's "Four Maries". She was now the wife of William Maitland of Lethington, the Queen's

Secretary. Maitland was known with dry Scots wit as "Michael Wylie", this being a vernacular rendering of Machiavelli. It was a richly deserved epithet, for the Secretary was a notorious intriguer and subtle diplomat, having been Scots ambassador at the court of Elizabeth. With a genius for manipulation and the indirect wielding of power, Maitland now found himself openly in the Queen's Party and very much her trusted advisor, agent and secret correspondent. The loyalties and interests of the Flemings were inextricably bound to Mary Queen of Scots.

When Mary had returned from France, and Lennox from England, it would have been natural for the queen to have placed Dumbarton Castle in Matthew Stuart's keeping. However, in a gesture which was guaranteed to cause profound offence, she had granted it instead to Lord Fleming, her step-cousin. It was a preference regarding which Fleming now had mixed feelings. On the one hand he found himself uniquely placed to be the man through whom the queen might regain her throne. On the other hand he felt very much a prisoner, confined to this little jumble of towers, cramped between the peaks of Dumbarton Rock. It had been a bitter winter and he could think of less draughty places to have spent it. Each day he grew more weary of the restrictions of his situation: the tiresome routines of the small garrison; the same faces and voices; the limited diet. He grew more tired of waiting. Waiting for the end of this truce which had been observed (if not meticulously) by both sides for fear of offending English Elizabeth. The King's Party praying that she would keep Mary in captivity, and craving the support of Protestant England in defence of the Scots Reformation. The Queen's Party praying that Elizabeth would release Mary and restore her to her Scottish realm. Fleming awaited word. He awaited action. He awaited, more than anything, the sight of a Catholic fleet sailing up the Firth of Clyde.

He was a man in hid mid-thirties, taller than average, slim and a little stooped. He had the same auburn hair as the Stewart monarchs and he was fashionably bearded. His weary and ruggedly handsome features gave an appearance now of almost permanent indignation. Indeed, he was indignant. None of this need ever have happened. If she had only listened to the good advice of sensible men. But Mary had never possessed sound judgement, forever trying to prove that she was in control, yet constantly and utterly dependent on some strong man – usually a rascal.

*   *   *

Fleming's mind went back to that terrible day when, after the humiliation of defeat at Langside, he and his monarch had spoken in the Abbey of Dundrennan. He had implored her not to leave her kingdom. It had yet been entirely possible to draw her supporters to her side, to fight again, perhaps to win. All had been far from lost, but no… her mind had been made up. Bizarrely she had chosen, of all things, to throw herself upon the mercy of a queen whose throne she notoriously coveted. He remembered the way in which she would enfold a person in a seductive warmth, with those magical eyes, make one feel like an intimate friend rather than a mere subject, then in an instant she would be cold and remote, every inch a monarch looking down that long nose at a lesser being. He had fallen for it every time. He always would…

It had been a Sunday afternoon, he recalled, in the month of May, almost three years ago, when they had embarked on the little fishing boat to the mocking sound of seagulls – Her Grace, Maxwell, Lord Claude Hamilton, Herries, and a clutch of servants – they might as well have been sailing off the edge of the world for all the sense it had made. But he had gone with her...

*   *   *

When Elizabeth had effectively made a prisoner of Mary, Lord Fleming had been permitted to return to Scotland. Dumbarton Castle had immediately become an issue, with the Scots queen being informed that Elizabeth forbade the Rock to be used as a point of access for French money and men. Mary, to her credit, had answered that if the Queen of England would not help her then she must seek aid from wherever she might receive it. Her Lord Fleming would hold the Rock, and the French would be most welcome. And so it had proved.

Of course, this had been a situation which was intolerable to the Regent Moray. In December of 1569 he had sent the Master of Graham on several occasions to negotiate the surrender of the garrison. The Keeper's hand, however, had been strengthened by the arrival of much-needed supplies from the town and so he had been able to hold out. The following month Moray had arrived to personally supervise the siege of the castle. He proved so efficient in his task that, by sealing off every means of entry to the fortress, Lord Fleming's garrison had been reduced to such straits that he had agreed to surrender if essential supplies did not reach him by a certain date. Mary, however, being well informed of these matters, had personally asked the French king to send aid. So again the Keeper had been playing skilfully and with a strong hand, for he knew that by then two French vessels, laden with food and munitions, were at anchor in Loch Ryan and that relief was near at hand.

Bitterly disappointed, Regent Moray had left Dumbarton and on the 23rd of January, in the High Street of Linlithgow, he was shot fatally by Hamilton of Bothwellhaugh. Scotland was without a ruler.

When the word reached the Royal Burgh of Dumbarton there had been mourning in the town and rejoicing in the castle. Fleming remembered the bitter cold morning, after that night of celebration, when they had lined the castle walls. He'd had a raw throat which burned like hot irons every time he swallowed. There had been a coldness in his bones that had nothing to do with the winter. To their amazement they had watched as, on the flat land surrounding the Rock, the late Regent's soldiers began to break camp in the morning mist. Dragging their cannon and siege engines, cavalry and infantry forming ranks and heading northward into the Vale of Leven. Fleming recalled that the castle garrison had not dared to cheer. They had just looked on silently mystified. Light snowflakes had begun to fall. By noon it had become heavy and lay thickly on the land, softening the edges of the deep ditches below. The fanciful among them had thought of a shroud. He remembered how, strangely, involuntarily, he had raised a hand as though to salute the last straggling infantryman, feeling not relief but a profound loneliness.

*   *   *

Reports reaching Lord Fleming had clarified the situation. The Earl of Moray had left Dumbarton in the first place because of serious developments in the capital. Sir William Kirkcaldy of Grange was the Keeper of Edinburgh Castle. He had been the general who'd commanded the victorious army of the Regent at Langside, but had now decided to support the Queen's Party. Although in theory Edinburgh's port of Leith was another potential point of entry where an invading army might have seized a bridge-head, in fact this would have meant sailing through waters which were very much under English control. Only the western approaches and Dumbarton offered a realistic prospect in that regard. However, Edinburgh Castle, dominating the capital as well as housing the Scottish Crown Jewels and ancient national documents, was of potent symbolic and psychological importance. Accordingly Regent Moray had sped eastward to see what might be done to rectify this unhappy state of affairs.

When word of his assassination had reached his forces surrounding Dumbarton's Rock there was shock and profound sadness. Not all of the Protestant lords were motivated solely by worldly greed. In most there was at least an element of spiritual concern. Lord James Stewart was known to have been principled and particularly sincere in his religion. Indeed, one Englishman compared him with those who led the people of Israel. Many regretted that his illegitimacy had prevented him from being their king. The first priority, after coming to terms with the loss of their leader, was to protect the young King James at Stirling from any attempt on his life, or any abduction. Hence the orderly withdrawal.

*   *   *

Looking down over the Royal Burgh, a cluttered sprawl of buildings, still dominated by the ravaged Collegiate Church, Lord Fleming reflected on the difficult period that had followed. The departure of the enemy forces had, of course, presented him with a golden opportunity to retake the town, and naturally he had done so, but there had been problems of discipline, morale and relations with the burghers. Of course, his soldiers, let loose after lengthy confinement in the castle, indulged themselves in excesses of drinking, wenching and brawling. That had required to be moderated. Ideally, he had hoped to win the townsfolk back to an allegiance to their queen, but for compelling military reasons he'd had to do some very unpopular things. It had been wise to accept that, sooner or later, the army of the King's Party would return and in all probability his own force would be driven back into the castle. With this in mind he had given orders for the fortifications surrounding the parish church to be dismantled so that they might not be of further use to the enemy. Unfortunately in the process damage was done to the church building and this had been interpreted by the citizens as deliberate, sacrilegious provocation. Breathtaking hypocrisy, he'd felt, coming from a mob which had so despoiled the Collegiate Church not so many years before.

Given that such damage had already been done, it seemed only practical common sense to use some of the broken masonry from these buildings to effect much-needed strengthening of the castle's own defences. However, there had only been so much stone available from the churches – they'd even used gravestones – and there had remained the requirement of building adequate stabling for the anticipated arrival of French cavalry. The materials for that particular enterprise had had to be taken from houses in the town itself. Of course, he'd chosen the properties of the most stiff-necked supporters of Moray, but, even so, it had hardly helped relations with the townsfolk.

*   *   *

He removed a velvet cap and ran his fingers through that auburn hair. The sun had come out again. The Leven was sparkling. The salt air was fresh. White clouds with grey bellies scudded across a cool blue sky. Through the small window of his chamber the Keeper could look northward and see the last traces of snow on the mountains around and beyond Loch Lomond. Their beauty failed to register on his consciousness because he was calculating, counting the months. Good Lord, it was a year... twelve months since Verac, the envoy from Charles IX, had first come. They had asked the French king to send an army to Dumbarton. He, Fleming, had assured His Majesty that, given a couple of hundred horsemen and three hundred infantry, he could have given a good account of himself in Queen Mary's and the Catholic cause.

*   *   *

Lennox had been appointed Regent – to please Elizabeth, of course. Very much her servant that one. Now more or less a madman. Totally unhinged by the murder of his wretched son. He had requested of Elizabeth that she send Sir William Drury, her Marshall of Berwick, to attack Dumbarton Castle. Instead she had ordered him to negotiate a truce between the King's and Queen's Parties. Knowing that Drury was by then at Glasgow, Lord Fleming and the Archbishop of St. Andrews had agreed to meet him at Kilpatrick, the village being rather loosely a half-way mark between Dumbarton and Glasgow. As the time approached they had begun to have second thoughts about the wisdom of leaving the security of the Rock. When Drury arrived at the designated rendezvous, he was naturally disappointed, not to say, mortified, to discover that the Queen's Party had not honoured the arrangement. Perforce, swallowing his not inconsiderable pride he, with a cavalry escort of no fewer than fifty, carried on along the north bank of the River Clyde in the baking heat of an exceptionally hot summer's day, toward the Rock, which could be seen through the haze shimmering in the distance. At a place about half a mile from the castle a messenger from the garrison informed Sir William that, if he were to continue with but a couple of his company, then Lord Fleming and the Archbishop would parley with him some short distance outside the fortress. Much against his better judgement, Elizabeth's envoy set off under a white flag.

It was not one of Lord Fleming's better days. He keenly resented the manner in which this English queen had taken it as read that she could impose her will on the affairs of the northern realm more or less as of right. It was bad enough that she was holding the rightful Queen of Scots in detention like some common criminal, but sending this arrogant upstart to lay down the law – for any understanding of negotiation as between equals was utterly alien to the English mentality – was quite insufferable. Fleming had prepared for the moment... had issued precise instructions.

As the three approaching horses pranced to just a few hundred yards from the castle walls – even their manner of riding seemed to suggest a kind of haughty superiority – the Keeper had glanced sidelong at the Archbishop, who stared straight ahead, for he had serious misgiving about what was to follow. Ignoring the almost huffy demeanour of his clerical ally, Fleming raised a gauntleted hand and nodded decisively to his most skilled cannoneer. Seconds later a falcene roared and belched flame. The shot fell a fraction wide, as intended, but some of the debris of the explosion showered insultingly, if not injuriously, upon the English emissaries. The men of Dumbarton Castle howled in derision as the puce-faced knight and his two lackeys galloped off in a manner quite entirely devoid of dignity. There would be, of course, a price to pay.

*   *   *

John Hamilton, Archbishop of St. Andrews, had been wise to have serious reservations about firing upon representatives of Queen Elizabeth. By way of reprisal, the town and castle of Hamilton, and all Hamilton properties and lands, had been put to the torch. It was a devastation which cost the lives of many common folk and brought utter ruin to hundreds.

*   *   *

Cattle was for centuries an important element of the Scottish economy. A Highland chieftain's wealth was calculated largely on the amount of cattle he possessed. The most famous breed was that of the West Highlands. Commonly black in colour, these were wonderfully adapted to the rough terrain of their native country. As early as the reign of James V, droves of these beasts were driven from Crown lands in Argyll to Stirling Castle by way of rent in kind. By the time of the civil war between the supporters of the Regent and those of Queen Mary, the Keepers of Dumbarton Castle were imposing duty on Argyll cattle which passed by the Rock on their way to Glasgow. Lord Fleming, however, had his own beasts. In the Forest of Cumbernauld, his ancestral lands, his stockmen nurtured a breed of pure white cattle which were (he claimed) unique in the British Isles. As a consequence of the insult to Sir William Drury, punitive raids were carried out in which these cherished beasts were slaughtered.

*　　　　*　　　　*

In August a ship arrived from France carrying ammunition for the garrison of Dumbarton Castle... but no soldiers. The following month saw the return of the envoy Verac. His vessel brought much appreciated supplies of bread and fruit... but no soldiers. That month a disappointed and frustrated Lord Fleming finally, and with a mixture of reluctance and relief, agreed to the six month truce.

*　　　　*　　　　*

Thank God for the truce. Without it, Fleming literally shuddered to think of what the winter months would have been like if they'd not been able to bring fuel into the castle. It had surely been bitter enough. Without fire it would have been simply unbearable. It was as well the enemy hadn't thought of that. As it was, it had been murderously difficult to maintain morale. Constant assurances that a French or Spanish fleet was just a few days away had begun to wear thin with the men. The drift back to the town's drinking dens had been impossible to check. That very morning, indeed, the desertion of one of the archers had been reported, one of the Highlanders. Anyway, it was now March of 1571. The Keeper of the castle sat in a locked chamber almost stifling with the blaze of a log fire. Velvet cap and fur-trimmed robe were cast aside. Seated with Lord Fleming around a cluttered table in that cramped little room were the Archbishop, John Fleming of Boghall, a kinsman of the Keeper, and an Englishman, John Hall.

The man Hall was a singular individual. He hailed from Warwickshire and had been a clerk for the Earl of Shrewsbury, Mary's gaoler. He had been the unlikely ringleader of a plot to effect the Scots queen's escape. The idea had been to somehow remove Mary from Chatsworth House and get her to the Isle of Man by way of Liverpool. Where she would go after that had not quite been worked out. The whole ill-considered scheme had fallen apart and the plotters fled… Hall to Dumbarton. He had certainly, if less than competently, proven his loyalty to Mary and was thus a trusted member of Lord Fleming's immediate company.

In the flickering light from the log-fire, the Keeper examined the faces of each man. Hamilton looked decidedly smug. Fleming of Boghall and the Englishman bore expressions of mystified anticipation. From the jumble of rolled parchments Lord Fleming picked out a particular document, and, with a triumphant air, he wagged it under the noses of his associates before handing it to John Hamilton.

"Gentlemen, I think it would be most fitting if my Lord Archbishop were to acquaint you with the content of this communication."

The churchman tried hard to conceal his glee with a look of ecclesiastic gravity.

"Friends… Her Grace is well served by loyal servants and supporters here in Scotland, in England and in the courts of Europe…"

In fact, Mary had several significant players on the chessboard of European politics. There was, for example, John Leslie, Bishop of Ross. This was the man who had counselled Mary, on her return from France, to overthrow the Scottish Reformation with the backing of the Catholic Highland clans. He was now, as a Commissioner at the "conference" called by Elizabeth, attempting to prove the Scots queen's innocence in the murder of her husband. He was also a prime mover in the ambitious venture of the Florentine banker, Ridolfi. But the Archbishop was speaking of his own nephew. Lord Claude Hamilton was the second son of Chatelherault, the Earl of Arran. Now in his early thirties, having as a younger man been in clerical orders, favoured by the Pope with the revenues of Paisley Abbey and later appointed Dean of the Ecclesiastical College at Dunbar, he had played a bold part in Mary's escape from Lochleven Castle. After the defeat at Langside he had accompanied his queen on her flight into England and now, it appeared, was serving her in a diplomatic capacity.

The Archbishop looked up from under dark eyebrows.

"…This report is from my kinsman, Lord Claude. On behalf of Her Grace, he has been in negotiation with the Duke of Alva, who, as you know, is presently in Flanders leading the armies of Philip of Spain. It would appear that an agent of His Holiness the

Pope, a certain Florentine financier by the name of... Ridolfi, has taken letters from Her Grace to His Holiness, to Alva and to Philip. In these letters Her Grace has requested that the Duke invade the British Isles with a Spanish army which would place her on the thrones of England and Scotland. For her part, Her Grace would ensure that both realms would be restored to the true Catholic Faith."

Fleming of Boghall listened politely. He had heard this sort of talk before. The Englishman, Hall, was agog... Hamilton's thin lips pursed as he savoured his next words.

"My friends... I can tell you that His Holiness, King Philip and the Duke have each expressed their favour for this... enterprise."

He looked steadily into the eyes of his listeners. Wind gusted against the castle's walls and the log-fire flickered wildly.

"Even as I speak, an army of invasion is being prepared in Flanders. I need not tell you that it is impossible to overestimate the importance of Dumbarton Castle as a point of entry for this expedition."

He held them now in the palm of his hand.

Chapter Ten
Prayer and Proposition

In six hours of darkness and extremely uncomfortable solitude, Duncan Robertson had an eternity in which to think about what he was doing and what he should be doing. An endless conflict of thoughts and emotions went round and round in his head. He should be with Margaret Lafferty. He didn't even know if she were still alive. She might have left this world as he had been tramping the miles from Dumbarton to this Drumquhassil. Had there been a particular moment... any special place... when he had felt any inward sense of her passing ? She might have breathed her last as he huddled in the freezing darkness of this horrid stone chamber.

There was a conflict between his wanting to anticipate her death, to try to begin the process of coming to terms with the devastation that such a reality would bring, or to cling desperately, pathetically to some frail hope that she might survive.

It was easier to be doing than to be waiting. At least it had been easier during the physical activity of walking. A kind of running away in one sense. He was essentially a man of action, but was the action part of the process of revenge for one living or for one no longer living ? And if, by some miracle, she were to live, did he have a future with her ? Were there any grounds for such hopes ? Had she given any real hint that she had feelings for him which might amount to a basis for a lasting romantic relationship... or more ? He was horrified and ashamed to discover that, even in such circumstances, he was irresistibly drawn to erotic thoughts about her. He found himself constantly trying to bring her face to his mind, yet he could do so only imperfectly. He couldn't capture that special something in her features, that expression of personality, of strength and beauty combined, which spoke directly to his heart and soul and made her uniquely wonderful – uniquely meant for him.

No... he must stop this. These dreams would make it all the more unendurable when he was confronted with the news of her death. In that cold, silent darkness it was impossible not to speculate about the nature of death. Not the actual process of dying which, of course, was different from individual to individual, from circumstance to circumstance, but the matter of the "hereafter". The awesome mystery which was so much the greatest ache of the human condition. The not knowing. The woman born blind trying to imagine the glories (and the horrors) of sight. The man born deaf seeking to comprehend the beauty (and the ugliness) of sound. Death – the unanswerable question regarding which the Church claimed to have the answers. The destinations of the soul of which the Church held the keys. Heaven and Hell.

Duncan shuddered. He could not bear to dwell on the possibility, however hopefully remote, of Margaret's soul suffering the never-ending agonies of Hell, or even the centuries of Purgatory.

Torments described only too vividly and horrifically by the Church.

He was eventually and mercifully released from these morbid introspections by the sound of raucous voices, the thump of booted feet upon flagstones, and the scrape of rusted metal bolts. He was at once assailed by a hideous shriek, as the dungeon door swung on its hinges, and by the blinding light which poured into his cell.

Two burly retainers strutted confidently toward him, grabbing him under the arms and hauling him without ceremony to his feet. Two equally beefy and belligerent henchmen stood just outside the cell. Duncan found himself being roughly manhandled up a spiralling flight of steps, emerging at length into the main hall of Drumquhassil tower-house. Other than being vaguely aware of a blazing fire and a long table cluttered with the remnants of a breakfast, Duncan took in little of his surroundings. His attention was arrested by two figures who stood in the centre of that stone chamber. Each had a loaded crossbow levelled at the prisoner's chest.

The tall, lean figure of John Cunninghame bore a lazily amused smirk on his wolfish face. Several paces to his right stood the other man whom Duncan felt he should know, but couldn't quite place. The Laird of Drumquhassil gesticulated briefly by wagging the crossbow so that two of his guards took up positions on either side of the door through which they had entered. The other pair stood a few yards on either side of Robertson, allowing a clear field of fire. Cunninghame spoke.

"I am, as I think you well know, Cunninghame o' Drumquhassil. This is Robert Douglas, a kinsman o' the Earl o' Lennox, Regent o' this realm."

Although the Cunninghames were a Lowland house, the accent was strangely Highland, perhaps because the estate here was located on the Highland Line close to clans such as the Buchanans and MacGregors. The speaker nodded in the direction of the table, where there lay, among the platters and goblets, Duncan's bow, quiver and dirk.

"You are an archer from Fleming's garrison at Dumbarton Castle…"
The laird's head wagged in the direction of the man Douglas.

"Robert thinks you came here to kill me. What say you to that ?"

Duncan remembered now where he had seen this Douglas. He had been one of Cunninghame's entourage at the Collegiate Church. He'd clearly made inquiries about the bowman who'd been in conversation with Canon Carmichael. He was a dark, heavy man, probably, Duncan guessed, of early middle years. Whereas Cunninghame, the treasurer, wore clothes appropriate to hunting, and no visible trappings of high office, Douglas was colourfully attired in courtly garb. The Highlander answered the laird's question.

"Far from coming here to kill you or any other – and in spite of the rudeness of your hospitality – I come bearing a gift."

Duncan spoke with a proud defiance which he did not feel. He knew that one ill-chosen word could bring about his immediate death. These men were answerable to no one, and there was, after all, a state of civil war, truce or none.

The Douglas snorted loudly. The guards shuffled impatiently. Cunninghame's eyebrows raised questioningly. The slack mouth sneered.

"A gift ? And just where are you hiding this gift ? You were closely searched last night, I'm assured. There was not a thing o' value on your person... unless we count your weapons. No, man, you'll have to do better than that to save your hide. First, tell me... exactly who are you ?"

"I am Duncan Robertson from Glen Finlas. By rights I should have served with Colquhoun of Luss in the army of the Regent, but... circumstances took me to Dumbarton Castle and Lord Fleming instead."

Robert Douglas hooted.

"Colquhoun of Luss... that reluctant convert."

Cunninghame strode across the hall several paces toward Duncan.

"I care not a snap o' the fingers who your brothers fought with. 'Circumstances'... Merciful Jesus, you are guilty o' treason... you and every traitor in every nook and cranny o' Dumbarton Rock... treason against your rightful king – James the Sixth o' Scots! For that alone you should be shot this instant and flung in the Endrick and that would be a fitting end to you."

Some of the sleepy insolence had given way to what seemed to be genuine indignation. The wolf was angry. He glanced meaningfully toward Douglas and raised the crossbow in his own hands.

"So... Robertson. You have five seconds in which to say something which will save your life... One..."

Duncan was drenched in sweat. His bowels churned as he tried to anticipate the feeling of two crossbow bolts entering his stomach. He looked Cunninghame straight in the eye.

"I can give you Dumbarton Castle."

*　　　*　　　*

This morning it was Virgil, and Jocky o' the Slates was footering with what appeared to be a loose tooth.

"By destiny compelled, and in despair, the Greeks grew weary of the tedious war..."

Through the school-room window he could see the distant stretch of the Ochil Hills, but George Buchanan's mental eye was focussed on the Plains of Troy. As ever, he addressed his little class as though he were talking to an adult audience.

"Noo, ye'll mind that ane o' the purposes o' the Aeneid was to demonstrate that Rome had been founded by a Trojan... Aeneas having been a member o' the royal house o' Troy."

He pierced Jocky with a glare and the amateur dental examination at once ceased.

"It's a' doon tae Homer and Greek mythology. So... we hae seen that Aeneas has been cast upon the African coast. He's enjoyin' the hospitality and the... attention... o' Dido, the Queen o' Carthage, and at yon banquet, ye recall, he's gi'en an account o' the fall o' Troy."

The old master was continuing his theme of combining the literary with the military. Young King James seemed to be able to cope with the concept of warfare more readily if it were presented to him within a poetic context. This tale held him fascinated. The large, brown eyes glowed. The lips were licked as he listened. Buchanan struck a pose and continued.

"Here is a maist revealing choice o' words. Virgil speaks o' the Greeks being opposed by the Fates – yon's a better translation. Ye see, the Fates would determine the destiny o' a man, or a city, or a state. An' this brings us back tae the inescapable paradox o' predestination versus free will."

As always, he realised only belatedly the hopelessness of developing this line of thought. Pursing his lips and rubbing his claw-like old hands, he pressed on, raising his voice over a fearful racket of the King's Guard drilling on the Outer Close.

"Aye... well. Noo, whit follows is a fine example o' wits succeeding whaur brute strength and force o' numbers hae failed. The Trojans hae thir doubts. Thir wiser heids warn them tae expect deception. But then appears just ane Greek – Sinon. He is able tae persuade the Trojans tae tak the Horse within thae walls... walls which hae withstood the Greek army a' this time. An' Sinon is able tae release the secret band o' Greek soldiers fae the belly o' the Horse... In sic way Troy is taken."

Buchanan exchanged a look with little James. The master's features were arranged in as near an approximation of mischievous humour as was possible. The comparison was far from exact, of course, but the similarity between the capture of Troy and the events Buchanan had himself set in motion afforded him a certain amusement.

"Ye must understand the significance o' the Horse. Ye see, the Horse was the symbol o' the city o' Troy. This is what gi'ed it special meaning tae them. It was like their heraldic badge. Certain folk and places tak emblems fae beasts. His young Grace wha sits amang us, he is known by the Lion o' Scots. The city o' Rome micht be said tae have been represented by the She-wolf that suckled Romulus and Remus."

Again the knowing smirk.

"An' closer tae hame, we hae the likes o' the Elephant... symbol o' Dumbarton."

                    *   *   *

Robert Douglas looked frankly and offensively disbelieving. Cunninghame of Drumquhassil narrowed his eyes, broke into a lopsided grin, and drawled sleepily,

"You will give me Dumbarton Castle ? Sure, Dumbarton Castle belongs to my king. Make yourself clear, man."

The crossbow was still levelled at Duncan's solar plexus.

"I can lead a body of men into the fortress... by stealth. They could overwhelm the guard... capture the castle."

The richly-clad Douglas looked perplexed. John Cunninghame whistled soundlessly and followed the progress of a wood louse along the edge of the breakfast table. He handed his crossbow to one of the guards and folded his arms across his chest, one palm gripping each shoulder.

"Dumbarton Rock is impregnable. The Earl o' Moray tried for months to break it down or starve the garrison out. The present Regent has failed again and again to enter that castle. What, in the name o' Jesus, d' ye mean – you can lead men into it ?"

Duncan experienced a rush of exhilaration, instinctively realising that his life was saved.

"I have lived among mountains all of my days. I know rocks. How to climb them. I have an eye for the right places for hands and feet. I tell you, over these long months I have studied every lump and bump and crack and tuft of the Rock, and I know a sure way over the wall. I know exactly how it is guarded, where there are strengths and weaknesses. Believe me, I could get your men in there just as easily as you could mount a horse."

In his sudden burst of confidence he was exaggerating outrageously, but his words were certainly making an impression on his listeners.

"Supposing you could do this... why would you do it? One o' Fleming's rebels, long-committed to treason, what brings you to me with this... offer?"

To Cunninghame's evident irritation, Douglas butted in.

"A right loyal house, these Robertsons of Finlas Glen, I'm thinking. Some brothers fighting for the king, another in the service of the murderess, Mary, now turning his coat..."

Cunninghame silenced him with an impatient gesture.

"Let him speak, man..."

This was a critical moment. Duncan had given most of his thought to the question of how he could best convince Cunninghame that he could gain entry to the castle, not why he should seek to do so. He had an instinctive, almost superstitious, desire to leave any mention of Margaret out of this. Quickly reasoning that Canon Carmichael, who must have considered Douglas very much a religious and political foe, would have imparted the barest minimum of information to him, Duncan hoped that they would know nothing of Margaret or his own interest in her. He was by nature an honest man and unskilled in dissembling, so very much without premeditation, he blurted out a version of the truth.

"I... bear a grudge. I seek revenge against Lord Fleming. He had my wife whipped. She was accused of theft. Accused falsely... I would have him pay dearly for it. This is my way..."

He could have bitten out his tongue. What a stupid thing to say.

"Falsely... hmm ?"

Robert Douglas was not endearing himself to Duncan Robertson.

"Falsely, unjustly, spitefully!" The Highlander replied angrily.

Cunninghame was eyeing Duncan shrewdly, searchingly. The Laird of Drumquhassil had not been slow to realise the incalculable potential if the archer was sincere and could fulfil his boast. Also he was thinking of how few weeks there were until the truce was over. Duncan's stomach rumbled noisily.

"Forgive me my base suspicions, Robertson. A man comes armed and under cover o' darkness to my modest home here in such unsettled times as these. Is it so ill o' a careful man to take precautions ?"

The insolent smile reached the eyes this time. The laird's open hands were spread before him in a gesture which appeared to indicate that he intended no harm. He let out a roar for servants, which took Duncan quite by surprise and, to his great embarrassment, caused him to flinch visibly. Instructions were given to provide the "guest" with more appropriate – but still secure – accommodation and a suitable breakfast. Shortly thereafter, Duncan found himself in a small, locked, but comfortable chamber. As he sipped weak beer and devoured bread, cheese and cold meat, he peered through the narrow, barred window. In the distance heavy rain-cloud kissed the distinctive contours of Dumgoyne Hill as it towered over the birthplace of George Buchanan.

*   *   *

Canon Carmichael had prayed himself empty. He felt a great, silent numbness. The silence of God. All through that long night the young priest had implored the Almighty to spare the life of Margaret Lafferty. He had uttered a seemingly endless river of spoken words which had trickled into incoherent mumbles, then into soundless pleas, until words and mental images lost meaning to him. The very concepts of intercession and healing became strangers to his understanding. Now, as he sat at the foot of her cot, staring vacantly at the crucifix which bruised his hand, he became aware of a terrible physical thirst. Painfully, stiffly, he rose to his feet. The slight sound of his movement through the sick-room was enough to disturb one or two of the fitfully sleeping patients. They moaned weakly and stirred uneasily. But Margaret Lafferty was still.

In the cold dawn light, the priest drank deep from the well in Saint Mary's orchard. The water chilled his stomach, but the quenching of the drouth revived his mental processes to the point that he began to torment himself by questioning the efficacy of prayer – the old, old question of how the desire of man could possibly change the Will of God. Why did he answer some prayers and not others ? Why did he grant healing for some and not for others ? Why did he permit the innocent to suffer ? Was he listening ? Did he care ? All questions which men and women had asked since the beginning of time. All questions for which the Church had clever answers. The young priest knew them – he knew them by heart. But they did not satisfy him. They were unconvincing and he wrestled with a spirit of rebellion. Yet he lived with the trick which had been mastered by most of the clergy – private doubt and public certainty.

His mood was matched by a bleak, grey sky and the cold, damp air. Sounds of the beginning of another working day reached him from the High Street and the various vennels: hammering, raised voices, a crying child. He could smell wood-smoke and the salt water of the two rivers. Just as it occurred to him that he should do a round of his other patients, Canon Carmichael noticed Brother Andrew walking towards him through the leafless trees. Given the nature of his faithless musings, the young priest felt a pang of guilt at the approach of his spiritual superior. At first he thought the older man had read his thoughts.

"We do well, Canon Carmichael, to turn to the Fathers of the Church. Not just for spiritual comfort, but in practical things also."

In Brother Andrew's eyes there was the warmth of a sad smile. From somewhere within the folds of his habit he handed a scrap of folded paper to the younger man.

"This comes to us from Saint Ambrose… or perhaps from God."

As the canon unfolded the note and began to read he wondered what on earth bees, of all things, might have to do with his present predicament, as he read on, though, his dark eyebrows were raised in surprise, and he looked in the direction of the hospital building with just the faintest spark of hope.

*   *   *

The two riders drew rein on the eastern bank of the meandering River Endrick at a spot just opposite the old moat of Catter. The sight of the ancient gallows-hill of the Earls of Lennox struck the right note of gravity. Half-way between Drumquhassil and the village of Drymen, the pair had come to discuss the man Robertson's proposition in some privacy.

"Don't you think it could be some sort of trap ?"

Douglas was almost petulant.

"Obviously that was my first thought, but I don't really see how. These rebels are locked up in Dumbarton Rock... or they will be again, as soon as the truce ends. They can hardly arrange an ambush."

"But, what do we know about Robertson ? I think we should find out a bit more about him before we swallow his story. It doesn't seem a very likely tale to me."

There was a gleam in Cunninghame's eye. He could see the enormous significance of the capture of Dumbarton Castle. Further, he could see great personal benefits arising from it.

"Look, Robert. Take the Rock, and the realm is secure. The Reformation is secure. Wee King Jamie is secure... and you and I are favoured men. Already we have been granted gifts o' the Crown, through the Regent. If we seize this opportunity wi' both hands, man, there's no telling what would come our way in royal gratitude. Hesitate or fail and there's no telling how Scotland will end up – back under the Papacy wi' Frenchies ruling the roost again."

Passion had brought colour to Cunninghame's face, but Douglas twisted his own features into an expression of scepticism.

"If it's not the French ruling the roost in Scotland, it's sure to be the English. Kinsman or no, I can see fine well that our Regent is but a tool of the English..."

Cunninghame cut him off savagely.

"Better it should be the Protestant English than the Papist French, man. Can ye no' see it ? One day oor Jamie could be King o' England. Then think o' what such as you and I could be."

Robert Douglas hawked and spat in the direction of the fast-flowing Endrick.

"There are over many 'ifs' and 'buts' in this for my liking, John. There is something false about Robertson. I feel it in my bones. No, I don't trust the man. Something about this stinks. We should at least make some sort of inquiries about him. We could send a messenger to Colquhoun of Luss. He should know something of him... I could go back to Dumbarton and..."

Cunninghame waved a gauntlet in a gesture of frustration.

"Christ's bowels. We have nae time for 'investigation'. The truce ends in three weeks. If we are tae gain full advantage it would be well tae act immediately thereafter. Anyway, what harm can one closely guarded, unarmed man do ? Your fears mystify me. What have we to lose, man ?"

The sweet notes from a single piper in Drymen drifted on the wind, but neither man heard them.

"The harm is in what he might lure us into…"

The Laird of Drumquassil had heard enough. In disgust he reined his horse around. He shouted back over his shoulder.
"You've become too soft, in your silks and lace. You sound like a feart auld wife."

Leaving a mortified Douglas, the laird spurred away. He would have an escort saddle-up, and he would take the man Robertson to the Regent in Glasgow this very day.

Chapter Eleven
Bread and Bullets

John Knox was "half dead". These were his own words. He had signed a letter to Cecil, Elizabeth's Secretary of State, – "John Knox, with his one foot in the grave."

*   *   *

He had been a Catholic priest. He had trained in Theology as a student in St. Salvator's College at the University of St. Andrews. There he had been exposed to the Protestant ideas which had flourished since the martyrdom of Patrick Hamilton in 1528. But Knox, in his student days, had remained loyal to the Church of Rome. On attaining his degree, because there were no vacancies for parish priests he had become a "notary apostolic", which was to say – a Church lawyer. Like so many folk, Knox was disturbed by the nature and extent of the corruption which he saw in the Roman Catholic Church in his native land. Gradually, after conscientious Bible study and listening to travelling Protestant preachers, at around the age of thirty, John Knox embraced the Reformation. One of his major influences was George Wishart. So impressed had Knox been with Wishart that he had volunteered to be the preacher's bodyguard, famously carrying a two-handed sword in that capacity.

One afternoon in January of 1546, after preaching in Knox's hometown of Haddington, Wishart sent the bodyguard away. Around midnight the preacher was arrested by the Earl of Bothwell. At length the prisoner was handed over to Cardinal Beaton at St. Andrews. A Church court found the defendant guilty of heresy. Beaton watched from a window as George Wishart was burned at the stake.

That May a group of Fife Protestants avenged Wishart by butchering Cardinal Beaton in his castle.

Beaton's murderers found themselves trapped within the walls of St. Andrews Castle. An army obedient to Lord Governor Arran and Marie de Guise besieged the fortress, but the so-called "Castilians" within were joined by some hundred and twenty Protestant supporters. These included John Knox. It was at this time and in these circumstances that he embarked on his career as a preacher. For over a year the Castilians held St. Andrew's Castle, confident that a Protestant English fleet would come to their rescue. In the event, the ships which came were Catholic French. The Castilians had little option but to surrender. Taken prisoner, Knox and most of his fellow Protestants were made to serve as slaves on French galleys. After a year and a half of this brutal treatment, the preacher's health had broken down and he was released. In Scotland Knox would have been a marked man, so he made for London. The Church of England was crying out for competent Protestant preachers, and the Scot was swiftly appointed to the ministry of St. Mary's Parish Church in Berwick-upon-Tweed. In 1551 Knox moved to Newcastle, and in the following year he was invited to become a Church of England bishop. He declined.

When the Roman Catholic Queen Mary I of England came to the throne in 1553, she initiated a period of religious persecution during which hundreds of Protestants were forced to flee the country and around two hundred and eighty were burned at the stake. Knox went first to Dieppe, and from there to Geneva, where he was greatly influenced by Calvin, author of "The Institutes of the Christian Religion", and one of the great leaders of the Reformation. It was in Geneva that the Scots preacher encountered Presbyterianism at first hand. In 1554 Knox was called to serve an exile English congregation in Frankfurt. He ministered to them for a number of months but was dismissed because of a typically Protestant quarrel over the Prayer Book and the form of service. He then hazarded a visit to Scotland in the following year and was there charged with heresy, being summoned to appear before John Hamilton, Archbishop of St. Andrews. However, the then Regent, Marie de Guise, aware of the increasing strength of Protestant opinion and fearing that the arrest of John Knox would provoke civil disorder, advised Hamilton to withdraw the charge. The reformer responded by taking the opportunity to preach publicly in the capital.

He was soon back in Geneva, writing revolutionary pamphlets which incited nobles and common folk alike to rise up and depose wicked and idolatrous rulers. These were sentiments which, though they were a reaction to the martyrdom of so many of Knox's co-religionists, were rejected by many Protestants, including Calvin. In November of 1558 "Bloody Mary" died and the Protestant Elizabeth I was crowned Queen of England. She was, however, no friend of Knox, being infuriated by his revolutionary writings. In Scotland at this time the Reformation impulse was gathering strength. Marie de Guise was increasingly unpopular since her daughter, the Princess Mary, had been married off to the French Dauphin. Walter Myln, a priest turned Protestant, was burned for heresy. Angry mobs were beginning to vandalize Church property and destroy religious images. It was in this extremely volatile situation that Reformation leaders asked Knox to return to Scotland.

He arrived at Leith in the month of May, on the very day that Marie de Guise summoned Protestant preachers to Stirling to give an account of themselves. Naturally, there were fears for their fate. Knox preached thunderously, from the pulpit of St. John's Kirk in Perth, as usual condemning idolatry – a term which seemed to include the veneration of images, the Pope, the Virgin Mary, the Mass and most Catholic ritual. Some time after the service an altercation between a priest and some Protestants proved the catalyst which set off mob destruction of the holy statues of St. John's Kirk and the general looting of the Grey and Black Friaries of Perth. Knox denounced this behaviour as being the work of "the rascal multitude", but his theoretical revolution was becoming a reality. Revolution brought out ugly elements of human nature, but for those at the bottom of the social scale it was an irresistible temptation, when circumstances afforded them an opportunity, to drag down clergy who had long lorded over them, abusing spiritual power with threats of hellfire and hypocritically living in relative luxury at the expense of the poor. Nevertheless, the widespread and routine destruction of religious architecture and art became a deplorable aspect of the

Reformation which was clearly beyond the control of responsible leadership. A grave embarrassment, to say the least.

There was an armed stand-off between a Franco-Scottish army led, for Marie de Guise, by the Duke of Chatelherault on the one side, and the supporters of the Reformation on the other. It ended in a stalemate. The Congregation – as the reformers called themselves – arranged a great meeting for the eleventh of June in St. Andrews. The Archbishop, Hamilton, was mortified and led an army to the burgh with the stated purpose of capturing Knox dead or alive. The great orator, though, had during his time as a galley-slave sustained himself with the dream that one day he would return and preach again in St. Andrews. He did so with impunity and the Congregation went on to capture Stirling and Edinburgh.

In July the armies faced each other again at Leith, outside the capital. In a negotiated settlement Marie de Guise agreed to freedom of religion and the Congregation agreed to hand over Edinburgh and accept her authority. Each side was playing for time. The Regent was awaiting French help, and the Protestants were hoping for English help.
In August Henri II died. Francois and Mary were now king and queen of France. The chances of French aid for Mary's mother increased significantly, to the horror of the English, and the Duke of Chatelherault was induced to defect to the Congregation. The Scots Reformation leadership met in Stirling in October and it was decided to depose Marie de Guise. At a further assembly in Edinburgh her suspension as Regent was officially announced. Scotland was now effectively governed by a council of the Congregation. Yet there was a moment when it looked as though

the Scottish Reformation would fail. Early in November of 1559 its self-seeking lords were squabbling. The rank and file were losing heart and drifting away. The Congregation abandoned Edinburgh, allowing Marie de Guise and her French soldiers to retake the capital.

John Knox turned the tide. From the pulpit of Stirling's Kirk of the Holy Rude, he preached a sermon so powerfully inspiring that the chastened leadership pulled themselves together, rediscovered common purpose and sent that wise serpent, Maitland of Lethington, to the court of Queen Elizabeth. The result was that in the first month of 1560 an English fleet sailed into the Firth of Forth. The following month the Treaty of Berwick was signed, effectively putting an end to Scotland's "Auld Alliance" with the French and introducing a new relationship with England which, though now preferable, would never be an equal partnership. Conflict ensued between English and French armies on Scottish soil. Marie de Guise died of heart disease on the eleventh of June, respectfully attended by Lord James Stewart and the Earl of Argyll, prominent leaders of the Congregation. Negotiation followed, which led to the Treaty of Edinburgh, according to the terms of which French and English soldiers would leave Scotland, the Scots would accept the sovereignty of Mary and Francois, but religion would be a matter for the Scots Parliament. On the tenth of July the Parliament assembled in Edinburgh. It enacted the legislation which effectively made Scotland Protestant. The nation would no longer acknowledge papal authority and the saying of the Mass would be illegal. The Scottish Confession of Faith was presented to, and approved by, the Parliament. This document set out the essentials of the Kirk's understanding of Christianity. It had been written by a committee of six ministers which included

John Knox. The same men wrote the First Book of Discipline, which was effectively the rule-book of how the Kirk was to be run. Ministers would be elected by congregations. The Superintendents, who were to run the nation's ten dioceses, were to be elected by ministers and elders. The ministers would be assisted by elected deacons and elders. Poor relief was to be provided by the Kirk. The reformers wanted every believer to be able to read the Bible. Accordingly it was the intention, or at least the hope, of the Kirk to ensure that all children received a basic education. But that was easier said than done... Also the range of subjects studied at Scots universities was to be significantly extended. The first General Assembly of the Church of Scotland was held that December, the month in which young Francois II died suddenly, leaving Mary Queen of Scots no longer Mary Queen of France.

The leaders of the Congregation asked her to come home to Scotland. Perhaps surprisingly, given the circumstances, they retained a certain loyalty to their young Catholic queen. She returned to the land of her birth on the nineteenth of August 1561. The citizens of Edinburgh welcomed her with the singing of psalms. Mary insisted on having her own private Mass, though it was now against the law. Although she agreed, for the time being, to accept the religious status quo, the great Protestant fear was that she would sooner or later, by one means or another, return Scotland to the bondage of Rome. It would have been entirely natural for Mary to have wished to bring her realm back into the fold of the "true kirk of God", as she believed. Indeed, she would have regarded it as her Christian duty. A confrontation between the queen and John Knox was inevitable. It was necessary. Mary herself initiated it. She summoned him to appear before her in the Palace of Holyroodhouse. There she accused him of, among other things, necromancy. The essence, however, of what separated these two was reached when Knox maintained that she had been raised on the false doctrine of the Catholic Church, and Mary asked –

"Ye interpret the scriptures in one manner and they interpret it in another. Whom shall I believe ?"

An eminently reasonable question.

Knox answered that she should believe the word of God. Which many would consider to be no answer at all.

Many Scots of all classes entertained the hope that Mary would eventually be persuaded to embrace the Protestant Faith. Knox never believed it for one moment. He distrusted her profoundly, convinced that given the chance she would become another "Bloody Mary". He preached against her uncompromisingly throughout her reign. He caused great offence, not just to the queen herself, but to many Protestants, with his repeated insistence that it was the right and the duty of subjects to depose a monarch who was ruling wickedly. This was really a very similar position to the one taken some two hundred and forty years earlier in the Declaration of Arbroath, which asserted the right of the Scots to get rid of any king who failed to defend national independence, but here the context was religious rather than patriotic.

After the murder of King Henry, when Mary was a prisoner in Lochleven and her personal rule had become a shambles, John Knox preached from the pulpit of Stirling's Kirk of the Holy

Rude on the occasion of the Coronation of her son, the little Prince James. The preacher – unlike George Buchanan – could not have envisaged the enormous eventual significance of the event.

*   *   *

Like the earl of Lennox, the leader of the Scottish Reformation was now in his mid-fifties, which was considered old at that time. He had suffered a stroke, which had rendered him speechless, a circumstance naturally interpreted by Catholics as God's judgement on the wickedness of the reformer's utterances. His silence proved, however, to be temporary. He climbed back into the pulpit of Edinburgh's St. Giles Cathedral and cried out for the death of Mary Queen of Scots.

Now, towards the end of March 1571, a General Assembly of the Church of Scotland had just been held. There were many in the Kirk who strongly disapproved of Knox's extreme bitterness toward Mary, and protests against this element of his preaching were nailed to the door of the cathedral. In a written response Knox stated that she was "...an obstinate idolatress, one that consented to the murder of her own husband, and one that has committed whoredom and villainous adultery." Two men who wholeheartedly agreed with this judgement were George Buchanan, King's Tutor, and Matthew Stuart, Regent of Scotland. But Knox – with his memory of the French fleet which had captured St. Andrews Castle and delivered him into bondage – perhaps more acutely than any of the leadership of the King's Party, remained gravely concerned about the possibility of a Catholic invasion which would, as he wrote "...restore Satan to his kingdom in the person of his dearest lieutenant." Knox had been fully informed of the French supplies which had reached Dumbarton Rock just a few months earlier. His secretary had referred to the envoy, Verac, as "a notabill pyrate", and had recorded the very details of the cargo: "some oranges, some reasins, some bisqueat bread, some powder, some bullet…"

*   *   *

On the long, undignified miles from Drumquhassil to Glasgow, Duncan Robertson brooded resentfully on the fact that, although he was the willing donor of a gift, the value of which was beyond calculation to the leaders of the King's Party, he was being treated with all the gratitude accorded to a common criminal. He was securely bound on horseback and closely hemmed in among Cunninghame's usual escort of a dozen riders. With the weather typically changeable for the season, alternating between drenching squalls and spells of almost exhilarating sunshine and blue skies, they galloped at a steady pace south-eastward through Strathblane, stretching between the towering Campsie Fells on the one side and Kilpatrick Hills on the other. Past Dumgoyne and through the little community of Strathblane itself, they rode on, pennons of Cunninghame black and white fluttering brightly in the fresh breeze, through Mugdock, Baldernock, Bardowie, then southward over the old Roman Wall down towards the town of Glasgow itself. Duncan found himself impressed by the fine horsemanship and discipline of the escort.

No matter how often he had experienced it, and even after these long months on Dumbarton Rock, Duncan, being a Highlander, was always almost shocked by the way in which the hill country suddenly opened out to the far horizons of the flat Lowlands. Although daylight began to fade, the towers of Glasgow Cathedral were visible to the riders for several miles. Logically, the Bishop's Castle was located a stone's throw from the great Gothic edifice of St. Mungo's, built, according to tradition, where the saint had founded his church a thousand years earlier. The town was, to all intents and purposes, really a very long High Street which ran from the cathedral more or less parallel with the Molendinar Burn, down to the River Clyde. They rode in by the heavily-guarded Kirk Port. Cunninghame and his colours being well-kent, they were not challenged but admitted by the gate-house. The escort led their mounts to the bishop's stables while Cunninghame, a still-bound Duncan, and four guards were ushered into the so-called "Bishop's Palace" of the central keep.

Duncan was no connoisseur of palace, or even castle, architecture, but he registered the fact that here was a chamber somewhat larger and more richly adorned than any in Dumbarton Castle or Drumquhassil. The detail of his surroundings were neither here nor there, because his attention was taken up almost exclusively by the personalities present. By the doorway there stood two pike-bearing guards wearing the royal livery. At either side of a huge fireplace which contained a crackling blaze sat two men who seemed elderly to Duncan's young eye. Standing around the room were a handful of what appeared to be officials and secretaries. Cunninghame's guards were dismissed and the Laird was announced.

"John Cunninghame of Drumquassil, my Lord, Collector-General... and... another."

The functionary eyed Duncan's rope-bound wrists askance and faltered somewhat. Cunninghame took over. He was not a man to whom deference came easily. Even so, he was addressing the king's grandfather, present ruler of Scotland, and – more to the point – his own recent and very generous benefactor. His attempt, however, to school both voice and features to an attitude of respectful humility had but indifferent success. His sideways grin and lazy drawl were too much a part of his nature to be dissolved at will.

"My Lord Regent, allow me to introduce Duncan Robertson from Glen Finlas. Archer... until recently... he tells me, in the company o' Lord Fleming."

This had been accompanied by a curt nod of the head which passed for a bow. Cunninghame, as ever, got straight to the point.

"He assures me he can lead a body o' men intae Dumbarton Castle."

The effect of these words on the Regent was remarkable. He spun around in his finely-carved chair and looked at his fireside companion with something close to superstitious awe.

"How, in the name of God, could you have known... ?"

The grey-bearded man in the black cowl waved a hand and tutted in irritation. It was essential that George Buchanan rationalise this development as much as possible from the outset. His actual modus operandi was liable to be misinterpreted. Witchcraft, as it would in all probability be regarded, was a capital offence.

"Och, Man… Lord Regent… when any sma' body o' men has been cooped up thigither a' yon time, wae a' the rigours o' siege an' winter, tae say nought o' sheer boredom… Man, they grow right sick o' the sight o' ane anither. There are a' manner o' tensions an' offence ta'en ower the sightest wee thing. Aye, mountains made oot o' molehills ye may say. It was only a matter o' time afore wan o' them broke ranks. Och there's nae great wisdom tae it."

The Regent would have given the matter rather more thought, and the Tutor a more rigorous interrogation, had he not been agog to hear precisely how this man who now stood before him intended to go about the business of opening up Dumbarton Castle to him. However, before he could level any questions at the prisoner, Buchanan forcefully interrupted.

"Na, na, na… we cannae hae the man bound like yon. No' like some felon, an' no led tae us like a dancin' bear…"

Duncan was struck by the fact that the elderly speaker was looking at him with something strangely akin to recognition.

"As Drumquhassil says, this man hauds the keys tae the kingdom."
Drumquhassil had said nothing of the sort and was about to underline the fact, when the Tutor waved him silent and called over one of the guards.

"Hae yir dagger oot, Man, an' cut thae ropes awa'."

The guard looked uncomfortably at the Regent, who nodded impatiently. Actually, by his own standards, Matthew Stuart was in, not a cheerful, but a less depressed state of mind than had long ordinarily been the case. The knee, ravaged by gout, had remained swollen, inflamed and an infernal agony to bend, or upon which to put weight. Also to his horror and dread, he had begun to experience the first twinges of the same symptoms in the foot of the other leg. He had always feared that he would sooner or later be affected in both sides so that he would have been totally unable to move, except by being carried around on a chair. Mercifully, when he had awoken the previous day, the knee had significantly improved and the foot felt quite normal. Accordingly he now dared to hope that he would soon be free of pain and able to enjoy freedom of movement again. The effect of this, at least in the short term, had been a decided lift in his spirits.

Drumqhassil pushed the guard aside and began to untie the knots of Duncan's binding himself.

"There's nae cause tae spoil a guid bit o' rope."

Quite the prudent treasurer.

When Duncan had been released from bondage, the officials and secretaries were shooed out of the chamber with dire warnings ringing in their ears as to the extreme confidentiality of what they had just overheard. A bench was hauled over by the fire-place, and Duncan and Drumquhassil were invited to seat themselves alongside Regent and Tutor. The former spoke first.

"Now, Robertson, you really can do this ? You're quite sure of it ? Because I warn you, if you trifle with me, I'll have the head off your shoulders. I'll not be made a fool of."

Duncan took a long, steady look at the man who had been thought of for so long by his comrades-in-arms on the Rock as The Enemy. Old, tired, suspicious… and clearly not a man to be crossed.

"I know the Rock intimately, my Lord Regent. I know the garrison. The times and places when and where the guard is strong or weak. I can climb sure-footed as a deer. I can lead a party of your men – if they are men wisely chosen – over the wall and into the castle. It will be up to them after that."

Duncan glanced toward the other figure by the fire and was sure that he detected, somewhere in the grey beard and beady eyes, a wry smile of encouragement. The Regent pursed his lips, considered for a moment, then directed his next question to Drumquhassil.

"Is he a Papist ?"

A strange question from a man who had been a Catholic nearly all of his life and who, in his heart, still probably was.

"Oddly enough, my Lord, I hadna thought tae ask him."

Duncan, mortified by being spoken of as though he were absent, or a dog, was on the verge of blurting out an ill-considered answer when George Buchanan made a timely interjection.

"My Lord Regent kens right well that in the Highlands there are no' just the same clear-cut and theologically stark distinctions between Christ's Truth as preached by the Reformed Kirk and the misguided superstitions which hae been perpetuated by the old Kirk. Och, it'll tak a wheen o' years afore the licht o' true doctrine penetrates intae a' the glens. A' in God's guid time... Aye."

The Regent gave him a sour look, but decided to proceed to questioning which was closer to the point. Like Cunninghame and Douglas before him, Matthew Stuart knew that motive was the crucial issue here.

"Why ? What has made you come to me with this ? Why have you turned against your own side in such a way ?"

Duncan, of course, had known that he would be asked this again. He'd had time to consider his answer. He realised that he had to stick with his original – and almost true – story. Any backtracking or changing of his tale would certainly increase rather than lessen suspicion.

"Lord Fleming ordered my wife to be whipped, my Lord – unjustly for a crime which she had not committed. I am bound in honour to avenge her."

The Regent glanced at Drumquhassil then at Buchanan, trying to gauge any response in their features. Buchanan was nodding quiet acceptance. The tax collector's face was a blank of indifference.

"What was this crime of which your wife was unjustly accused ?"

"It was said that she had stolen a silver cross, my Lord."

"And she hadn't ?"
"She came upon it honestly. She found it while tending some roses, my Lord."

Strangely, it was this mention of roses which inclined the Earl of Lennox to instinctively feel that Duncan's story had the ring of truth.

"Where is your wife now ?"

Again, Duncan had anticipated this question, and he darkly suspected the reason for its asking. Of course, Margaret being his "wife", he actually could not have answered truthfully even had he wished. He knew not if she were alive or dead. Above the ground or below it. Silently he prayed for forgiveness and answered.

"She is unwell as a result of the whipping, my Lord, and being cared for by my family in Glen Finlas."

He realised that this was an answer fraught with danger. Some messenger might be sent to Glen Finlas to question his father. What sort of answer could he give ? He'd be totally bemused. Duncan's priority was to ensure that they didn't involve Margaret... if she were still alive. Of course, a few more enquiries at St. Mary's... He clung to the belief that the Regent would not want to waste time on what were largely irrelevancies. There would be no time and no very good reason for investigation. He'd want to capture the castle. Quickly.

The mention of Duncan's family brought something to the mind of Drumquhassil.

"Robertson tells us he has brothers that are wae Colquhoun's company, my Lord. Now, if your mind was running to thoughts o'... security, maybe it would be a simple matter to have the brothers held in custody, as it were, to just make quite sure there'd be no... breach o' faith, shall we say?"

Buchanan tut-tutted and bristled in an obvious display of disapproval. A burning log collapsed in the fire-place, embers glowing and a shower of sparks flying. Duncan held his tongue. He intended no "breach o' faith", so Will and Alasdair should come to no harm. In fact, if things turned out as Duncan intended, then all the Robertsons would be in good standing.

Matthew Stuart well knew how often in time of civil war brothers found themselves on opposing sides. As though reading the Highlander's thoughts, he spoke.

"You will be richly rewarded, if you do this thing successfully, man, Robertson."

The red glow from the fire reflected on the Regent's forehead and the long Stewart nose, adding drama to his intense features. It enhanced the richness of his royal purple robe. Gently he caressed the gold pendant which hung on a chain over his breastbone. A diabolical glint flashed in the dark brown eyes.

"Aye... that would fairly settle the bitch. There'd be no way back into Scotland for her then."

Buchanan allowed a slow smile to reach his lips. He knew that with those words the matter had been settled. But then he'd always known.

*   *   *

If there was consolation anywhere in the life of Matthew Stuart it was in the love of his wife. When their son Henry married Mary Queen of Scots, Elizabeth of England had been so furious that she imprisoned Margaret, Countess of Lennox, in the Tower of London. In an act of compassion, Elizabeth released the Countess after the murder of her son. Margaret was unable to join Matthew in Scotland, but she commissioned one of the finest jewellers in the land to create a magnificent gold locket elaborately decorated with an Indian emerald, Burmese rubies and enamel. Margaret was fifty-five years old and had been blessed with almost twenty-seven years of devoted marriage. She sent the heart-shaped locket to Matthew essentially as a token of her enduring love for him. The jewel was complex and had different levels of meaning. It was decorated with many symbols and bore several inscriptions in Scots. The ideas of Faith, Hope, Victory and Truth were symbolised. The various words and images, however, expressed two profound concepts – the love of Margaret and Matthew, and the heartfelt conviction that their grandson, James, would one day sit on the thrones of both Scotland and England, thus rewarding the couple's lifelong efforts with ultimate victory. The Regent wore the jewel on his breast constantly.

*   *   *

Servants entered the chamber bearing platters of steaming food, beakers of wine and large jugs of ale. Fresh logs were heaped on the fire. Minstrels were told that their services would not be required. It was a meal fit, appropriately enough, for a king. Duncan, now being treated with the courtesy due to an honoured guest, ate sensibly of salmon, bread and boiled eggs. He abstained from the wine, but thoroughly appreciated the ale, which was of superb quality. During the meal George Buchanan engaged Duncan in conversation. Having spent his childhood in Killearn and Flanders Moss, the King's Tutor was well acquainted with Loch Lomondside and this gave the pair a subject of mutual interest. Then they went on to discuss the relative merits and demerits of the bow and arrow as compared with the arquebus. The Laird of Drumquhassil lounged back, his legs stretched out as he gnawed the meat from a bone, looking more wolfish than ever, sharp eyes and keen ears taking in everything. At length, when they had eaten their fill and were contentedly sipping from their goblets, the Regent brought them back to the business in hand.

"So... we will act. You will be given your chance, Robertson. Now, the truce expires in... less than three weeks time. So we will aim to strike immediately thereafter."

He glared around the company defying contradiction. There was none.

"Now, numbers of men ? What say you ?"

Cunninghame spoke first.

"We have reckoned that Fleming has a garrison o' fifty men on the Rock."

He looked questioningly at Duncan.

"Three dozen. A dozen archers. A dozen hagbutters. The rest arquebusiers and officers."

The Regent shook his head and twisted his mouth wryly.

"Three dozen men... with the fate of a kingdom – maybe two kingdoms – in their hands."

Buchanan, striking one of his poses, was about to launch into a learned comparison from the history of the Greeks when Duncan made a contribution.

"The men... our men... must be of the best sort. Well disciplined, physically strong, able to move silently and invisibly..."

Cunninghame snorted sarcastically.
"Oh I like it – 'our men'. That didn't take ye long, Robertson. But ye don't ask much, dae ye ? Silent and invisible men ?"

Again the old master came to the archer's assistance.

"Ye ken fine well what's meant, Drumquhassil. Ye've stalked the deer oft enough yirsel'. Possessing the skills o' the stalker. That's what ye mean, is it no', Duncan ? Just that ?"

Duncan confirmed that this was the case. The Regent resumed command.

"Right. If they have three dozen, we'll want to outnumber that. More than thirty-six, but few enough to move silently and not attract attention to themselves."

Cunninghame spoke.

"Aye, well. It canna be much more anyway. Because we'll hae a job gettin' many men o' the quality ye require at sic short notice."

George Buchanan adopted an avuncular manner.

"A hunner men, nae less, will be needed. An' hae nae worries as tae whar they'll come fae. I hae a certain centurion in mind."

Matthew Stewart and John Cunninghame eyed him a little indignantly. The Regent leant back in his chair, put his right hand to his beard, considering, then said,

"Are we running ahead of ourselves ? Should there be a proper Council of War, involving the appropriate officers of King James's government ?"

"Tcha... there's nae time for that. Blethers an' argument. Anyway, the fewer folk who ken o' this, the better. That's the thing. Prepare swiftly and secretly."

All nodded agreement with the Tutor. Through the thick walls of the Bishop's Palace the bells of Glasgow Cathedral could be heard chiming in the night. The Earl of Lennox was rubbing his gold locket again. Drumquhassil was thinking of one of the serving women who had brought in the meal. Duncan was beginning to feel sleepy with the unaccustomed food and ale. It had been a long day. Buchanan continued.

"I can suggest just the very man to lead this expedition, my Lord Regent. An' he's no' sae very faur fae here..."

Chapter Twelve
The Bible and the Dagger

An atmosphere hung over the schoolroom. The Old Master was pointing to a chart which he'd hung from the wall. On the chart he'd sketched reasonable representations of a tree, a small bird, a bell and a fish with a ring in its mouth. In the Tutor's hand the wooden pointer looked for all the world like a magician's wand. He addressed his pupils with a stony expression.

"Noo… we spoke o' the Horse o' Troy an' the She-Wolf o' Rome… even oor ain Elephant o' Dumbarton. The thing is, behind the symbol there is often a story… a myth or legend o' some kind."

The pointer rapped insistently on the chart.

"This morn I'll be tellin' ye aboot the stories behind some symbols associated wae Glasgow… from which town I'm just returned. I hae tae start wae the legend o' Saint Mungo… or mair properly – Saint Kentigern. Noo, we hae tae be on oor guard here. The stories that are telt o' Kentigern cam tae us fae a monk ca'd Jocelyn. He was writin' in the twelfth century, a guid six hunner years efter the life o' the saint. Noo, Jocelyn claimed tae hae his knowledge fae an auld Gaelic manuscript, an' maybe he had, but we maun bear in mind that thae monks wrote in sic a way as tae uphold the claims o' the auld Kirk o' Rome. So we maun gang warily."

The penetrating stare scanned his clutch of attentive pupils. The little king looked huffy.

"Aye, warily, but behind maist o' thae legends there is likely some kernel o' truth. Noo, we're telt that Saint Kentigern was brought up by Saint Serf o' Fife at Culross. The lad was schooled in the Gospel after the fashion o' the auld Celtic saints. When he was of an age, he set out by himsel' and it cam aboot that he met an auld man ca'd Fergus. The auld man died an' oor Kentigern had the body put on a cairt that was drawn by a pair o' wild bullocks. Noo Kentigern – they'd hae us believe – let thae bullocks wander at will, draggin' the mortal remains o' the man Fergus, until they ca'd a halt at the place o' a grove o' trees by a bit burn."

The Master laid the pointer down and folded his arms. Fixing his eyes steadily on the class, he drew a deep breath and continued.

"I'll tell ye a bit mair o' this grove. They say that Saint Ninian – wha gets the credit o' being the first Scottish evangelist – had consecrated this grove some twa hunner year earlier. Noo, if this was the case, it's mair nor likely that the grove had ane time been a sacred site o' the auld Druids… Anyway, Kentigern buried auld Fergus there an' by an' by he built a simple wee kirk an' gaithered a congregation o' sorts. An' this was the wee seed fae which the mighty St. Mungo's Cathedral was eventually tae spring. The burn is kent tae us as the Molendinar, and aroon it grew the toon o' Glasgow."

The black-cowled figure paced the room theatrically, clapped his hands together, rubbed them and carried on.

"There's likely a fair bit o' yon that we can credit, but mind thae monkish tales aye mak claims o' miraculous deeds which we are wise tae regard wae extreme caution. That's no' just tae say they're a' blethers, mind. We maun never rule oot the authentically miraculous, but… caution."
The Tutor tugged at his old, grey beard and eyed young Jamie searchingly. The boy glowered back with silent defiance. The Master rapped the chart with his pointer.

"Wan such yarn concerns an incident fae Kentigern's boyhood, when he was under the tutelage o' Serf. It seems the auld saint kept a pet bird… a wee robin."

James stirred uneasily in his wooden chair. His face began to colour.

"Noo, a bunch o' young rascals got haud o' the puir wee thing an' squeezed the life oot o' it."

Buchanan glared menacingly at each pupil in turn, saving an especially malevolent scowl for His Grace King James the Sixth of Scots.

"Allegedly the boy Kentigern took haud o' the deid bird an' restored it tae life."

He let the words hang in the air.

"It's a richt pity Kentigern hadna been wae us a week since."

All the boys were squirming, but James was close to tears. By an uncanny and awful coincidence, there had been an occurrence during the previous week in which Jocky o' the Slates had brought his tame sparrow into the schoolroom. James had been envious and had demanded that Jocky give up the bird to him. Jocky, quite naturally, had refused and a brawl ensued in the course of which the sparrow had been killed. Buchanan had been furious and James had been shown in no uncertain terms that his royal status did not place him beyond punishment. Now, looking at the wee boy struggling heroically to maintain his composure, the old man's heart softened and he felt a little ashamed of himself.

"Aye… well…" He swallowed uncomfortably and turned toward his chart.

"What's past is past." He cleared his throat noisily and rapped the image of the fish firmly with the pointer.

"We'll no' bother wae the tree an' the bell. They're of nae great interest when a' is said an' done. Na… but ye see the fish – a salmon it is – has a ring in its jaws ? Aye, yon'll gie us plenty tae think ower."

A quick glance at the little king showed him that the lad had regained some emotional ground and was expressing silent defiance again. Good for him.

"As the story comes doon tae us, in Kentigern's day there was a King o' Strathclyde ca'd Ridderch wha had his stronghold at Dumbarton Rock. Noo, the Rock was his fortress – Dun Breatann – the Gaelic for "Fort o' the Britons", but Ridderch had his palace up the Clyde a bit at Partick. Ridderch's queen was ca'd Languoreth, and she was… weel, ower friendly, we'll say, wae ane o' Ridderch's heid warriors."

The Tutor peered round to see if the boys were taking this in. Approximately satisfied, he continued.

"We're telt that wan day King Ridderch found this warrior sleepin' by the side o' the river. The warrior was wearin' a particular ring on his finger that Ridderch had gein tae Queen Languoreth…"

Small boys being small boys, he was never going to get away with it. It was Willie Murray who asked the inevitable question.

"Maister Buchanan, Sir, what dae ye mean by 'ower friendly' ?"

"Since ye ask, young Murray, I mean she wis the kind o' wummin that was inclined tae gie oot certain favours tae ither men that should hae been gied tae nae man but her lawfu' wedded husband. An' if ye ask what I mean by 'certain favours", ye'll spend the rest o' the day on yir hauns an' knees scrubbin' oot the kitchen flairs."

The threat accompanied by one of Buchanan's most belligerent looks was quite enough to put a stop to awkward questions – if not to muffled sniggering.

"Aye... the king had found the queen's ring on the warrior's finger. He took it fae the sleepin' man's haun' and in a fit o' spite threw it intae the Clyde. Noo, some time later, when he'd calmed himsel' an' gien the matter sober thought, Ridderch demanded o' Queen Languoreth, in front o' a' the court, that she show him the ring. If she failed to do this, she'd be pit tae death."

He tapped the image of the ring on the chart.

"Of course, Ridderch kent fine well she could dae nae such thing. This was his way o' forcin' the truth oot o' her. Well, in a panic Languoreth went tae Kentigern for help. She telt him the fu' facts o' her mischief, an' they wad hae us believe that Kentigern, hae'n pity on her, gied word tae ane o' his monks tae dae a bit fishin' by yon bit o' the Clyde. Sure enough the monk pulls oot a salmon and brings it tae Kentigern wha taks the ring fae the fish's mooth... an' this is supposed tae have saved Languoreth fae Ridderch's wrath."

The Tutor picked up a large Latin Bible in his right hand and waved it aloft.

"Of course, it's plain enough this story has its origin in the Gospel o' Matthew, whaur the Lord and his disciples are in Capernaum, an' the collectors o' temple tax try tae trick him. He tells his disciples tae fish in the lake, an' they catch a fish that has a coin in its jaws. Then they pay the tax wae it. Och, ye'll hae seen that."

Young heads bobbed affirmatively.

"Maist likely, thae tales o' Kentigern's supposed miracles were written tae mak him seem a' the mair holy. We maun hae an open mind on that score. Yet, quite apart fae thae kinds o' embellishment, this tale contains elements that deserve oor keen attention."

Dramatic pause.

"Consider the wider political situation. Ridderch – wha's factual enough – was the chosen war-leader of the Strathclyde Britons. In his day, there existed four British kingdoms in the south o' the land we noo ca' Scotland. These were: Strathclyde; the Rheged; Manau; and Gododdin. These were the peoples wha were gien effective resistence tae the pagan Angles and Saxons wha were invading the land o' Britain. Now, mark weel, Ridderch was a Christian king. He gied protection and encouragement tae the missionary endeavours o' no' jist Kentigern, but, we are telt, Columba himsel'."

Young James was no stranger to this subject matter. His teacher regarded it his duty to impart to the infant king as much knowledge as possible relating to the foundations of his kingdom. To teach him, or as he sometimes put it with that enigmatic smile... remind him.

"So we have a potent dramatis personae gaithered thigither at this particular time and in this particular place. King Ridderch, the victorious general, and his faithless Queen Languoreth – we may credit yon bit o' the tale, for we need na look sae far in oor ain time tae find the like – the twa saints, Kentigern and Columba. Ower an' above which, we hae it fae ither sources, nane ither than

Merlin was in yon company. I'll hae ye picture it. The michty Rock o' Petracloithe – Dumbarton... ancient capital an' fortress o' Ridderch's Strathclyde. Upstream at Partick, was his palace, built on a hill whaur the River Kelvin flows intae the Clyde. Here we encounter Ridderch and Languoreth, for a' the world Arthur an' Guinevere, Columba an' Merlin, regardin' whom there are that monie coincidences that some tak them tae be ane and the same man. Na... it's nae coincidence that Jocelyn composed his work on Kentigern aroon the same time as certain ithers were scribin' their romances on King Arthur."

Buchanan was not disappointed by the level of concentration he was receiving from his class of four. Jocky o' the Slates, Willie Murray, Wattie Stewart and King James were all but hypnotized.

"'Deed aye. If we just sift oot a' that monkish invention, political distortion an' romantic blethers, we discover a richt gold nugget o' truth. Am I right, yer young Grace ?"

The large brown eyes in the little round face eyed him warily.

"Oh aye, Maister Geordie, you're right... as ever."

Buchanan frowned, wondering if his royal pupil had developed a sense of sarcasm, even at such a tender age. He turned back to roll up his chart, muttering to himself.
"The past, the present and the future are a' but thread interwoven in the tapestry o' time."

*   *   *

About a mile from Partick stood the tower-house of Jordanhill. When George Buchanan recommended Thomas Crawfurd of Jordanhill as the man to lead the Dumbarton Rock raid, he was, as it were, pushing at an open door. Crawfurd had commanded the Lennox men for the earl at the Battle of Langside. He was a sincerely religious man and had been one of the earliest supporters of John Knox. The Regent would probably have chosen Crawfurd anyway, but for more prosaic reasons than the poet.

Born sometime around 1530 in Kilbirnie, Ayrshire, Thomas was the sixth son of Laurence Crawfurd. While still in his teens, Thomas fought at the Battle of Pinkie. In 1547 the Duke of Somerset, in yet another English attempt to bully the Scots into submission, led a large, professional army into East Lothian. It was confronted, on the bank of the River Esk near the coastline, by a well dug-in Scots host led by the then-Regent, Arran. Somerset, however, was well supported by the artillery of an English fleet and this proved the decisive factor. The Scots were routed and Thomas Crawfurd was taken prisoner. Fortunately he was ransomed, and shortly thereafter he went to France where he became a member of the Royal Scottish Guard of Henri II. During ten years on the Continent, Crawfurd gained an excellent education in matters military and courtly. In 1561 he was one of the gentlemen who returned to Scotland with the widowed Mary Queen of Scots.

It was at this time that Crawfurd became impressed with the preaching of John Knox. Such was his fervour for the Bible that one French observer recorded the fact that he had seen Crawfurd "in his tent by the light of a military lantern, turning over the pages of the Sacred Book with his dagger." Thomas became a servant and friend of King Henry. When the young king lay ill in Glasgow – suspected of having been poisoned – it was Thomas Crawfurd he sent to meet Queen Mary when she was on her way to see her ailing husband. She treated Crawfurd with the same haughty disdain that she had shown to Cunninghame of Drumquhassil earlier in Stirling.

The king's father, the Earl of Lennox, understandably entertained suspicions as to Mary's intentions with regard to his son. Lennox asked Crawfurd to pay particular attention to the exchanges between the royal couple. This was later presented as evidence to Elizabeth's commission, the purpose of which was to establish the innocence or guilt of Mary in the matter of the king's murder at Kirk o' Field. When Thomas appeared in front of the commissioners, he declared that it had been clear to him that the queen was trying to lure King Henry to Edinburgh, and that he, Crawfurd, had warned him strongly against this, fearing that the king's life would be in danger.

When Mary married Bothwell, prime suspect of the regicide, there was widespread outrage. A number of the Scots lords formed a confederation with the intention of removing Bothwell – who was described by Buchanan as "an ape in purple" – and avenging the murder of the late king. Mary's forces met those of the Confederate Lords at Carberry Hill near Musselburgh. Bothwell theatrically offered to settle the matter by single combat but, when it looked as though this suggestion might be taken up, Mary promptly overruled it. Negotiation ensued and an agreement was reached which resulted in Bothwell escaping from the field and Mary being taken prisoner. Lochleven and forced abdication followed.

After her escape from Lochleven, Mary's supporters gathered around her, and the armed forces of the Queen's Party were confronted by those of the King's Party at Langside, just south of Glasgow. Mary's half-brother, the Earl of Moray, acted Regent for young James. The actual generalship of the king's army was left to the experienced Kirkcaldy of Grange. Thomas Crawfurd led the Lennox contingent. Mary's force was led by the Earl of Argyll who, in spite of having superior numbers, managed to lose the battle, MacFarlane archers chasing his retreating forces from the field. In defeat Mary panicked and foolishly fled into England. Thomas Crawfurd would well understand the business of the Robertson brothers fighting on opposing sides during this battle, for his own brothers, Hugh and Patrick, had fought for Queen Mary.

*   *   *

Although Bothwell was generally believed to have been the murderer of King Henry, there were certainly others who had been involved in the conspiracy. It came to be alleged that when Mary sought advice from her chief advisors as to how she might get rid of her husband, a secret meeting had been held at Craigmillar Castle. At this conference the plausible Maitland of Lethington had drawn up a bond the meaning of which, though not expressed directly, was that the king would be murdered, but the queen need not be given prior knowledge of the details of the plot. Lethington was a smooth operator who had manoeuvred effortlessly from one side to the other on several occasions during and since the reign of Mary. He had served her as Secretary, then he had sided with her half-brother, the Earl of Moray. He had been among those who were behind the murder of the queen's favourite, Riccio, yet had managed to ease his way back into Mary's favour. When she fled to England, Lethington was with the King's Party and had been one of a team sent to the English commissioners to demonstrate Mary's involvement in the murder of her husband. Thomas Crawfurd, who had also been giving evidence, had, however, observed that, far from persuading the Commission of the queen's guilt, Lethington had seemed very much to be acting in Mary's interest.

Crawfurd of Jordanhill had been more than just a servant to King Henry. They had been friends. The king had treated him with loyalty and respect. Thomas saw and admired Henry's many qualities and talents. An attractive and charming young man, he had been excellent company. Of course, he'd had faults, and Thomas had been well aware of them. But it was hardly surprising that so much power and adulation, attained so quickly by one so young, should have gone a little to his head. Thomas felt strongly, however, that had the queen not treated Henry in such a treacherous and humiliating manner, he could well have matured into a fine king. When Henry's strangled body had been found in the garden of Kirk o' Field – the house having been blown to pieces by a secret store of gunpowder – Thomas had wept.

In August of 1569, a royal servant called Nicholas Hubert – more commonly known as "French Paris" – had been questioned in St. Andrews by George Buchanan. Hubert claimed to know, among other things, that Bothwell, Lethington and James Balfour (whose brother, Robert, had been the proprietor of Kirk o' Field) were the principals behind the king's murder. Hubert had been involved in the conspiracy himself to the extent that the queen had actually seen him "begrimed" with some of the gunpowder which was to blow up Kirk o'Field. Accordingly he had been hanged, but arising from his testimony Lethington was called to account at a meeting of the Privy Council in Stirling Castle that September.

The Earl of Lennox had allowed Thomas Crawfurd to present the damning evidence on that occasion. With heartfelt emotion Crawfurd had flung the accusation at Lethington. That sophisticated courtier had pursed thin lips, superciliously looked down his long nose at the soldier before him, and denied that charge. For once his clever talk availed him nothing. He was arrested and taken to be imprisoned in Edinburgh Castle. Even so, his luck had not yet run out. In charge of the castle was Kirkcaldy of Grange, the general who had so successfully commanded the Regent's forces at Langside. It was Lethington's subtle persuasions which caused Kirkcaldy to change sides and join the Queen's Party. So it had come about that, in March 1571, Maitland of Lethington was roosting in the Marian citadel in Edinburgh, while his brother-in-law, Lord Fleming, held the other Marian fortress in Dumbarton.

*   *   *

Thomas Crawfurd of Jordanhill was an attractive and impressive man. Tall, by the standards of his day, he was athletically built. He enjoyed and excelled in many of the outdoor and martial pursuits which he had shared with King Henry. His dark hair was swept back and fell to shoulder length. He was bearded and his handsome features could express kindness or cruelty depending on circumstance. He carried a natural air of authority lightly, managing men skilfully and well. He dressed expensively but well within reason, favouring – when not in the field – doublets of crimson and black. With his experiences on the Continent, he had exceeded even the high standard of education which was typical for a Scotsman of his class. Even so, he was essentially a man of action, and now he had a chance to lead his men in a military action which would endure proudly in the pages of history.

Chapter Thirteen
Honey and Heresy

Canon Carmichael was in an agony of doubt and indecision. He was wrestling, though whether with God or the Devil, he did not know. He desperately wanted to talk to Brother Andrew about the ideas and the longings which were tearing him apart, but that would have required a degree of plain speaking which was frankly inadmissible. Put bluntly, the young canon wanted to renounce holy orders. He wanted to be free. Free to marry.

A miracle had taken place. That was the only way he could describe it. Margaret Lafferty was healed.

When Brother Andrew had given him that writing of Saint Ambrose, he had been astonished to discover that it concerned the medicinal qualities of honey. When translated from the Latin, it had read:

The fruit of the bees is desired of all and is equally sweet to kings and beggars and is not only pleasing but profitable and healthful, it sweetens their mouths, cures their wounds, and conveys remedies to inward ulcers.

He had read it again and again… "cures their wounds…"

Religious houses commonly kept bees. Beeswax made the vast amount of candles which were used by the Church. Honey was used to make mead. It was fortunate that, even after the destruction of the early years of the Reformation, St. Mary's had managed to maintain the upkeep of a few of her hives. Accordingly, Canon Carmichael had been able to apply honey to Margaret's wounds almost immediately. Any delay would surely have proved fatal. Within a matter of hours the patient's temperature had returned to normal. She had regained consciousness and been able to sip a little water before falling into a deep, natural sleep. In the course of just two days of regular applications the process of healing the wounds themselves and ridding her entire body of toxins was well underway. Indeed, she was healing more quickly than the bruising, from the crucifix, on the canon's hand. Margaret was awake, lucid and ravenous most of the time. She was visited in the hospital regularly by Margaret Kennedy. Canon Carmichael had, with a reluctance of which he was heartily ashamed, told her of the faithfulness and concern which had been shown by Duncan Robertson, but of course neither he nor Margaret Kennedy could shed any light on the Highlander's subsequent, sudden and mysterious disappearance. It was vaguely assumed that he was somehow detained on duty in the castle, much to Margaret's unspoken disappointment.

Canon Carmichael considered the healing to have been miraculous simply because he could understand how the honey might have successfully treated the actual flesh-wounds themselves but, even when he took into account the Irish girl's youth and evident stamina, he would never reasonably have expected any salve applied externally to overcome the poison which had so affected her whole system that it brought her to delirium and the point of death. Brother Andrew shared his assessment and gloried in it.

It would be some time before Margaret regained her strength sufficiently to be able to return to her friend's lodging. In the meantime the young canon was more than willing to give her every possible attention. They had spent hours talking and getting to know one another, Margaret speaking fondly, and sometimes emotionally, about her family and childhood in Creeslough, while her physician spoke a little of his own Lanarkshire background but mostly just listened... and fell utterly and hopelessly under her spell. The vitality and the challenge in those eyes... the temptation of those lips...the woman's smell... Of course, he had desired women, had secretly lusted after their bodies, and despised himself for it, but never before had lust been transformed by love into something transcendent, so obviously natural, wholesome and... heavenly.

Or was this really the terrible illusion about which he had been so sternly warned ? Was that which felt God-given and pure really diabolical and filthy ? It seemed so ironic that Saint Ambrose, through whom this miracle had surely come, had written so eloquently on the importance of virginity. This miracle, the effect of which seemed to be that the young priest was finally brought to the very precipice of revolt against the Church. He had entertained doubts for a long time. Theological doubts, moral doubts. Not doubts about the love of God. Not doubts about the Life and Death and Resurrection of the Lord Jesus Christ. But doubts about the infallibility of very obviously fallible men.

Doubts about certain interpretations of Holy Scripture. Doubts about wealthy and worldly popes, cardinals and bishops preaching poverty and obedience. In truth, he admitted to himself in a secret corner of his mind, doubts he shared with the reformers...

He despised the Protestant lords for their hypocrisy and greed. He held in utter contempt the Protestant mob for their brutish, sacrilegious vandalism. But the actual leaders of the Reformation – men like the Swiss Zwingli, the German Luther, and the French Calvin – they had all been Roman Catholic priests. They had all been motivated by doubts like his own. He sensed their sincerity and quietly – perhaps enviously – admired their courage. They had liberated themselves from the tyranny of hypocrites... and been free to marry. Knox, at the age of fifty, had married a sixteen-year-old. The canon recognized that he'd had doubts for a long time, but he'd been able to overcome these doubts with a spirit of humility. He'd accepted that in such matters he was but a child. There were those who knew better than he. There was all the authority and tradition of the Church. The matter had been fully addressed and dealt with at the Council of Trent. For a priest to marry was anathema. If he was honest with himself, the wild beast of his rebellious rage had been unleashed as a result of his... infatuation with Margaret Lafferty. This was Adam tempted by Eve.

He'd poured over Holy Scripture and found it ambiguous. He could find passages in the New Testament which appeared to support the celibacy of the priesthood, and he had found other passages which appeared to encourage marriage, even for priests. The disciples had surely been married men... but, of course, the Church had its answers for that. Was his rebellion like that of the apostles against the Scribes and Pharisees, or was it the rebellion of Lucifer against God ?

Yes, many of the leaders of the Church could be justly compared with the "painted sepulchres" of the Gospel. They demanded that young priests, such as himself, live lives without the comfort of women, but they had their own concubines, their secret – or not so secret – marriages, their children – often appointed to privileged positions within the Church – like the much lamented Cardinal Beaton, with his wife, his five sons and three daughters...

Yet a humble and obedient Canon Carmichael would have bowed in acceptance of all of it... except for Margaret Lafferty. Although it went against his every natural instinct, all of his upbringing and religious training bore down on him with the fear that she was luring him on to the eternal fires of Hell.

Absently he thought again of Saint Ambrose, whose symbol was, of all things... a whip.

*　　　*　　　*

It was amazing – and a little shameful, she reflected – just how quickly she had begun to take her recovery for granted. Canon Carmichael said it was a miracle... so a miracle it must have been. He had said it was from Saint Ambrose, but she believed it was from himself. If anyone had brought her back to life, it was Canon Carmichael.

From her cot in the long hospital building of St. Mary's, Margaret Lafferty could see through just one narrow window. It was shuttered, not glazed, but every so often the shutters were opened to allow cool, fresh air to ventilate the ward. Then her limited view included, by chance, the head and shoulders of Ben Lomond, nearly twenty miles to the north. She was not impressed. To her eye it compared unfavourably with Muckish Mountain, to the west of her own Creeslough. Even the rainbows here in Scotland lacked the vivid, glowing magic of their counterparts in Tyrconnel. Absence had made her heart grow fonder. Of course, she had more on her mind than homesickness. If women were forbidden fruit for priests, priests were forbidden fruit for women. And all the more desirable for it.

She was appalled at the thought of how she must look to him. She had managed to bathe, of course. All apart from her back – he attended to that – gently, skilfully, often. How much of her body had he seen ? Her breasts, certainly. As a priest and a physician he would look at her without lust, she hoped… and hoped not. She had managed to wash her hair and Margaret had brought her a comb…

It had been wonderful being listened to by him, sharing such personal, precious memories. Of course, he didn't have the Gaelic, like Duncan Robertson. There was a strange one. To have paid her court – for that was obviously what he had been doing – in his shy, awkward, altogether charming way. To have shown such concern for her and then… what ? Could he really not get away from the castle ? Previously he'd seemed to be able to come and go, if not quite at will, then with a certain degree of freedom. He couldn't just have forgotten about her. Not when she'd been so close to death. She thought of his strong hands... his dimpled chin... the lilt in his beautiful Highland voice.

She was a virgin. Because of the teaching of her church, because of her upbringing and the social morality of her community, she was a virgin. In spite of a close run thing during her abduction, and numerous approaches, subtle and brutal, by men of various ranks, ages and qualities, in the castle and the Burgh of Dumbarton. That she remained a virgin was probably another miracle. Was it only because he was a priest that Canon Carmichael had that thrilling aura of authority ? If he had been a sailor, or a farm labourer, or a merchant, or a soldier... would those eyes still make her feel like a silly girl at one moment and a smouldering woman in the next ? Would she want to give herself to him if he were not a priest ?

If Margaret Lafferty had known that Canon Carmichael was on the very verge of abandoning his calling on account of her she would have been horrified... and ecstatic.

*   *   *

Just three days had elapsed since Duncan's nocturnal march to Drumquhassil. Now he found himself looking out through the window of yet another locked and guarded chamber – this time over the banks of the River Clyde. He was in the towerhouse of Jordanhill. In the castle and in the grounds which surrounded it, there was much purposeful activity. Thomas Crawfurd and his officers were preparing their men for the imminent raid on Dumbarton Rock...

Since those first awful hours in the dungeon of Drumquhassil, Duncan had been given little time or solitude for reflection of any sort. It had all been endless questions, planning, repetition... The Regent and his lieutenant were thorough men – the former obsessed and the latter professional. But now, with time to think, Duncan had begun to wonder about himself. What sort of man was he ? What could be said about his sense of priorities ? He'd left Margaret Lafferty unconscious on a cot in St. Mary's to escape into this... adventure, when all he should have been thinking about was being there with her, by her side, praying for her. Willing her to live with every breath, instead of running away with a heart filled with hatred and revenge. While men sharpened swords and daggers, while they tested hagbutts and polished armour, while they made ladders and tested ropes, while they screwed up their courage by breast-beating and displays of bravado, Duncan Robertson could think of nothing but whether Margaret Lafferty was alive or dead. He had to know. He somehow had to find out. How could he find out ? Of course he was a prisoner. The last place they'd let him go now was Dumbarton. Even if he blurted out the truth – told them about Margaret and where she was – they wouldn't send anyone to find out for him. They wouldn't have time for a distraction of that sort. What if they found out she was dead ? Would they even tell him ? Would he be of any use to them in a state of collapse ? They'd tell him what he wanted to hear. Anyway, it would all be over soon... and maybe he'd be dead himself.

*　　　*　　　*

Monsieur Verac, special envoy of the King of France, stood upon the highest peak of Dumbarton Rock and peered westward over the Firth of Clyde. It was another morning of mixed weather – sunshine and squalls. Managing, in spite of the restrictions of circumstance, to maintain the very highest standard of personal appearance, the spry little Frenchman was immaculate in black doublet, trimmed modestly with gold, and a snowy white ruff. His black beard was neatly trimmed. The dark brown eyes keen. He was the very picture of refinement and dignity. His patrician, aquiline nose smelled a rat. There was something in the air. A certain expectancy. Lord Fleming had taken on a conspiratorial manner. An ill-concealed impatient smugness. He was frequently locked away with his little circle of confidantes, and he spent more time than hitherto pacing the battlements, peering downriver. Verac was no fool. There had been some development of which he had not been informed.

It occurred to him yet again, as it had occurred to others, how incredible it was that so very much might depend on these thirty-five men. These bored, weary, argumentative and ordinary, yet extraordinary men. The sense of excitement certainly had not been communicated to them. As Verac looked down into the cleft between the two great peaks he could see little groups of them going about their business in the usual listless manner. All of this was such a far cry from what the little French ambassador was used to – kings and queens and courtiers and magnificent palaces and chateaux and splendour and extravagance. To be sure, this Scotland had its rugged beauty, when the rain wasn't pouring and the winter gales weren't howling, when the mists gave way to brief blue skies and one could see the lakes and mountains, but it was all so... raw, so... comfortless. And the people. What a strange and astonishing people were these Scots. For the most part wretchedly poor, yet proud as Lucifer. He never failed to be amazed by the intellect and the poetry he encountered even in the common folk of this burgh. Not that a single one of them regarded themselves in any way common. All, from ragged Highland drovers to tavern wenches seemed to genuinely consider themselves in some way related to the country's aristocracy. Verac was used to associating with the rich, the powerful and the sophisticated echelons of European society, but he was a man who was interested in people... all people irrespective of their social standing. He had come to know some of these men in the garrison quite well. His English was fluent and he had a good understanding of Scots. Even the Highlanders, whose native tongue was, of course, the Gaelic, spoke Scots much of the time. He turned and looked deep down into the jumble of little towers, walkways and fortifications, singling out some of the visible personalities for consideration.

*   *   *

Malcolm MacGregor was a member of the garrison of Dumbarton Castle because of a sense of personal indebtedness to Mary Queen of Scots. In matters of religion he believed that through his faith in the Lord Jesus Christ he would not perish but have eternal life. He had been brought up with the Gospel, and he didn't care whether it was preached by a minister or a priest.

Clan Gregor claimed descent from the family of Kenneth MacAlpine, the king who had first ruled over a united Scots-Pictish kingdom back in the ninth century. Accordingly, the MacGregor motto was 'S Rioghal Mo Dhream – My Race is Royal. At one time the clan had possessed extensive lands in Glenorchy, Glenstrae, Glenlochy and elsewhere. Over the centuries, however, their powerful and aggressive neighbours, the Campbells, had usurped much of these lands, driving the MacGregors as far afield as Tayside, Balquhidder and the Trossachs. Dispersed and marginalized, Clan Gregor had become known as Clann a' Cheathaich – The Children of the Mist, living on their wits and often having to give allegiance to other chiefs. The Campbells had used guile and had been shrewd enough to adapt to changing times. They had employed legalities in a way which had been alien to clan society, and MacGregor land which had been held by the sword was lost to Campbells by the pen. Campbell aristocrats had made themselves popular at court, obtaining powerful offices of state, Earls of Argyll becoming Lords Justice General. Abusing this power, Letters of Fire and Sword, which outlawed Clan Gregor, had been obtained through the Privy Council in 1563. Effectively criminalized, all by the name of MacGregor were then fair game – anyone could hunt them down and kill them, if they had motive and means. In the year 1566, it was Mary Queen of Scots who had tried to put a stop to this genocide by issuing an order that Clan Gregor be given land and cattle at Loch Rannoch. It had been a futile gesture – in 1570, with Mary now imprisoned, the clan chief, Gregor Roy, had been "legally" beheaded by the Campbell Laird of Glenorchy. Even so, MacGregors had cause to love Queen Mary. She was the only monarch who had shown compassion for them, and Malcolm MacGregor the forester from Strathcashell would not forget it. When the queen had escaped from Lochleven and rallied supporters to her cause, Malcolm had taken his bow and arrows, left Loch Lomondside and joined her army at Langside.

Joseph Brock was a tall, gaunt and prematurely grey man of some thirty-five years who had been a farmer in the Parish of Kilpatrick.

When Lord Claude Hamilton – Mary's agent who had sent the all-important Ridolfi letter to his uncle at Dumbarton Castle – had been but seven years old, the lands granted to him by the Pope included those of Kilpatrick. In this way Joseph Brock had become his vassal. The arrangement had included a duty of military service and, as the years passed, duty had turned to mutual loyalty. Accordingly, when Queen Mary had escaped from Lochleven, and Lord Claude had provided her with an escort of horsemen, the man from Kilpatrick had been one of their number. Subsequently he had been with the queen's cavalry at Langside, being lucky to escape with his life. Several around him had fallen to MacFarlane arrows in the flight from that field. Here, on the Rock, he served as a hagbutter. As a trusted man, he had been allowed to visit his wife and two daughters at his home village, not four miles eastward, during the period of truce. With the possibility of renewed hostilities any day now, Brock knew not when he would see his loved ones again.

Jeremiah Leitch Young had been a prosperous fishmonger of Paisley. He joined Lord Fleming's company because of religious conviction. Young was devoutly loyal to the Church of Rome, and a militant opponent of the Reformation. Although bitterly disappointed that a Catholic monarch had not brought about a reinstatement of the Old Faith in this realm of Scotland, the merchant had left his worldly interests in the hands of a brother and committed himself wholeheartedly to the cause of Mary Queen of Scots. A red beard which flowed abundantly to his stomach gave him an Old Testament gravity. Chilling, light-blue, piggy eyes stared out under the brim of a high hat. Although absolutely abstemious, Jeremiah had the florid complexion of the habitual drinker. His once-fine clothing was now stained and ragged. A deep and uncommunicative man, he had been trained as an arquebusier. Indeed, it had been he who had fired the controversial shot at Elizabeth's envoy. He made his comrades-at-arms nervous because they darkly suspected that Young seriously craved martyrdom, and would be a reckless hazard to them in combat.

John Carpenter might have been a handsome man had it not been for the fact that his face was badly pitted with pock-marks, and that his eyes were unnaturally dark, almost black, giving him a sinister appearance. His dark, curly hair was oily, and his thick lips seemed always to be wet. Although he was not tall or visibly muscular, he had a certain physical strength. He was that sort of bully who is careful to impress his superiors. He made himself useful to the officers of Lord Fleming's garrison by taking on most of their disciplinary responsibilities. Such officers seldom care how their blunt instruments get results, as long as they are not personally inconvenienced by the methods of subordinates. Remarkably, in spite of being a member of the pro-Catholic garrison, Carpenter had managed to ingratiate himself with the minister of the burgh's reformed kirk. He was deferentially attentive to Lady Fleming when the occasion arose. Most of the men under his command feared him, and it is often the case that men feign a liking for a bully simply to keep on the right side of him. So it was that Carpenter was superficially popular. In the drinking dens of Dumbarton he was a 'hale fellow well-met', but shrewd enough not to be a drunkard. He chose his victims cunningly in such a way that his lickspittles usually egged him on, invariably agreeing with him that the persecuted individual had been "asking for it". He indulged in petty criminality – demanding money with menaces, theft, blackmail, and made a point of involving others in a way which ensured that he was never brought to account. An unmarried man, he was the sort that many women found attractive. He did not lack female comforts. He was the second son of a small Cumbernauld landholder, so he had originally entered Lord Fleming's service in a feudal way. Though a bully, John Carpenter was not altogether a coward, and he found that soldiering suited him very well.

Chapter Fourteen
The Priest and the Victim

John Hamilton, Archbishop of St. Andrews, was a sinner – which is to say, he was a man.

*   *   *

He was the illegitimate son of James Hamilton, the first Earl of Arran. The earl had been the son of Mary, sister of King James III. Arran's eldest legitimate son, the second earl, who was also called James, was the great grandson of King James II. Accordingly, on the death of the Stewart Duke of Albany, he became heir-presumptive to the Scottish throne. When James V died, Arran became Regent for the infant Mary. The weakness of his dynastic position was that a question hung over the legitimacy of the marriage of his parents. He assisted in marrying off the child queen to the French Dauphin, and was rewarded by being created Duke of Chatelherault. He exchanged the regency with Mary's mother, Marie de Guise, on the strength of a promise that, should Mary die childless, he would take the throne. However Mary, on marrying into the French royal family, secretly signed over the Crown Matrimonial (which she later denied to her second husband, King Henry) to the Dauphin. Arran changed his religious and political allegiances repeatedly in his efforts to establish a Hamilton dynasty, but when Mary married Henry Stuart the House of Lennox won that battle. So it came about that the civil war, which was about to recommence, was as much a continuation of the clash between the Houses of Hamilton and Lennox as between the Queen's Party and the King's Party.

*   *   *

Arran had been Governor of Dumbarton Castle and various Hamiltons had been its Keepers. Although the castle was the oldest recorded fortified site in Britain, and predominantly military, from its earliest times it had also had a spiritual focus. The ancient chapel on the Rock, dedicated to Saint Patrick, was said to have been founded by Saint Modwenna, who lived in the sixth century. In the very heart of the Rock, deep between the two peaks, was situated the "chalmer between the crags" – the chamber between the rocks. It was this building which was now being used as Saint Patrick's Chapel, and it was in this deep sanctuary that John Hamilton, Archbishop of St. Andrews sat alone at midnight.

He was now fifty-nine years old, fleshy and visibly debauched. There were pock-marks on his olive, almost Mediterranean complexion. The hair under the clerical cap had been black and was still dark, but with silver at the temples and in the eyebrows. The features were dominated by a large, almost disproportionate and predatory beak. The eyes were brown. There was little compassion in them. The upper lip was thin. The lower lip pouted in a feminine way. The chin was pointed and there was a blue shadow of stubble. One did not have to take account of the purple cassock and the episcopal ring to recognize that this was a man to be reckoned with, a man of power – reduced to roosting on this seagull's nest.

John Hamilton was born in 1511. As a child he was placed in the care of the Benedictine monks of Kilwinning. At the age of fourteen he received the royal gift of the abbacy of Paisley. He was educated at the universities of Glasgow and Paris (even Knox was grudgingly to acknowledge his intellect). When he returned to Scotland, in his early thirties – and by this time in holy orders – his half-brother was Regent. Accordingly John found himself Keeper of the Privy Seal and then Treasurer of the realm. He became a firm supporter of Cardinal Beaton and an enemy of Protestantism. An enemy, but not a fanatical persecutor. But there had been the old man...

The chapel was dimly lit by candlelight. Within its thick stone walls he was conscious of the vast mass of rock which surrounded him and the infinite darkness of the night. He felt a terrible loneliness. He'd had no choice. Always there was free will, but he'd had no choice. The diabolical errors of the Protestants were spreading like a disease which might soon have infected the whole realm. An example had had to be made...

He'd been appointed Bishop of Dunkeld. Then, by the favour of Marie de Guise, Archbishop of St. Andrews, Primate of Scotland. Of course there had been corruption within the Church. None had denied it. Financial corruption. Sexual corruption. Spiritual corruption. Had not St. Paul, himself, written in his Letter to the Romans – "For I do not the good thing, which I would, but the evil, which I would not, that I do." ? Yet the Church still prayed

"Thy will be done even in earth, as it is in heaven." Reform had to come from within the Church herself. The True Church – the only Church.

The Lord Jesus Christ had chosen his apostles. He had given them their Commission – "Go therefore, and teach all nations, baptizing them in the Name of the Father, and the Son, and the Holy Ghost." He had caused the Holy Spirit to come upon them at Pentecost. The apostles had appointed bishops and passed on to them their apostolic power with the laying on of their hands. In like manner these bishops appointed other bishops in an Apostolic Succession.

The Lord had chosen Peter as leader of the apostles – "And I say also unto thee, that thou art Peter, and upon this rock I will build my Church…" He had given to Peter the keys of the kingdom of Heaven. Peter who became the Bishop of Rome – the first of an unbroken succession of popes reaching from the very breath of Christ down through these fifteen hundred years to the present Holy Father, Pope Pius V. These were the Shepherds. The Shepherds and the Flock. The One, Holy, Catholic and Apostolic Church. The Ark of Salvation. Only the Catholic Church had the true teachings and traditions and sacraments as handed down from Jesus, through the apostles and through the bishops. Only the Catholic Church had inerrant doctrine as established through the Magisterium – the teaching authority of the great councils of the Church – Nicaea, Constantinople, Ephesus, Chalcedon… the bishops in conference, speaking for Peter through the Pope, and guided by the Holy Spirit.

The old man had been a priest. So many of them had been priests. From Lunan, by Aberdeen, they'd said, and one-time schoolmaster in Linlithgow. It had been just a matter of days after the young queen had married the Dauphin in France. But the old man had been a heretic. Leading poor folk into diabolical error. It had been a terrible thing... yes, terrible. But by burning that one man's mortal body... how many souls had he saved from an eternity of hellfire ?

Only the Church had the right and the duty and the power to reform herself from within. That process of due and proper, internal reform had been well underway. There had been the Council of Trent which had addressed many of the abuses – the sale of indulgences, the moral conduct of monks and nuns, even of cardinals and bishops, concubinage and illiteracy of the clergy – these things had been decisively dealt with. The Holy Father, himself, had done much, by his personal example and through the authority of his office, to rid Rome of immorality and put an end to certain clerical vices.

Here, in this realm of Scotland, bishops and abbots had set programmes of reform in motion. He, himself, had initiated reforming councils over a period of ten years. In order that common people could have a clear understanding of the Church's teaching he had personally laboured to produce his Catechism. In plain Scots vernacular that was read out to all of the faithful on Sundays and Holy Days, it had explained the Ten Commandments, the twelve articles of the Creed, the seven Sacraments. It had given sound guidance in the manner of prayer, the Pater Noster, the Ave Maria... Of course, none of this had satisfied the Protestants, for the simple truth was that they had not been honestly interested in reform. They had sought rather to foist a false and perverse religion of their own prideful devising on guileless souls. Their insistence that Scripture alone was their source of authority, and that every man should read and interpret the Bible for himself, was a devil-inspired madness that would lead to as many heresies and as many separate "kirks" as there were Protestants – their leaders detested each other – but then these people claimed that every "believer", be he butcher, baker or candlestick maker, was a priest – even women.

There had been other burnings. Beaton had presided over most of them. Walter Myln had been his name ... the old man. Eighty-two years old, it had been said. But still a heretic. Still a danger to countless souls. It had been done outside the Dean's Court at St. Andrews. This had been... thirteen years ago. It seemed like so much less – but then such a lot had happened in those years. The memory was so uncomfortably vivid. It was as though the very smell of burning flesh still stank in his nostrils. The sound of the roar and crackle of the flames... But it had been for the good of the many...

They'd managed, though, to poison enough minds, to corrupt so many of the lords – ravening for Church lands – that eventually they'd seized control of the realm. They had rejected the authority of the Pope and banned the Mass. It was hard to imagine more Satanic doctrine than this. By the will of Christ and through his words expressed undeniably in the Gospels, Peter was chosen to be the leader of the apostles and the shepherd of Christ's flock. A divinely appointed and sustained and inspired leader who in his own person, and in the persons of his successors, would represent that authority – the keys of the kingdom – which was required for true doctrine and the essential unity of the Church. Saint Peter had been martyred in Rome. Had been Bishop of Rome. That the bishops of Rome held primacy, and that they were the successors of Peter – Vicars of Christ on earth – was beyond question. Yet in their wicked, rebellious arrogance these Protestants rejected that authority – and in rejecting Peter, they rejected Christ.

St. Patrick's Chapel was a small, windowless chamber. Cut into the thick stone wall behind the altar there was what appeared to be a small, cube-shaped cupboard. In fact it was the Sacrament House, the purpose of which was to contain the Blessed Sacrament – the consecrated elements of the Mass. Normally such a tabernacle would have had some form of external decoration, but in this time and in this place special circumstances surely prevailed. The civil war was, of course, in large part between the forces of the Roman Catholic Church and those of the Reformed Kirk. For long, all symbols of the Old Faith had been at risk of destruction. The Protestants presently had the upper hand, politically and militarily. Their "Scots Confession" of 1560 asserted that – "To adore or venerate the sacrament, to carry it through streets and towns in procession, or to reserve it in a special case, is not the proper use of Christ's sacrament but an abuse of it." Given that it was not utterly impossible that at some time in the future the sacrilegious vandals of Protestantism might break their way into even this citadel, the archbishop had considered it prudent to arrange matters in such a way that the sacred purpose of this chamber might at sudden notice be transformed to the appearance of wordly usage. At a glance, then, the Sacrament House would be taken for an ordinary cupboard and remain, hopefully, inviolate. Within the tabernacle, on the left, there was a large Cross carved into the stone slab which formed the side of the ambry. This had, in fact, been salvaged from the destruction which the Protestant mob had visited upon St. Mary's some ten years previously. It was the only visible hint as to the "cupboard's" true purpose.

The objections of the Protestants – in so far as they were comprehensible – to the Mass were, they claimed, that the bread and wine should be eaten and drunk, but not kept to be worshipped as idols. Also that the priest came between Christ and the worshipper, claiming to offer up, repeatedly, that sacrifice which Jesus had made with entire sufficiency, once and for all, on the Cross. Such, at any rate, was the archbishop's understanding. What he considered a contradiction and a hypocrisy was the fact that, although the heretics claimed to believe that the bread and wine became, by the power of the Holy Spirit, in some sense the body and blood of Christ: "A life-giving power from the flesh of Christ is poured into us." as Calvin had put it – though not by transubstantiation – yet they objected to it being reverenced accordingly.

The Council of Trent had emphatically restated the truth of the permanence of Christ's presence in the Eucharist... and the absolute propriety of venerating the reserved Sacrament. As for the sacrificial nature of the Mass, scripture could not be clearer or more conclusive. Jesus gives himself as the new Passover Lamb. "Take, eat; this is my body, which is broken for you..." "For this is my blood of the New Testament that is shed for many, for the remission of sins..." Jesus is at once Priest and Victim. His sacrificial offering of himself is the very heart of the Sacrament...

Hamilton sighed wearily. What was to be gained from, yet again, trying to enter into the thinking of these wilfully blind heretics ? The candles were burning low. Although wind moaned around the Rock, the flames were steady. He had hoped... the Church had hoped, that the return of a Catholic queen would have heralded a reinstatement of the True Faith throughout the realm. In the event, Mary had been a bitter disappointment. She had refused to ratify the "legislation" by which Scotland had allegedly been made a Protestant state, and that refusal had rendered the entire exercise illegal and fraudulent. Beyond that, however, she had done little or nothing to advance the Catholic cause in her realm. He had remained loyal to her because she was rightful queen and a Catholic monarch. He had given her his support at the critical times in her rule – and such times had been frequent. She, for her part, had humiliated him.

In 1563 she'd had him imprisoned for saying the Mass. She – who had insisted on her own personal right to have Mass – had granted authority for the Primate of Scotland to be gaoled for saying Mass. Three years later he had been given his place to officiate at the baptism of Prince James in the Chapel Royal of Stirling Castle. It had been an extravagant affair. Mary had been intent on impressing an international audience, and on this occasion it had been her policy to emphasize her Catholicism. The royal baby had been baptised "Charles James" and it was in relation to the baptismal ritual that Mary had inflicted her second humiliation upon the Archbishop.

John Hamilton was flesh and blood. He had human weaknesses. Like most men he lusted after women, and like many men he lusted not only in his heart... There was a woman in his life. A

woman with whom he had been in love for many years. Grizzel...
Grizzel Semphill. She was the widow of a Provost of Edinburgh.
She had borne him three children. He loved his children as he
loved their mother. Even so... he lusted after other women. Many
other women. He even had discreet arrangements with certain
women of the Burgh of Dumbarton. He prayed sincerely and
habitually for the power to resist such temptation, but that power
seemed never to reach him. He bore God's punishment in his
body. He had undergone painful and expensive treatment, but he
was diseased. It was true.

An element of the Catholic ritual of baptism required the priest to
spit saliva into the child's mouth. Mary had forbidden this,
allegedly referring to the Archbishop as "a pocky priest".

She had restored him to his consistorial jurisdiction solely, he
suspected, in order that he might find a way of annulling her
marriage to that despicable youth, the Lennox Stuart. Of course,
he, as a Hamilton, had been only too keen to seek some means by
which he might have dragged a Lennox from the throne, but it
had proved impossible. Only the Holy Father had the authority to
pronounce nullity where royalty was concerned. In the event, of
course, more drastic methods had been required to rid the queen
and the realm of that thoroughly loathsome young man.

Of course, there had been her infatuation with Bothwell. A
coarse, godless, and dangerous brute... though not without his
uses. But to marry the man who was widely understood to have
murdered her husband, had not been just folly, but insanity.
However, it had been an act of madness which John Hamilton
had been happy to encourage. Bothwell would never have lasted

long on the throne... and that would have left it empty for a Hamilton. The archbishop had been needed to facilitate another divorce. Yet another embarrassment. Bothwell's union with Jean Gordon, sister of the great Catholic lord, Huntly, had, naturally, been an obstacle to the queen's desire to make Bothwell her own third husband. Considerable difficulty had arisen in this delicate matter because in order to marry Jean Gordon in the first place, Bothwell had required a dispensation, there having been a degree of consanguinity between himself and his intended bride. Unfortunately, in retrospect, it had been Archbishop Hamilton, himself, who had been induced to obtain the papal dispensation. Now he had been landed with the mortification of having to declare the nullity of a marriage which he had declared valid in the first place. Then, in the face of public outrage, Mary had married Bothwell... in a Protestant ceremony. The story had been put about that Bothwell had raped her, but it had also been reported that Mary had announced that she hadn't cared if she'd lost France, England and Scotland – she'd go with Bothwell to the world's end in a white petticoat before she would leave him. The archbishop had no idea if she had said any such thing, but it sounded to him very like the kind of ill-considered nonsense she may well have come out with. In the event, of course, she'd let Bothwell go to the devil... on his own.

In spite of having been used and abused in these ways, John Hamilton had continued to serve her, standing by her side at the Battle of Langside, then beseeching her not to flee into the hands of the heretic Elizabeth of England... And here he was, serving her yet. All these harsh months cooped up on this bare, windswept rock. Serving not just Mary Queen of Scots, serving not just His Holiness Pope Pius V, or the Catholic Church, but serving, to the best of his wretched and unworthy ability, the Lord Jesus Christ.

In the small, silent chamber, by that fading candlelight, the archbishop read and reread the letter which had come to him from his nephew, Lord Claude Hamilton. That precious document which informed the reader that the Duke of Alva, with the approval of the Holy Father and the King of Spain, was in the process of preparing an army which would put Mary on the thrones of England and Scotland. He read it with intense analytical caution, first looking for shadows of doubt, then looking for the light of hope. Finally, hesitantly, reaching for a conclusion of assurance. In his mind's eye he could see the sails of the ships which would, one bright Spring morning, appear on the Firth of Clyde. Sails which would bear the crossed keys symbol of St. Peter – the keys of the kingdom. Ships which would be packed with Catholic soldiers who would swarm onto this rock and from it reclaim the realm of Scotland for the One, Holy, Catholic and Apostolic Church. From the depths of his heart and soul, John Hamilton, Archbishop of St. Andrews, Primate of Scotland, prayed for that day. Long into that night he prayed.
"...and upon this rock I will build my Church; and the gates of hell shall not overcome it."

The poetic association between these words of Jesus and the archbishop's physical and spiritual situation on the mighty Rock of Dumbarton had not, of course, escaped him. Not a day had gone by of these long seasons of his enforced residence here that he had not reflected on this striking significance. God had willed that he would be placed here – the leading Catholic of this realm guarding the gate to the kingdom.

John Hamilton had done much that was good. To an admirable extent he had used his undoubted talents in the service of God and of his fellow men. But he was painfully aware of his failings... and there had been the old man. Of course he had been given an opportunity to recant and had refused. When it had come to the actual execution it should, in the accepted manner of doing these things, have been the responsibility of the secular powers, but the Provost of St. Andrews took no part in the matter, and the archbishop had had to order his own men to attend to the actual burning. To make matters worse, the mob had demanded to hear the old man speak... and he had died bravely.

Some of the candles had gone out and smoke spiralled upward from the molten wax. The archbishop peered at a gold crucifix which stood before him on the altar. Even Christ had felt forsaken. He listened to the silence and thought of the infinity of darkness which stretched between him and his God. That awful loneliness... He thought again of his excuse for burning Walter Myln, and he remembered other words from scripture –

"And Caiaphas was he, that gave counsel to the Jews, that it was expedient that one man should die for the people."
The last candle spluttered into extinction and left John Hamilton in utter darkness.

Chapter Fifteen
Inspiration and Revelation

George Buchanan's thoughts had also turned to the night of Christ's arrest and trial.

"If I then your Lord, and Master, have washed your feet, ye also ought to wash one another's feet. For I have given you an example…"

"Noo here, ye see, we hae, fae the highest possible authority, baith exhortation and example. It is the expressed will o' God that thae who are chosen to lead should be the servants o' their people… and should gie them guid example."

The sun was rising over the Ochil Hills behind them. Tutor and king were alone on the west-facing battlements of Stirling Castle, looking out over the awakening expanse of Flanders Moss toward the distant mountains of Loch Lomond. Young James eyed his mentor with his accustomed expression of respect and wariness.

George Buchanan was writing a book. It was – of course – in Latin, and for the benefit quite entirely of wee King James. De

Jure Regni Apud Scotos – the power of the Crown in Scotland. It would prove, in fact, a revolutionary work and eventually be banned by the king in his maturity, but for the time being it was in the process of being created, and its author was, in a manner of speaking, thinking aloud. Its central themes were that sovereignty lay with the people, and that the people had the right, indeed the duty, to depose a tyrant. Difficult ideas to present to a Stuart king – especially to a four-year-old Stuart king.

The old man seemed suddenly to be aware of precisely where they were standing. He paused and permitted himself one of his digressions.

"Och… was it no' fae here…? Aye, it was. It must hae been, what… sixty-three year past, yon Italian charlatan – ca'd himsel' an alchemist – Damian, aye, John Damian, that was his name. He took a len' o' yir grandfaither, James the Fourth… claimed he was a freen' o' Da Vinci. Well, this Damian took a notion that he could fly…"

Little James looked up as though he'd misheard. The Tutor continued.
"Fly like a bird, nae less. Aye, he made himsel' a pair o' wings an' took flight fae this very spot… sae I've been telt."

The royal eyes were like saucers.

"He flew… like a birdie ? Fae here ?"

The boy looked out over the flat lands of the Carse of Stirling.

"Where did he fly to ?"

Old Buchanan smiled wryly and tugged at the grey beard which he'd allowed to grow recently quite beyond its usual length.

"Aye, well… it's said his stated intention was tae fly the length o' France. Of coorse, there was nae question o' that."

He allowed himself a cackle.
"But he must hae managed a wee distance. Ye see, yir young Grace, the story goes that he cam doon intae a midden. Weel, if yi but glance doon, yi can see fine… he'd hae tae have flown a measure jist tae get clear of the rocks o' the castle escarpment here. There wid hae been nae midden doon there. Na… charlatan or no', his bit wings must hae carried him a fair length."

James was beside himself and began to flap his arms and prance about in an excited manner. When he commenced to clamber on to the parapet, his master grasped him unceremoniously by the scruff of the neck and hauled him back to safety. Imagining for an awful moment how he would have fared if he'd been responsible for the monarch plunging to his doom some three hundred feet below. Buchanan experienced a disturbing bout of palpitations before shaking his liege lord by the shoulders and roaring furious admonition at the child. When pupil and master had calmed down and a thaw in their relations was underway, James cautiously asked what had become of the bird-man, Damian.

"Och… well… As I said, he cam doon in a midden an' broke his leg by a' accounts."

He paused for a heartier cackle this time. It grew into a hacking cough. When he'd recovered he wiped his beard with the back of a hand and went on.

"He telt the king that it had a' been because he'd used hens' feathers fir his wings. They'd sought the midden. But if he'd used eagles' feathers they'd hae soared tae the sun. Mind you… there wis never any word o' him tryin' it again wae eagles' feathers…"

It seemed to dawn on the irascible old sage that he'd wandered, yet again, from his lesson. He thought for a moment if he might turn this business of Damian's flight to some relevant purpose, and with a little imagination he surely may have done so, but he could not be bothered with the effort. In truth, his mind, this day, was very much elsewhere. He picked up more or less where he'd left the subject.

"The king is servant o' his people. Aye mind that, yir Grace. It is his duty tae rule in the interests o' his people – a' his people, no' jist himsel', or his lords. Rule in justice tempered wae mercy. Such power as is invested in the Crown must no' be abused."

The small features in that pale, round face looked doubtful – it was little wonder – and the king was tight-lipped. The black-cowled poet considered that his earlier biblical allusion had been on the weak side, so he took an example from the reign of Bruce, Scotland's Hero King.

"Take yi noo the Declaration o'Arbroath itsel':

"Him, too, divine providence, the succession to his right according to our laws and customs which we shall maintain to the death, and the due consent and assent of us all have made our prince and king…"

"Note that right well, yir young Grace – our laws and customs… the due consent and assent of all of us – Ye see, the decision rests wae the people."

The Tutor pursed his lips gravely, gave the little king a steady, serious look. The infant's response matched his own. The lad didn't like the sound of this. Buchanan drove his point home.

"Yet if he should give up what he has begun… we should exert ourselves at once to drive him out as our enemy and a subverter of his own right and ours."

"Yon couldna' be clearer. The people hae baith the right, aye, and the duty, to depose a king whae has strayed into grievous error."

He raised the old grey chin and glowered skyward as though defying the Almighty to contradict.

"These are the solemn and maist significant words, as inscribed in a letter tae the pope – wha was considered the ultimate authority in thae days – in the year o' oor Lord, thirteen hundred and twenty, tae establish recognition o' Scotland's independence. There could be nae mair weighty authority – ither than numerous references in Holy Scripture, which I'll set oot in due course – for the principle o' the sovereignty o' the people."

James sniffed huffily. With admirable nerve, and fixing the greatest Latin poet in all Christendom with the kind of imperious look that certain infants can manage wonderfully well, he asked,

"Was I no' chosen by God, Maister Geordie ? Am I no' the Lord's anointed ?"

It was not that the old curmudgeon was short of an answer. Heaven forbid. But, for some reason, he sniffed back just as huffily, and changed the subject. The pair were walking back through the castle's Lower Square, in the direction of the Prince's Tower – a company of the Royal Guard having been brought to attention as their monarch passed – when Master Buchanan began to speak of other things.

"This last wee while we hae been touchin' fae time tae time on certain matters o' whit we might ca' myth or legend. Naturally we hae spoken o' Arthur and Merlin. We hae mentioned auld saints such as Kentigern and Columba. We hae spoken o' Troy and... och, well, monie such things. Noo, when we're dealin' wae the past... far past, distant... then we see, as Saint Paul put it, through a glass darkly. That is tae say, yir young Grace, whether we are availin' oorsels o' the riches o' the Greek Myths, or the Arthurian Romances, or thae hagiologies o' the Celtic Saints... or even the Old Testament..."

He looked around warily. Not so long previously he would have been in dire trouble for the suggestion he was about to make.

"We must aye tak care no' tae read them in a naïve and literal manner. Which is tae say – they are stories that point in the direction o' truth, without bein' jist exactly, fully and precisely whit happened."

By now they were climbing the flight of steps which led to the school-room in the Prince's Tower. There was no formal class that morning. None of the other pupils were in attendance, for this was no ordinary day. The Regent was expected…

"Ye hae seen fir yirsel' the hash that's been made o' Arthur and Merlin. Inventions, distortions, anachronisms an' the like…"

From the school-room window he cast a glance down toward the Round Table on the sward.

"Places have a' been muddled up. Personalities have been miscast and misrepresented. Elements o' the doonright fantastic have been pit in. But something o' the essence o' the thing comes through in spite o' it a'. A general gist o' deeds and purposes."

He observed from the expression on James's face that, as usual, the boy was taking in more of his meaning than would usually be expected of a child of that age.

"As we baith ken, there is real history behind the tales telt aboot Arthur an' Merlin, but often enough a story will be crafted tae express an idea that canna be pit ower any other way. Such a story wid be a myth, an' there's nae real folk or places, in an historical way o' things, gien rise tae it. The tales o' the Roman and Greek gods are fair examples o' yon. An' truth tae tell, the Bible – the Old Testament, that is – has its share o' such. Then again, we hae prophesy. When stories are telt o' things that are tae come aboot in the future. Again... or mair than ever... we must treat such matter wae caution. Aye, great caution."

The thick door of the school-room was bolted. There was no guard directly outside. The walls were thick. Buchanan was free to speak his mind.

"These matters... whether we are dealing wae past deeds, eternal truths, or future events... are the proper preserve o' the poet. It's tae the poet that inspiration comes. If the poet is inspired enough, revelation may follow. But the poet receives images, feelings, symbols... his art is no' precise. By the very nature o' inspiration and revelation the poet expresses what comes through him in a kind o' code. He imparts hints, pointers. He may call a warrior a lion. He may call a century a day. He may call the plague a hag. He may express hope by a star..."

The wee king instinctively drew meaning from such talk. He was himself destined to be a poet, and his tutor knew it.

"Prophecy is a particularly chancy business. No' jist fae the point of view o' accurate prediction, but for the safety o' the prognosticator. Folk expect clarity. When powerful persons don't hear what they want tae hear, or when things turn oot different fae their interpretation o' prophesy, then the poet is likely tae suffer their wrath."

The sound of shouted commands, marching boots and rattling weapons from without was another indication that men were being prepared for the imminent expiry of the truce.

"Noo, yir Grace, I consider it appropriate, aye, and fitting, that I acquaint ye wae certain matters appertaining tae events o' the immediate future and the mair distant future. Events and outcomes relating to your ain realm and reign."

Buchanan assumed one of his more pompous poses. Nose in the air. Lips pursed.

"A' this o' poetry and prophesy is pertinent. It's tae the point. I hope I hae made it clear that it's no a' jist blethers. It's a' a matter o' proper interpretation o' the images and symbols and such facts as hae come tae the poet in inspiration. Noo... heed closely tae this. There was a man ca'd Thomas Learmonth o' Ercildoune. He lived in the Border country in the days o' Wallace and the Bruce. The story goes that one day Thomas was in the forest, by the Eildon Hills, and he met the Queen o' Elfland. She was right bonnie, and the long and the short o' it is Thomas was fair enchanted wae her. He followed her intae Fairyland, where he stayed for seven years. When he left she had granted him the gifts o' poetry an' prophesy."

"And is a' that true, Maister Geordie ? O' Elfland and fairies ?"

The little brow was furrowed. James hoped that it wasn't just signs and symbols.

"Well, yir Grace. Ne'er despise a belief in fairy-folk. There is mair, much mair, in this world than maist folk see and hear aroon' them."

It wasn't an answer, but it was better than James had anticipated. His tutor continued.

"It's said that Thomas was incapable of speaking falsehood – hence his nickname – 'True Thomas'. He prophesied much that came to pass – such as the tragic death o' Alexander the Third, wha' fell fae a cliff, ye'll mind, an' the terrible Battle o' Flodden… But here's tae the point."

The old man rubbed his hands together and beamed with satisfaction.
"Tales o' Thomas are oft mixed up wae stories o' Arthur and Merlin. It seems that Thomas visited what was supposed tae be the grave o' Merlin in Drumelzier – a place near Peebles – ye ken. There, at that spot, he penned a maist significant prophecy which we do well tae heed wae utmost seriousness."

The grey beard bristled. The beady eyes glinted. The predatory nostrils flared.

"When Tweed and Powsail meet at Merlin's grave,
  Scotland and England shall one monarch have."

"Note… aye, note wae care – 'When Tweed and Powsail meet…' No' If Tweed and Powsail meet.' Ye see that outcome is assured – Union. One monarch – two realms."

He let that hang in the air to some dramatic effect.

"Regarding matters mair immediate. Thomas disappeared in later life, thought tae have returned tae Elfland. Monie believe… aye, and insist, that Thomas – like Arthur before him – lies sleeping just, awaiting the time when the nation will need him to lead an army in battle. It has been said, yir Grace – and heed this closely – that Thomas sleeps yet in the Hill o' Dumbuck, but a mile fae Dumbarton Rock. It is said that Thomas will lead yon army oot fae Dumbuck an' defeat the forces o' evil on the banks o' the Clyde."

Their eyes locked together in a depth of instinctive mutual understanding which was uncanny between a four year old boy and an old man. So absorbed were they that they failed entirely to register the sounds of distant excitement which signified the arrival of the Regent.

"Mind this well the morn, yir Grace – Thomas and Dumbuck."

Chapter Sixteen
Fortitude and Fear

It had been the Lord's Day. Now the sun was setting magnificently. Layers of heavy, dark cloud contrasted with a varied range of golds, scarlets and violets. Such skyscapes were common over the Clyde. Evening was falling and Glasgow was subdued. A chill breeze blew off the river and the town's craftsmen, merchants and humbler folk were mostly indoors kindling fires, but any sizeable body of men, particularly military men, cannot assemble in a public place without attracting a certain amount of attention. There were twenty cavalry and seventy infantry. John Cunninghame of Drumquhassil led his horsemen, and Thomas Crawfurd of Jordanhill, in overall command, led the foot-soldiers. Each infantryman was armed with a sword and dagger. On a leather strap, hung over his back, each carried a heavy musket. Each man's head was protected by a steel helmet. All of the soldiers wore, from left shoulder to waist, a sash of red and white – the heraldic colours of the Earl of Lennox – over a metal breastplate. Duncan Robertson's bow, arrows and dirk had been returned to him. He wore no helmet or armour of any sort. His green and blue checked plaid set him apart from the others.

All of these men had attended public worship that day, and not a few of them were still reflecting on the sermon which had been powerfully delivered by a reformed minister in a part of the cathedral. The text had been – on the instruction of the Regent – Isaiah chapter fifty-four, verse seventeen –

"But all the weapons that are made against thee, shall not prosper: and every tongue that shall rise against thee in judgment, thou shalt condemn. This is the heritage of the Lord's servants, and their righteousness is of me, saith the Lord."

The Regent had left Glasgow for Stirling early that morning. His place, he had announced, should now be with King James.

The force had mustered outside the Bishop's Castle. The infantry had followed the cavalry downhill by the High Street to the Mercat Cross. Thomas Crawfurd, who was handsomely mounted, rode over to Cunninghame.

"It's by nae means impossible that one, or mair, spies will hae gaun on afore us for the Rock wae word o' this company o' oor's for the ears o' Fleming and Hamilton. Sae get ye on after any such wae your bit cavalry here. Mak ye certain that nane reach Dumbarton by this road tae spoil oor advantage o' surprise. All depends on it."

Cunnighhame gave Crawfurd one of his more roguish lop-sided grins.

"Ye don't imagine fer one minute that yon hadnae occurred tae me ? There's no' a soul will leave the toon by the West Port this night but we'll have him bound, gagged and led at the point o' a dagger tae a suitable place o' confinement. If sae much as a whisper reaches Dumbarton Castle, it'll be nae fault o' my bonnie boys."

Crawfurd returned grin for grin and the pair shook hands through their thick gauntlets.

"God be with you."

"And with you."

Cunninghame's horsemen trotted off, two-abreast, with their customary style and discipline. They headed westward along the north bank of the Clyde. When the cavalry had ridden out of sight, the infantry marched after them, out of the West Port along the Dumbarton road. For five long, monotonous hours they trudged along the open road and through little communities such as Partick, Yoker and Kilbowie, under the cover of darkness. Only the officers knew where they were headed, and why. The Kilpatrick Hills lay off to their right and the wide river stretched out on their left, when they reached the garrison of Dunglass Castle, a tiny fortress on the Clyde shore, just two and a half miles to the east of Dumbarton Rock. Ahead, the distinctive silhouette of a distant hill became visible through the gloom.

"D'ye think it looks like a sleeping soldier ?" Thomas Crawfurd laughed gently as he asked the question of his Ensign, Captain Alexander Ramsay.

"Yon's an auld tale... but, aye, I dare say it has the look o' a man lyin' on his side. That wid be the heid and yon wid be the shoulder..."

The two men were mounted at the head of their column of infantry. Between them, also on horseback, rode Duncan Robertson. Ramsay was a red-faced, ginger-bearded desperado in his late twenties. He had been at Crawfurd's right hand for a number of years and had acquitted himself conspicuously at Langside. He smelled of whisky.

"We'd do well to speak respectfully o' yon place. It's said to be o' the fairy folk."

Duncan took heed of the man's words. He also knew better than to slight the sith. Instinctively he crossed himself. The other two looked at him askance. Ramsay was about to make some sarcastic remark but thought the better of it. In truth he and Crawfurd would have done the same, not so many years before.

Duncan had spoken little on the journey. Most men were nervous, if not actually afraid, prior to military action. When Duncan was anxious he was not talkative. He was thinking of the fact that in a few hours he hoped to kill a particular man, that he might have to kill men he had known and liked. That he might well be killed himself. He thought much of Margaret Lafferty. Apart from these things, the Highlander, though he could ride a horse, seldom did so, and after fifteen miles in the saddle he was sore.

At length the company reached the hamlet of Milton of Colquhoun, in the Parish of Kilpatrick. Towering above the tiny community, in the darkness, there loomed another mighty rock. This hill emerged from the surrounding landscape in a less dramatic way than the nearby Dumbarton Rock, but at over five hundred feet it was considerably higher. This rock was also basalt and the hill had the appearance of some massive crouching beast. Some believed that it was from the shape of this formation that Dumbarton had taken the elephant as its heraldic symbol. In the night it was felt as a vast, sinister and powerfully disturbing presence. This was Dumbuck.

*   *   *

While the Regent's soldiers had been marching westward that evening, Margaret Lafferty had sat on her cot in the hospital building thinking of Creeslough and her family. There were only two other patients, and when they slept she had cried a little. She longed for her mother. She had been in the hospital for over three weeks now. Her wounds were healing wonderfully well, but there was the ache of homesickness in her heart. Soon she would have to leave and find work and lodging in the burgh. Strangely, she had not seen Canon Carmichael at all that day. Margaret Kennedy had attended to her in his absence. Brother Andrew had looked in on her once, looking very distracted. As she wiped her tears on her sleeve, she heard the singing coming from the Church itself – that almost supernatural sound. Faintly through thick stone walls and through the trees of the orchard. Whispering to her in the night –

Salve Regina, mater misericordiae:
Vita, dulcedo, et spes nostra, salve...

There were only six singers. She knew this. But they could have been a host of angels.

*   *   *

While Margaret had listened to this heavenly music, Canon Carmichael had been unburdening himself to Brother Andrew. In the quarters of the spiritual leader of the Collegiate Church of Saint Mary, the young priest had broken down and made his confession... his terrible confession.

*   *   *

That night Mary Queen of Scots won at cards.

*   *   *

Thomas Crawfurd had chosen the farmhouse of Dumbuck as his base of operations for the raid on Dumbarton Rock because, at just a mile and a half from the castle, it was not too near and not too far, because it was relatively isolated and because the proprietor was a loyal and dependable subject of King James. Here, at midnight, the seventy men who had marched from Glasgow made their rendezvous with a further thirty led by a certain Captain Hume.

In front of the farmhouse, under the massive, overbearing rock of Dumbuck, the men were assembled. At a short distance in each direction, ten of Cunninghame's horsemen guarded the road to the west and to the east. From horseback Thomas Crawfurd, looking every inch a leader of men, addressed his hundred in a voice which would have done credit to John Knox.

"This night I speak to you, not as soldiers under orders, but as friends and willing men. The midnight hour has passed. The truce o' these past months is now expired and we find oorsels again in a state o' war. A war in which brother is turned against brother... father against son. To different men it is a conflict about different things – those of us loyal tae King James against thae who wid hae Mary Stuart back on the throne... oor Regent, Lennox, against the Hamiltons... but tae maist, an' right truly, it is a war o' religion. We in this realm o' Scotland hae, this past dozen years, been liberated fae the corruptions, cruelties an' wicked superstitions o' the Church o' Rome. We are free tae worship God in a true an' proper fashion. That freedom came by the Grace o' God, but was paid for dearly in martyrs' blood... Is there amang ye one who wid hae back the tyranny o' pope an' priest... o' Inquisition an' the stake ?"

There was a profound growl of dissent. Crawfurd thrust a gauntleted fist in the direction of Dumbarton Rock.

"Yonder stands the gate by which the pope's armies could yet enter our land an' return us tae bondage. There are some here who want tae avenge the murders o' King Henry an' the Regent Moray... count me among them. By taking the Rock fae Fleming we would take it fae Catholic Mary an' deal a death blow tae her hopes o' ever rulin' this realm again."

Mutterings of approval greeted these words. Crawfurd gestured with a thumb toward Duncan Robertson, who had sat set-faced and staring into the darkness above the heads of that body of men.

"Here is the man who will lead us to victory. Here is the man who will guide us into that stronghold which has stood beyond our grasp a' these months. I trust him... you can trust him. I believe he has been sent to us by the Lord. It will not be an easy thing.

The rock is high and steep. They will be on their guard. Men will die this night. But I tell you this... We owe it to Patrick Hamilton, to George Wishart, to Walter Myln and a' the ithers who gave their bodies to be burned in the fire that we might hae True Religion in this land. We owe it to Christ Jesus, who gave us his innocent body on the Cross for oor salvation."

By now Crawfurd's voice was hoarse with heartfelt emotion.

"We owe it to the God that created us in his ain image tae hazard oor lives tae secure his true Reformed Kirk in this realm. If there are any amang you who are feared, let them turn away. You are free men... mind it."

There was total silence. No one moved a muscle. Then from memory, by way of prayer, Thomas Crawfurd began to recite the eighteenth psalm –

"Surely thou wilt light my candle:
the Lord my God will lighten my darkness.
For by thee I have broken through an host,
And by my God I have leaped over a wall..."

Many of those present, knowing the words, joined in.

"For who is God besides the Lord ?
  Or who is mighty save our God ?
  God girdeth me with strength,
  and maketh my way upright.
  He maketh my feet like hinds' feet,
  and setteth me upon mine high places..."

Duncan found that he had joined in quietly in the Gaelic.

"Thou hast also given me the shield of thy salvation:
  and thy right hand hath stayed me,
  and thy loving kindness hath caused me to increase.
  Thou hast enlarged my steps under me,
  And my heels have not slid…"

… Therefore I will praise thee, O Lord,
  among the nations, and will sing unto thy Name.
  Great deliverances giveth he unto his King,
  and sheweth mercy to his anointed,
  even to David, and to his seed forever."

The "Amen" from a hundred throats echoed like a peal of thunder from the rock of Dumbuck… causing the hairs to rise on the back of Duncan Robertson's neck.

*   *   *

Having praised the Lord, it was time to pass the ammunition… These men were going to be applying themselves to the sort of prolonged physical exertion that should not be undertaken on empty an stomach – most of them had already marched fifteen miles – so first they were fed. When a simple but nourishing meal of coarse bread, cheese and small beer had been finished off, the officers split the company into teams of twenty and began to instruct the men on the details of the operation. It was a cloudless night. Stars shone distinctly but there was no moon. Even so, there was no point in giving enemy look-outs the gift of bright clothing, so all of the Lennox sashes of red and white were discarded and the soldiers – all of whom wore otherwise drab clothing as a matter economic necessity – were ordered to smear their faces with dirt and dull their breastplates with mud, the latter being easier said than done. Then ladders and grappling-hooks were issued to the leading party.

Fifty men were chosen to spearhead the initial rock climb and entry into the castle, with the other fifty remaining at a short distance from the foot of the rock as reinforcements. The terrain to be covered was uneven, boggy marshland. It was thick with reeds which grew in places to the height of a man's head, punctuated with occasional birch trees, and it was riddled with ditches. This was a difficult enough stretch of country to pass through in broad daylight. In almost total darkness it was to prove something of a nightmare. The shoreline itself would have made much easier going, but it was wisely ruled out as being too exposed. A number of ropes were tied together to make one enormous length of cord. The men would proceed in single file, roughly three or four paces apart where practicable, and each would hold onto the cord. In this way it was hoped that none would go astray. Hagbuts were slung across the men's backs, leaving their hands free to negotiate the reeds and – eventually – the Rock.

In fact, it was almost three in the morning before the first men set out. At their head was Duncan Robertson, the guide, with the rope tied around his waist. Behind him was Thomas Crawfurd, then Captain Alexander Ramsay. Next came the men who carried the ladders and the grappling-hooks. Following on, clinging to the great snake of rope, came the rest of the foot-soldiers. Cunninghame's twenty horsemen had taken up a position on the road, something near midway between the farmhouse of Dumbuck and Dumbarton Castle.

The men in the marsh were conscious mainly of the feel of the ground under their feet – fearing to sink into bogs, or fall into ditches – the salt and sulphur smell of the shoreline, the awareness of the wide river nearby in the darkness and, most importantly, the man in front of them. Although the night was cold, before long they began to feel the heat of exertion and sweat under their layers of clothing and armour. The heavy hagbuts grew heavier. Swords caught in reeds. Ankles twisted excruciatingly on hummocks, driftwood and boulders. Yet near silence was maintained.

At one point, Thomas Crawfurd looked up into the heavens. Seeing those millions of stars, it brought to him a sense of perspective, and he thought, like many a man before and since, of the tiny insignificance of himself and his concerns, of this little kingdom and even perhaps this world, until he remembered that he and the men around him were significant to… were indeed loved by… the Creator of everything in those heavens. They mattered. This thing they were doing mattered. Even when measured against infinity.

*   *   *

Archbishop John Hamilton was looking at the same sky as Thomas Crawfurd – the same stars, at the same moment. But he was thinking very different thoughts.

There was a sense in which the Archbishop had much to hope for – much to be optimistic about. In a short time – a few weeks, perhaps – the ships would come. After a short and successful campaign, Scotland would once again be a Catholic realm. As the nation's leading churchman, and one of the heroic garrison of Dumbarton Rock, John Hamilton would surely be the man of the moment. Returning Scotland to the One, Holy, Catholic and Apostolic Church would be a tremendous achievement for its own sake – for the sake of innumerable souls. It would please God. There would be great rejoicing in Heaven. The Pope would reward him with a cardinal's hat. He would be free to leave this bare prison and enjoy the fruits of victory and grateful recognition. But these were not the thoughts which filled his head that night. He was in the grip of a terrible depression. He was filled with an irrational sense of impending doom. Looking into the depths of the ink-blue sky, he identified the constellation of Orion – the Hunter. He twisted his thin lips into a bitter, ironic smile. He felt like a hunted man. His head ached. His body was covered with painful sores which tormented him mostly at night. He could find no relief in wine – it lay sour in his stomach and failed to cool his blood or soothe his mind – he was unable to sleep. Insomnia and a fevered imagination had driven him from his bed in the north-facing Wallace Tower. He had climbed up onto the eastern summit of the Rock. From there he had peered through the night, down over the sleeping little burgh, beyond, through the hills of the Vale of Leven, into the impenetrable darkness of the Highlands.

He was slowly dying. He knew it. The disease was spreading through his body and twisting his mind. Old pleasures were now beyond him. Satisfaction eluded him. Each month he seemed to age a year. He knew that self-pity was a sin, but he could not help feeling wretchedly sorry for himself... even to the point of tears. Surely God had some great consolation in store for him. He needed to pray.

*   *   *

There had been at least one man who had wanted to accept Thomas Crawfurd's challenge to decline involvement in this attack. One man who had wanted to have no part of it.

Hunter Miller, tallish, slim, balding and supple in his middle-years, a one-time hawker from the village of Kilbarchan in Renfrewshire, was not afraid of cold steel or hot musket balls. He had seen action on several occasions, keeping a steady nerve and acquitting himself with honour each time. He had been one of those of the right wing on the field of battle at Langside who had spearheaded a counterattack which had broken the ranks of Mary's army and turned the tide of that conflict. No, Miller was not afraid of military action... he was terrified of heights.

As white knuckles gripped his section of rope, and he floundered his way through the bogs of the Clyde-shore, the sweat on his furrowed brow was not entirely caused by physical effort. Had he been given prior knowledge of the nature of this mission he would undoubtedly have fortified himself with strong drink. However there had been nothing other than weak beer at Dumbuck, and he was now filled with horror at the prospect of climbing these hundreds of feet of rock on narrow ladders. As his mind's eye made near reality of various scenarios in which he would panic and disgrace himself, Miller was nearly vomiting with nerves as he squelched forward through the reeds, his body doggedly obeying the will rather than the instincts. When he had been given the chance to escape, like so many men in such circumstances, he had lacked the courage to be a coward.

*   *   *

John Hamilton came down from the top of the Rock and, in full clerical vestments, made his way in the darkness down the narrow and precarious stairway which ran through the central cleft. In the Chapel of Saint Patrick he sat between the Sacrament House and the altar. For a while he stared, deep in thought, at the golden Crucifix. Then he prayed. He prayed for Scotland. He prayed for the garrison… and he prayed for himself. But there are times when a man – even an archbishop - feels that God just isn't listening.

*   *   *

Some thirty miles to north-east, George Buchanan was closeted in another small chamber on another fortified rock. He too was wide awake. That evening he had meditated at some length on certain of the psalms. He had then spent an hour in the Church of the Holy Rude in fervent prayer. Now he was in his own little room, the door carefully secured again. Once more there was the single lit candle and the goblet of pure, clear water. Yet again the cowled figure was breathing slowly… deeply. On this occasion, however, spread before him on a wide table, was a large, rectangular piece of cloth. It was white and it bore a red diagonal cross. In the quarters there were four red roses – the Rosy Cross, in a manner of speaking. Buchanan sat erect, spine straight. The palms of his hands were pressed flat on the surface of the emblem, about eighteen inches apart. Again he looked into the bright, steady candle-flame and visualised the Rock of Dumbarton with uncanny clarity.

*   *   *

As well as innumerable ditches, the raiding party had to negotiate two substantial burns, each of which they discovered to be bridged by the trunk of a felled tree. When they were only a matter of a few hundred yards from the Rock, which now appeared to them like a huge rugged, black dome looming into the night sky, Duncan, in the lead, came to a clearing in the reeds to find himself on the bank of the second burn. It flowed swiftly through a deep gully which appeared to be, perhaps, about ten yards wide. In fact it was very difficult to estimate the width, the far bank being obscured in the darkness. Duncan was about to set out carefully on the rounded surface of the tree trunk when a fantastic thing happened. The Highlander's eyes widened and he took a pace backward, almost knocking over Crawfurd who was close on his heels.

"Mercy of God… what… what is that ?"

It may seem incredible, but it is a matter of record. There appeared before them, on the opposite bank, what appeared to be a brightly luminous figure. Some of the men took it for a ghost; others thought it was one of the fairy folk; Thomas Crawfurd came to believe it was an angel. Later it was rationalised as having been a "will-o-the-wisp" – an ignited pocket of marsh gas. Whatever it was, if it had not appeared precisely there and then, the raid may have come to ruin. In the eerie light which came from this phenomenon, Duncan and Crawfurd were able to discern that the tree-bridge was, in fact, in a state of near collapse. It would have borne the weight, possibly, of two or three men and then given way, with all plunging into the rushing burn below and dragging others with them on the rope. This would almost certainly have created an involuntary outcry which, now so close to the castle, would have alerted the guards. This damage must have occurred recently, for the bridge had been sound enough, to Duncan's knowledge, when he had left Dumbarton.

In the event, having been thus miraculously forewarned, half a dozen men, under the whispered instruction of Crawfurd, were able, by the skilful use of rope and ladders, to render the bridge fit for its purpose. It all took time, of course, working in near-silence and with great care. By the time they were ready to cross the bridge and venture onto the level and more exposed land beyond, the first hint of dawn-light was creeping up on them.

*　　　*　　　*

The last thing they wanted was to be attempting to scale the Rock in broad daylight, so swift movement became imperative.

"There will be no guard on this eastern side."

Duncan spoke with the authority of intimate knowledge.

"It is the opinion of the garrison's officers that this face of the Rock is impossible for men to climb, so they keep no watch here."

Crawfurd and his Ensign drew alongside Duncan, and Ramsay gave him a sceptical look.

"Aye, well… if ye ask me, it was nae matter o' chance that yon bridge was broken. I reckon they're expectin' an assault fae this airt."

He paused to take a swig of whisky from a small drinking horn while Crawfurd, ignoring his remark, took matters in hand.

"Right… if fifty men are caught out here, in this open ground when light comes, we'll be seen for sure. The best thing will be for the first company to get up right close to the Rock. Line up alongside it."

Crawfurd waved forward the ladder-bearing party, and he, with Duncan and Ramsay, sprinted over the exposed ground to the grassy bank at the base of the Rock. From this position they were not visible from any inhabited part of the castle. The main gateway was located around on the north-west facing side, looking over the river toward the burgh. The Rock itself screened them from the town which was, anyway, half a mile distant. Crawfurd glanced quickly upward then turned to the guide.

"Now, man, Duncan… it's up to you."

Grasping the archer's shoulder with a huge, gauntleted paw, Crawfurd looked him steadily in the eye and smiled a smile that spoke of trust and respect. Here was a leader who knew how to get the best out of men. Duncan, who found himself, as was so often the case, in the grip of mixed emotions, was unable to reply.

*　　　*　　　*

The Highlander chose a precise spot at the north-east base of the Rock. There, he informed Crawfurd, ladders would be required… long ladders. Accordingly, three sets of twenty feet each were lashed together to form one enormous sixty foot ladder. Precariously, this was eased up the jagged rock-face and the base was set into the grassy soil at the foot. Robertson taking the lead, the advance party began to climb. Perhaps if the twine lashing had not been completed in such haste, or if the foot of the ladders had been more securely fixed, there would have been no problem, but the combined weight and movement of five clambering men ascending with clumsy urgency dislodged the huge ladder, causing it first to sway alarmingly, and then it brought them all crashing to the ground.

It is not possible for a group of men to fall from such a height into a tangle of wood and bodies without making any sound. There were, of course, involuntary howls of alarm, fright and pain, the like of which would normally have been expected to arouse the doziest of guards – even those at some distance – but, as it happened, inexplicably, the garrison remained oblivious. Fortunately the ladders were capable of repair, and because they had fallen onto soft turf, none of the men was seriously injured. Duncan, who as leader had fallen from the greatest height, was lucky only to have been winded.

Precious time was used up in making the necessary repairs to the ladder. This time the twine lashing was tighter and more carefully knotted, and on this second attempt the climbers were ordered to ascend slowly, carefully and in a unified rhythm of movement.

They were aiming for a certain small ash tree which grew out of a cleft in the rock. When Duncan reached the top of the ladder he discovered, to his considerable exasperation, that they were some twenty feet short of the tree.

"I'm going to have to climb, myself, to the tree. I'll take the rope."

"I'll gie ye a hand, man."

Ignoring Robertson's protests, a secretly terrified and sweating Crawfurd followed, taking great care to use exactly the hand and foot-holds employed by the guide, the tangles of roots and grudged inches of rock ledge. At length they had one end of the rope securely bound around the ash tree, and the other tied to the top of the ladder.

They had now rendered it possible for the entire raiding party to climb, by ladder and rope, from the base of the Rock to the little tree. There remained, however, some thirty yards or so between the ash and that particular section of the defensive wall which was the target Robertson had selected for them. With their hearts in their mouths, the man from Glen Finlas and his companion from Jordanhill began to climb. They were hugely grateful for the fact that here they were not dealing with steep rock-face, but with a rounded slope of grass and bushes, the roots of which proved strong enough to give adequate climbing support. By the time they reached the base of the wall it was fully daylight.

*   *   *

As foul mischance would have it, Hunter Miller was not far behind the leaders on the ladder. In comparative darkness it had been possible for him to climb the ladder without feeling the sensation of height quite as acutely as he had feared. But now, in broad daylight, his senses bombarded his mind mercilessly with the awful reality that he was perched on a thin spar of wood hundreds of feet above the ground. More horrifying was the knowledge that there was available to him absolutely no avenue of escape. He could not get down that ladder because of all the men below him. He could not even hasten to the top because of those ahead of him. This was a nightmare from which he could not awaken. He would, in all seriousness, have welcomed a musket ball in the head to put him out of this misery. He was literally on the verge of tears. In his imagination he threw himself off the ladder. He felt sure he must. Hellish waves of panic engulfed him. He was whimpering... he was actually whimpering. His bloodstream filled with adrenalin that demanded physical expression, but the poor wretch had nothing to fight but fear, and nowhere to run but to certain death. Suddenly he realised that the man ahead of him was no longer there. He saw a pair of boots about a dozen feet above him. The man below him was angrily demanding to know why he wasn't moving. Miller's hands gripped the sides of the ladder with a fierceness he could not release. He was literally scared stiff. Petrified. Could move neither up nor down.

It was fortunate that Miller had not taken his panic attack on the sixty foot ladder, but on a shorter one which had been pulled into position above the ash tree. By excellent good luck Alexander Ramsay was the man below Miller. Perhaps, had he but known, he could have prevented this potentially fatal incident simply by filling the Kilbarchan man with whisky, but things were too far gone for that to take effect now anyway. Ramsay was rough and ready in his methods, but he was also quick-witted. He sized up the situation in moments and whispered orders – at the top of his voice, so to speak – for more rope to be sent up. When this was eventually passed to him, he was able, with enormous difficulty, to bind a rigid Miller securely by hands, waist and ankles, to the ladder. Then, with remarkable skills of agility, sheer whisky-assisted nerve and a little help from the man beneath him, Ramsay was able to turn the ladder around so that Miller was now, as it were, underneath it, and men were free to climb on the rungs past the bound and speechless Miller.

Finally, by the time Robertson and Crawfurd were able to raise a ladder near to the top of the defensive wall, yet another strange thing had happened. A dense sea mist – more of a fog actually – which might normally have been expected to settle over the marsh or the river at ground level, had actually surrounded the top of the fortress rock. Sensing the advantage this gave them the pair signalled to the chain of attackers on the ladders below with unmistakable gestures. Moments later, with the aid of grappling-hooks, they led the way over the wall.

Chapter Seventeen
Mercy and Justice

When Duncan Robertson went over the wall of Dumbarton Castle he had one overriding priority. He would kill John Carpenter. Lord Fleming would be captured and probably hanged – let that be as it may – but Robertson had to deal with the sergeant personally. On the ride from Glasgow, and even when he was fighting his way through the marsh, he had been picturing in his mind, again and again, the sight of those vicious weals on Margaret Lafferty's back. He had been reminding himself vividly of how these wounds had been inflicted and by whom. He had brought himself to accept that Margaret was now dead. He intended to take a life for a life.

The nearest sentry, as it turned out, was seated about one hundred yards to the west of the place where Duncan and Thomas Crawfurd climbed over the wall. In spite of the thick mist, the man spotted them at once and started to shout for assistance. Almost immediately half a dozen semi-clothed defenders appeared, clambering up from the direction of the Windy Hall in the cleft of the Rock. These men, being quite unarmed, began in desperation to throw rocks and stones in the direction of the attackers, who now numbered five, with men pouring over the wall behind them at a swift rate. Alexander Ramsay, face flushed and grinning with apparent relish, unsheathed his sword and charged toward the group of defenders. Three of them closed in on him, but the ensign had the advantage of his blade and the fact that he positively enjoyed combat. He swung his sword with skill, energy and even a certain impressive grace, while laughing and mocking the stone-throwers. Behind him he could hear increasing numbers of fellow attackers roaring their battle-cry –

"Lennox… Lennox… Lennox."

Duncan knew exactly where he would find Carpenter. Each man had an allotted station in the event of any attack. This was something which had been practised from time to time. Carpenter's place was on the roof of the Wallace Tower, the stronghold which commanded the castle's main entrance, and in which the Flemings and Archbishop Hamilton had their quarters. Duncan was confident that, from a certain spot on the northern slope of this summit, he would be able to pick Carpenter off. The Highlander entertained absolutely no notion of fair play or chivalry in this matter. He intended to give his victim as little chance as possible, and he would place himself in the minimum of danger.

Ramsay was soon joined by reinforcements, and three of the defenders were slain. Just as bloodstained weapons were being noisily drawn from lifeless bodies, the attackers heard an almighty rumbling behind them. Turning in astonishment, Ramsay and his comrades-in-arms saw that the sheer weight of the men, eagerly pulling themselves over the wall, had caused it to crumble and collapse, fortunately – yet again – causing no serious injury.

It became quickly apparent that there was no appreciable organised defensive effort. Crawfurd impressed his command upon those attackers who were now within the castle wall. Seemingly, from what could be discerned through the fog, some of the Queen's Party had secured themselves in the castle's major strengths, which were the Wallace Tower, the White Tower, which was on the western peak, and the Windy Hall in the cleft. Many others, mainly the half-naked common soldiers, were taking full advantage of the poor visibility to make good their escape by whichever route presented itself. The surprise of the attack had completely unnerved them.

Meanwhile, Robertson had unobtrusively detached himself from the main body of attackers and was working his way cautiously around the Rock in a north-westerly direction. The green and blue check of his plaid made excellent camouflage, and at length he settled himself into a position at the base on the inside of the defensive wall, from which, even through the damp mist, he could fairly clearly see the men on the roof of the tower. But there was no sign of Carpenter.

Duncan would have been able to distinguish the sergeant's figure, his style of movement, even his features... but he was definitely not on that roof. His usual company were there. Duncan could identify each man, but the orders were not being given by Carpenter.

*　　　*　　　*

Unlike most of the garrison, Lord Fleming was up and about, fully dressed, and clear-headed. At an early stage of the attack it was perfectly clear to him, from the general shouting and bawling, and the appalling sight of fleeing men, just what was afoot. It was the work of a moment to divest himself of his more obviously expensive garments and don a breastplate and helmet. His obvious escape route would have been via the main north gate. However, he naturally, but mistakenly, assumed that the enemy would literally be at the gate. Blaspheming, pushing servants aside, and leaving his ashen-faced wife and near-hysterical daughter to their own devices, he ran from the Wallace Tower, through the cleft, in the direction of the Portcullis Arch.

*   *   *

When a company of the attackers, led by Crawfurd, seized some of the castle's artillery and turned them on the towers in which the remaining defenders were holding out, the conflict, such as it had been, was effectively over. Dumbarton Castle had been captured for the King's Party.

*   *   *

As a bitterly disappointed and mystified Duncan Robertson made his way down from the summit of the eastern peak, he saw the figure of Lord Fleming as he dashed for the cover of the Portcullis Arch. The helmet and breastplate may have provided protection, but they proved a very ineffective disguise. In an instant Duncan put arrow to bow and adopted the characteristic stance of the Highland archer, with the rear leg bent, and drew careful aim. In fairness, it was a poor firing position and Duncan was out of practice. His arrow sparked harmlessly off the rock just as Fleming disappeared under the arch.

*   *   *

When four of Crawfurd's men finally managed to batter in the heavy, iron-studded door of Saint Patrick's Chapel, they were surprised to find a heavy, bleary-eyed, pockmarked figure, wearing a steel helmet and a jacket of chain-mail over purple clerical vestments. The man was almost comically attempting to hide a gold crucifix under his clothing. In such circumstances the archbishop's surrender was surprisingly dignified.

*   *   *

The prisoners – who included neither John Carpenter nor Lord Fleming – were herded into two closely-guarded groups in the courtyard between the Wallace Tower and the Windy Hall in that part of the fortress known as the Over Bailey. The common soldiers were gathered in one group, while the "quality" prisoners stood apart, their guards treating them with rather greater respect. The select band included the elegant and attractive Lady Fleming, her scowling daughter, Verac, the French ambassador, Fleming of Boghall, the Englishman, John Hall… and John Hamilton, Archbishop of St. Andrews.

Crawfurd of Jordanhill removed his breastplate and, from around his torso he unravelled a large flag, which he had borne thus on his person since they had left Glasgow. He folded this standard and handed it to the ensign Ramsay, who in turn, with a quietly spoken order, passed it to one of his men. One might have expected the principal flagstaff of Dumbarton Castle to be at the summit of the highest peak, but it was not so. In fact it was on the roof of the Wallace Tower, above the main gateway. Crawfurd had wanted to take the red and gold Lion Rampant, but this would have been appropriate only if the monarch had been there in person. It had been George Buchanan, strangely enough, not the Regent himself, who had insisted that the emblem of Lennox – the red diagonal cross, with four red roses on white – be raised above the captured fortress.

The victorious raiders – including a released and largely recovered Hunter Miller – formed up in ranks and listened respectfully as the Lennox standard replaced that of Fleming, and Thomas Crawfurd addressed all present.

"Wae a' due thanks tae Lord God Almighty, I hereby take this Dumbarton Castle for its rightful sovereign, King James Sixth o' Scots. God Save the King."

A hundred voices echoed these sentiments right heartily. Treating Lady Fleming to one of his most charming smiles, he continued –

"Some will receive mercy…"

Then with a very different expression he faced John Hamilton.

"…and ithers will receive justice."

*   *   *

A chip of rock, flying from the impact of Duncan's arrow, had actually ricocheted from Lord Fleming's helmet. Emerging from the other side of the Portcullis Arch, and now out of the Highlander's line of fire, the Governor had, to avoid a nearby party of the attackers, and at considerable risk, leapt from a high precipice of the Rock, thereby enabling him to flee the castle by the south postern gate. From there he had sprinted to the shore and, discarding breastplate and helmet, swum unnoticed to a small fishing craft. Once aboard he'd had little difficulty in persuading the skipper to set sail with haste.

*   *   *

Duncan had taken no part in the victory rituals and celebration. He couldn't face any of the prisoners. None of the attackers had been killed in the raid, but four of the defenders had lost their lives. One of them had been MacGregor from Strathcashell – his friend. Duncan felt that he might as well have wielded the fatal weapon himself. He would live with that on his conscience for the rest of his days. And for what ? Carpenter and Fleming had escaped... and Margaret was dead anyway.

*   *   *

At the moment when the Lennox flag was raised above Dumbarton Rock, in a stuffy little chamber in Stirling Castle, an exhausted George Buchanan finally slumped over the emblem on the table before him, and fell into a deep sleep.

Chapter Eighteen
Death and Resurrection

Whatever may have been thought of Lord Fleming's decision to abandon his wife and daughter, perhaps he should not have been too harshly censured for the loss of Dumbarton Castle. He had been in a difficult situation. For sound reasons of security he could not have let his men know that a Spanish fleet might be expected to relieve them in the near future, however such news may have boosted their morale. On the other hand, it might have been expected that, with the truce expiring and a resumption of hostilities being at least possible, if not indeed likely, then he would have made some effort to raise vigilance and preparedness for any potential raid. However, the fact had been that Lord Fleming's latest intelligence was to the effect that the Regent was totally incapacitated with both gout and injuries sustained as a result of falling from his horse. In short, the Earl of Lennox had been in no fit state to lead a military exercise. Admittedly the Governor had let discipline slip. Some of the men had taken the view that if the forces of the King's Party were soon to return and hem them back into the castle for some indefinite period, then they might as well make the best of the burgh's facilities, as it were, while they could. Accordingly, in those last hours before the truce ended, while the Regent's men were marching from Glasgow, the majority of the Rock's garrison had been disporting themselves to excess in the drinking dens of the town. Hence the state of hungover and unarmed ineptitude of the defenders on the morning of the raid.

*　　　*　　　*

On receiving confirmation of the mission's success, the Regent Lennox wasted no time in coming to the scene of the victory. The castle had been discovered to have been surprisingly well provisioned with food and wine, so the leadership dined grandly and the Regent insisted that Lady Fleming join them at table. In a graceful, perhaps chivalrous, gesture Lennox insisted that she keep all her valuables and expensive clothing – items which would normally have been regarded as victors' spoils – and, further, he granted to her certain of her husband's lands which would, in the usual run of events, have been forfeited. Lady Fleming accepted the gesture with quiet dignity but mixed feelings.

Any disappointment arising from the failure to capture Lord Fleming was largely ameliorated by the discovery of a certain important document. When the archbishop had been searched a letter had been found on his person. This was the communication from his nephew, Lord Claude Hamilton, which betrayed the fact that, through the Florentine, Ridolfi, Mary Queen of Scots had made approaches to Philip of Spain, the Duke of Alva and His Holiness the Pope, with a view to a Spanish invasion. When Lennox read this he was beside himself with an unholy glee.

"God, Thomas, do you know what you have done this day ? Not only have you barred the door of Scotland securely against any threat to your king and the Reformation, but this…"

He shook the letter in the air.

"…this will surely finish the bitch."

He was alone with Crawfurd in what had been the Governor's quarters.

"Elizabeth will have her executed for this. This is her death warrant."

Lennox was almost slobbering with satisfaction. Crawfurd had private doubts about Mary's fate. Elizabeth had shown a dogged reluctance to kill a fellow monarch. In spite of much pressure from her advisors clamouring for Mary's death – in spite of the logic of that course of action – she had already forgiven Mary for much. Time would tell. Lennox wasted no time in having a copy of the letter sent to Elizabeth's court by the swiftest messenger.

*   *   *

Duncan Robertson had another priority. As soon as was possible he had to go to Saint Mary's… to see Canon Carmichael and have his dreadful assumption confirmed. He told Crawfurd that he was going to see his "wife", and the commander insisted that he take an armed escort. Obviously Robertson was at risk from those defenders who had managed to escape and who might remain in the vicinity. When they reached the Collegiate Church, Duncan had little difficulty in persuading the escort to remain at a discreet distance. With a heavy heart he set out to find the priest. It had turned out a blustery afternoon, with spells of beautiful, clear blue sky and white, wispy cloud. As Duncan walked slowly through the wet grass of the orchard in the direction of the hospital, he had to pass a small graveyard close by the perimeter wall. There, he was not surprised to discover a fresh grave. As he stood there looking at the damp earth, he remembered Margaret telling him about her childhood in Creeslough, her hopes and her dreams. He remembered the hour they had spent together at Saint Shear's Well. A lump came to his throat and tears misted his eyes. After a while he became aware of a presence. He turned around. There stood Margaret Kennedy, the other Margaret. She wore an expression of concern and mystification.

" I wouldna' hae thought you'd shed tears ower him."

Duncan looked at the furrowed brow, and then her words registered.
"Him ? What do you mean ? Who… ?"

"Yon's the man Carpenter. Buried no' three days past. Him that whipped Margaret."

Duncan stepped back a pace and rubbed his brow with the palm of his hand.

"Carpenter ? You tell me it's Carpenter who is buried here ?"

"Aye… Died sudden, he did."

Robertson actually laughed. A strange yelp brought about by emotional strain.

"But... Margaret ? Where ? How ?"

The Kennedy lass smiled as comprehension dawned.

"Your Margaret is fine. She is well. Come... see her."

Margaret Lafferty was walking through the trees toward them. Her raven hair looking all the darker against her pale complexion and her long, white dress, but the eyes bright with life and happiness.

Duncan gasped at the sight of her. Ran to her and embraced her tenderly, sobbing uncontrollably.

*   *   *

John Carpenter had indeed died suddenly. He'd begun to experience severe stomach cramps and vomiting which had actually been the result of nothing more sinister than bad beer. However, understandably, he had sought medical help. Being one of the castle garrison, loyal to the Catholic queen, Carpenter knew that he'd be well regarded by the clergy of Saint Mary's. Also, like everyone in the burgh, he was aware of Canon Carmichael's healing powers.

*   *   *

On the day that Canon Carmichael had first set eyes on the terrible wounds on Margaret's back, he had asked, naturally but almost absently, who had been responsible. It had been Margaret Kennedy who had told him that the sergeant – Carpenter – had been the guilty man. Canon Carmichael knew Carpenter by sight. He was well known about the town. The priest had determined simply to treat the man with absolute, though unspoken, contempt from that time on, but when Carpenter had presented himself at Saint Mary's seeking treatment – thank God he hadn't come to the hospital itself, where Margaret would surely have seen him – Carmichael had faced a terrible choice. After examining the soldier curtly, he had prescribed a certain medicine.

One hour after taking the first dose of this potion Carpenter had started to feel dizzy. His vision began to blur. He became confused and unable to work his limbs properly. Soon he found it impossible to speak or even lift his chin from his chest. A great darkness came down on him. He fell into unconsciousness and was dead within minutes. His body was found in the doorway of a drinking den in the Boat Vennel. Some would think he had been granted a more merciful end than he deserved.

Whether John Carpenter's death came about by natural causes, by accident, or by the deliberate action of Canon Carmichael, would remain a secret of the confessional – known only to God and to Brother Andrew. But on the very dawn after the canon had made confession, Brother Andrew had sent him packing to a Catholic community in the distant Highlands.

Chapter Nineteen
The Sheep and the Shepherd

The copy of the letter from Lord Claude Hamilton found its way to William Cecil, Elizabeth's Chief Secretary of State and most respected advisor. The document alerted the English government to the existence of the Ridolfi Plot, so that later in the year they were able to arrest, at Dover, an agent of Mary's servant, the Bishop of Ross. In the possession of this agent further incriminating documentation was discovered. Swiftly the bishop himself was taken into custody and, under threat of torture, he poured out the confession which confirmed Mary's involvement in this latest attempt to dethrone Elizabeth. Norfolk, for his part, was executed, but, as Thomas Crawfurd had suspected, in spite of the clamour from her lords and parliament, the English queen refused to give the order for Mary's execution. Even so, in a very real sense, the letter discovered at Dumbarton Rock effectively finished Mary. From that point on there was absolutely no question of her ever being released. She would never occupy another throne.

*   *   *

Mercifully little James did not witness the hanging. Fine Spring weather continued to favour the Carse of Stirling, the Ochil Hills and the distant Highland mountains. The little king was on the battlements again, this time in the company of the Countess of Mar. The Earl of Mar being the traditional guardian of Scots princes, the stern Lady Mar was the nearest the boy had to a mother figure – he called her "Lady Minny". She had taken him to a small, grassy enclosure just to the north of the King's Old Building. There, under her steely eye, James and his schoolmates were being allowed to play leap-frog, their tutor, for the present, being occupied with other serious business. Even from the height of the castle rock, however, the boys could hear the roaring of a crowd in the distance. Lady Mar silenced their eager questions with a look that sent a chill up young spines.

*   *   *

They had wasted no time. Only three days had passed since John Hamilton had been captured at Dumbarton Rock. Some semblance of a trial had been rushed through to lend the proceedings an air of legitimacy, but it had, of course, been a travesty. The Archbishop of St. Andrews was declared guilty of being "art and part" in the murders of King Henry and the Regent Moray, and of being involved in a plot to kidnap King James.

When Moray had been assassinated in Linlithgow, the fatal shot had been fired by Hamilton of Bothwellhaugh from a window of a house owned by his uncle, the archbishop. John Hamilton confessed to having prior knowledge of the plot, but that was a far cry from bearing any responsibility for it. As far as the other charges were concerned, he denied them to the end. The noise the boys had heard was the Stirling crowd voicing its approval as the Archbishop of St. Andrews was hanged from the town's common gibbet. He was executed wearing his full clerical garb, and he died with dignity. Even before his capture, he had felt in his bones that his time had come. He may or may not have been involved in the murders in question, but he had been entitled to the benefit of reasonable doubt. He was a Hamilton and his Lennox enemies were now very much in the ascendancy; perhaps it had been as simple as that, but there were many who believed that he had been executed principally because he was the leading Roman Catholic in the land.

*   *   *

It was late in the day before James saw his old tutor. With the required body of guards at a respectful distance, Buchanan and the king were partaking of what had become their regular evening walk. The sage appeared rather less shabby than usual, sporting a new, fur-trimmed robe and a velvet cap in place of the habitual cowl. The grey beard was trimmed again, and if there was not exactly a spring in the old man's step, there was a definite sense of purpose as the pair arrived at the Round Table on the old tourney ground.

Buchanan, as a Lennox man, had been unshakeably convinced of the culpability of John Hamilton in the murders of the little king's father and his uncle. He had been glad to see the realm rid of one he considered to have been a thoroughly nasty piece of work. Yet the hanging, somewhat to his own surprise, had left a sour taste in his mouth. As the castle above became a dark silhouette, and the cloud-streaked sky turned to mother-of-pearl, he began, yet again, to speak his thoughts aloud, as though to an understanding listener.

"I'm fair sick o' it... Sick o' hate an' torture an' killin', a' in the name o' religion. I saw the life choked oot o' a man the day... an', God forgive me, I hated that man... but I'm sick tae the teeth o' it a'."

He paced on sightlessly, a perplexed James trotting in his wake.

"Mysel', I was lucky. I was hounded by yon Beaton an' imprisoned by the Inquisition, but I was treated wae kindness compared tae what was done tae many anither. Ye wouldna' believe the monstrous cruelties inflicted on innocent folk in the name o' Jesus."

His face contorted with anger and his eyes focussed on some terrible mental picture. Buchanan had quite forgotten whose company he was in.

"I had friends... good friends, tortured and burnt because they loved their God in what was deemed tae be the wrong way. This age is seein' hundreds... thousands o' burnin's, hangin's and drownin's o' Christian by Christian. Catholics burnin' Protestants. Protestants burnin' Catholics... Fair sick. Satan must be takin' rare satisfaction oot o' it a'."

He seemed to shudder, drew the new robe tightly around his old shoulders and suddenly realised where he was and with whom.

"Ach... forgive me, yir young Grace. I'm an auld blether. Ye heard nane o' yon, d'ye hear ?"

On their way uphill toward the Church of the Holy Rude, he made a conscious effort to lighten his mood. There was, indeed, much about which to be positive. His purpose had been achieved... and right gloriously.

"Wae yir grandfaither's men takin' Dumbarton Rock like yon, yir throne is secure yir Grace. Believe me – yir throne and the Reformation in this Scotland. There is nae thing now will stand between yirsel' an' the throne o' England in due course. The great Union which wise men hae long sought."

The old eyes gleamed with rediscovered purpose.

"Och aye... yi'll hae ither troubles, obstacles, enemies, for certain... but eventual success is assured. Trust me yir Grace. I know... I jist know."

As Buchanan strode, and James scampered, uphill through Stirling town, oblivious to common folk and Royal Guard alike, the tutor had his pupil's entire attention and partial comprehension.

"Ye'll be king o' one Great Britain, yir Grace. You will be the new Arthur. There'll be an end tae war between Scotland and England, an' yon will bring aboot prosperity. Ye'll found a right mighty empire ower an' above... the biggest empire in a' human history... a great commonwealth... a family o' races an' nations fae a' the world ower. Soldiers will march fae yon very castle and sail tae the ends o' the earth tae raise your flag."

The sage gesticulated enthusiastically, waving a pointed finger toward the rock against the darkening sky.

"The key tae a' this is Union. The first step will be your United Kingdom. Union must aye be encouraged ower enmity. Harmony ower discord. But, mind ye this, yir Grace... ideal unity should ne'er be a matter o' imposition... o' tyranny. There should be willingness, mutual advantage an' respect. It's a' a matter o' balance. There's sae much in Life that is a matter o' balance. Ye should strive for the kind o' unity that permits diversity..."

All around them the folk of the town were heading homeward, traders closing shops and stalls. After such a day – you didn't see an archbishop hanged every day – seeking a bite by the fireside and a blether over a dram or cup of wine. The captain of the Royal Guard, who was close enough to overhear some of Buchanan's outpourings, began to look perplexed.

"The Romans, at their best, had yon skill. They knew well when tae lay down the law and when tae leave well alane. The day is comin', man... yer Grace, when there will even be concord amang the powers o' Europe. Aye – the British, the French, Spaniards, Portuguese, Netherlanders, Germans, Italians, Danes... Irish – a' in one great union o' peace an' common purpose."

The captain had heard enough. He knew his duty. Geordie Buchanan was clearly either drunk or senile. Either way, he had no place being in charge of the boy king's education and well-being. This would have to be reported to the Earl of Mar...

As they reached the Church of the Holy Rude, the sight of God's House, as it were, seemed to remind the old master that there was a spiritual dimension to all of this. There was so much more he wanted to say, but darkness had fallen. It must wait.

"The morn, yer Grace, you an' I'll hae a word aboot the Holy Grail."

The captain of the royal guard shook his head sadly.

*   *   *

The morning was glorious. They stood, once again, on the battlements of Stirling Castle. The sky was blue and the sun shone. Birds were singing and the air was fresh and clean. The vast panorama of mountains, hills and plains spoke of all that was natural, good and healthy. The sense of springtime engendered an exhilarating thrill of hope and positive expectation which intoxicated. Even the habitually crabbit Buchanan responded to the mood.

"We hae spoken, yer young Grace, o' the Reformation. Secure noo, here in Scotland, thanks tae Big Tam Crawfurd an' his men. It will be a cleansin' and rejuvenatin' force. Liberating. No' jist here, mind. A' through the world in the centuries tae come. It'll foster a spirit o' democracy, individuality – for a' men are equal in the sight o' God… be they beggar or king – mind it well!"
He glowered down at his royal charge meaningfully.

"Here, yer Grace, there will be education. No' jist for lords an' the like, but for common folk. A man will be free, an' able, tae read the Bible himsel', in his ane tongue. Tae drink at the pure well o' the Gospel. He can think an' interpret an' discuss openly without fear o' persecution or the stake. There will be intellectual growth an' scientific advancement"

To the young king, much, if not most, of this was incomprehensible, however much good it did his tutor to get it off his chest.

"Maister Geordie, ye said ye wad speak o' the Holy Grail this morn."

The old poet spun around and started to pace purposefully back along to the small area of garden next to the Prince's Tower. When, rather breathlessly, he had reached it, and the wee king had caught up, Buchanan waved a hand in a throwaway gesture toward the Round Table, far below.

" I said that you would be the new Arthur... and so ye will – in a manner o' speakin', but ye'll be faur greater than he."

He paused and tried to gauge the boy's reaction to this. The brown eyes were wide.

"You will no' be a warrior. At least no' wae sword or spear. You will slay intellectual enemies wae the keen edge o' learnin'. Aye... education."

A bony finger stabbed in the direction of the schoolroom in the Prince's Tower.

"Printin' !"

The old eyes glinted sharply like cut diamonds.

"The Church o' Rome held tight on the monopoly o' the Word o' God. They kept the Bible in Latin, an' folk heard only whit the priests telt them. This was a' part o' their authority… their power. But wae the invention o' printin', books can be run aff in their hundreds and their thousands, an' neither pope nor monarch can stop them fae reachin' the common man. An' books, as I've telt ye, are soldiers…

"But, Maister Geordie… the Holy Grail ?"

"Och aye. The Grail, aye… well. Ye see, thon's a tale. A symbolic thing. The Grail, as ye know fine well, was said to be the Cup o' Salvation. The Cup that Christ used at the Last Supper, wae the wine that was his blood. The story goes that Joseph o' Arimathaea brought the Cup – the Grail – tae Britain, an' it got lost, sae Arthur's knights went on a quest for it. It was supposed tae hae a' manner o' magical powers. But it's a' blethers. Your Holy Grail will be quite otherwise."

The grey beard bristled and the velvet cap was pulled off as Buchanan tried to recover the thread of his thought.

"The Bible. It's the maist precious thing we hae. The Bible is God makin' himsel' known tae Man. The Gospels are Christ speakin' tae Man. This Book is the means o' Salvation. A man canna' believe in what he disna' know. The Bible is the true Holy Grail. But mind, it's a gey difficult book. In the future… through scholarship… folk will come tae learn jist how it was written – by ordinary men – och, inspired men, without doubt, but men capable o' error. Compiled and edited by fallible men, so that jist every word canna' be taken literally. The Bible is fu' o' poetry and symbol. It must be interpreted. Each man must conscientiously apply reason and discernment and pray for the guidance o' the Holy Spirit – aye, an' no' be too proud tae be advised by wiser men. There is nae mair serious job o' work – an' fraught wae danger – but at the end o' the day it's between each man and God."

"Maister Geordie, will I hae tae read the whole Bible ? It's an awfu' big book."

"Aye… the whole Bible, yer young Grace, an' it'll nourish yer soul, yer imagination and yer intellect as nae ither book ever will. Noo, the next thing – efter printin' – that was needed, was the Bible in the vernacular tongue. When a man has direct access tae the Bible, he has direct access tae God. Och, Erasmus put it in a bonnie phrase when he spoke o' the Scriptures, he said -

'I wish that they were translated into all the languages of all Christian people – that they might be read and known not just by the Scots and Irish, but even by the Turks and Saracens. I wish that the farm labourer might sing parts of them at his plough, that the weaver might hum them at his shuttle, and that the traveller might ease his weariness by reciting them.'

Thon says it just grandly."

James was watching a squirrel as it circled its way up the trunk of a nearby tree. His tutor carried on regardless.

"We already hae Bibles in English, of coorse... Tyndale gied us the first ane – an' was burned for it. That was jist the New Testament, mind. It was the man Coverdale wha produced the first whole Bible in English. Och, there have been ithers, as ye know. Noo we hae the Geneva Bible, but these are no' the best possible translations. They're gey questionable. Mind, a wrang word here or there can hae fell important and far reaching consequences o' theology. They can be improved on. Aye... much improved. A right guid, sound translation gi'en full royal authority, whit might be called... authorized."

The old grey head wagged impatiently in the direction of the Round Table.

"You will no' be remembered sae much as the founder o' that mighty empire – the English will tak the credit for that. No, as the new Arthur, your knights will be scholars, your Round Table will be the Conference Hall. You, Jamie... yer young Grace, will be remembered by your Bible. It will raise and refine the whole quality o' the English language – it'll hae tae be English, oor ain Scots will no' dae fir this, mair's the pity – an' it will be a wondrous unifying force for a' the Protestant English-speaking world."

Just at this almost climactic point in Buchanan's delivery, the pair were distracted by the commotion of Lady Mar personally leading King James's fellow pupils up the steps of the Prince's Tower to the school-room. She gave the tutor a look which would have shrivelled any person of normal sensitivities. He levelled flared nostrils at her with equal contempt. There was little love lost between these two. When she had disappeared out of sight and beyond earshot, the visionary continued.

"When I was a prisoner o' the Inquisition, yir Grace, I wis near a year in solitary confinement. Then I was sent tae a monastery and confined there fir whit they ca'd 'instruction'. Tae pass the time I translated the Psalms o' David fae the Hebrew intae Latin. This morn you will take the first symbolic step on the road tae yir greatest royal achievement – yer ain Holy Grail. In yon Prince's Tower ye'll sit an' begin the task o' translatin' the Psalms fae Hebrew intae English."

Buchanan paused and absently took in the contours of the Ochil Hills. He drew in a deep breath of fresh morning air, as though to fortify himself. He paused, rubbed his chin thoughtfully, peered around cautiously and continued in a quieter voice.

"I hae a final word tae say afore we go in by…"

The brow furrowed deeply. He would not find this easy.

"… I hae spoke o' the Reformed Kirk. O' the dire need for cleansin' an' renewal. I've gi'en ye some notion o' the great benefits which will derive, in the centuries tae come, fae the liberatin' effects o' Reformation, but… heed ye this, yer Grace, the Kirk is no' without fault. It will hae it's share o' mean mindedness and bitterness and sinfu' pride. Nae human institution is free o' imperfection. There will be wicked disputation an' shamefu' lack o' charity. There is great danger comes wae freedom. Much error. A terrible price must be paid.

But against that... ower thae centuries o' which I speak, the Reformation will dae the Church o' Rome a power o' guid."

The four-year-old listened respectfully, obediently, taking in but a fraction of his master's meaning.

"Yesterday efter I saw yon Hamilton... well, yesterday I got tae broodin' ower the terrible sin o' Christian hating Christian, o' the Children o' God bein' at ane anither tooth an' claw, mair like devils than Christ's ane beloved. It impressed on me that much mair important than political unity is that o' Christian unity. There should be but the one Body of Christ. That is God's certain will. Roman Catholic or Reformed, these must be seen as but different expressions of the one transcendent truth – the Kingdom of God."

Fortunately little James did not notice the single tear which was running down the old man's cheek and into his beard.
"I am as sinfu' a man as the next. I am fu' o' pride an' hatred... but I can see that there is a time for rebellion... a time for protest, for... revolution. But there is a season for healing, for reconciliation... for reunification. And that, too, will come."

He was almost whispering.

"Wha knows..." he forced a weak smile,
"...maybe someday the crowds o' Edinburgh will come oot tae cheer the Pope in the streets."

It was as well the captain of the royal guard was not within earshot. It would have been altogether too much for him.

"There will hae to be humility... an' acceptance o' authority. No' compulsion or imposition, mind you – yon does mair herm than guid. There's an awfu' difference between unity an' uniformity... but the time will come for a' God's children tae come together in one great Christian Body –

"Other sheep I have also, which are not of this fold; them also I must bring, and they shall hear my voice; and there shall be one sheepfold, and one shepherd."

Silently he took the boy's hand and led him to the school-room.

Epilogue

Of course, they had plenty to talk about. Margaret recounted the business of the "St. Ambrose Miracle" – as Canon Carmichael had insisted on calling it. She had been snatched from the jaws of death by the curative powers of honey... and perhaps some help from above. This, naturally, caused the pair of them to speculate at length about the mysterious disappearance and present whereabouts of the healer-priest. Brother Andrew remained tight-lipped on the subject, which, needless to say, only increased the mystification. Neither Margaret nor Duncan were aware that, prior to his untimely death, the man Carpenter had sought medical help from the canon. So, mercifully, there was no dark brooding on that subject, only the grim, mutual admission that neither of them was particularly aggrieved by the loss of the man at whose hands Margaret had so nearly lost her own life.

Duncan, for his part, gave an account of his activities – and his motives – from the time he'd deserted from the castle garrison until he'd embraced the "resurrected" Margaret in the orchard. He endeavoured to tell his story with a seemly modesty and yet leave absolutely no doubt that his had been the key – and heroic – role. Margaret's response had been suitably gratifying. The thought of a man being willing to risk his life in order to avenge her was naturally pleasing to her, but she was quietly relieved that he had not, in the event, been required to kill for her.

As for the four men who had died in the raid... well, Duncan tried –largely in vain – to assure himself that, if it led in the long run to more stability in the realm, then these losses might turn out to be for the greater good. The Robertsons of Glen Finlas stood high now in the estimation of the Regent and his government. Duncan's brothers, who had not been so much hostages as simply kept a close eye on, now basked in the reflected glory from the man who had won Dumbarton Rock. Indeed, the Regent had proved true to his word. Duncan was rewarded, and that right handsomely. Several acres of land on Loch Lomondside were purchased by the Crown from Colquhoun of Luss and granted to the archer from Glen Finlas.

Duncan and Margaret were making their way down the Cross Vennel, having just been in the company of Brother Andrew at St. Mary's. They had sought his advice and a favour. One of Margaret's priorities had long been to get some word to her family, home in Tyrconnell, as to her present whereabouts and well-being. Now that the Regent had effective control of the western part of the realm, shipping movements were no longer under the same restrictions as had previously applied. The chaplain had been able to advise her that a vessel – a tidy little merchant ship called The Patricia – would be sailing with the tide that day and that it would be calling in at Lough Foyle for Derry. Brother Andrew would use his influence with the captain of the little ship to ensure that Margaret's message would eventually reach her folks in Creeslough. Duncan had handed over a suitable financial encouragement. As to the message itself, well, neither

Margaret nor Duncan could write, and because a written message would be more accurately passed on – and more greatly valued – they had asked Brother Andrew to write a letter to Margaret's dictation. The chaplain had, of course, been happy to do so. Now, as the pair approached the Town Cross, Margaret had the said missive held preciously upon her person. Turning left at the foot of the vennel, they walked along the High Street, enjoying each other's company and the Spring weather which continued to be kind.

Originally, Margaret's intention had been to sail for Ireland and home at the first possible opportunity. She was, at last, free to do so, and, thanks to the kindness of friends such as Margaret Kennedy and Brother Andrew, she had been gifted the means to do so. There had, however, come about a considerable change in her circumstances.

They were now at the quayside, with all its bustle and smells and sounds: the catches of fish, the salt water, the seagulls and the raised voices of mariners. Irresistibly drawn to the dominating sight of the mighty fortress rock, just half a mile downriver, they each thought simultaneously of a certain special moment.

*   *   *

Just a day or two after the raid they had been walking together on the Rock. Duncan – with very mixed feelings – had been showing Margaret where the attackers had climbed, where they had come over the wall, where the artillery had been captured… and so on. They had reached the Portcullis Arch, and the Highlander was showing the Irish lass the very scratch on the rock where his arrow had so narrowly missed Lord Fleming, when Margaret – perhaps understandably – had changed the subject rather abruptly.

"Duncan, you have been kind... kindness itself. It was a wonderful thing that you did for me. I will never forget it... or you..." she flushed as she spoke, "...as long as I live."

Duncan's heart had pounded in his chest as Margaret drew close to saying what he so dreaded to hear.

"I have so enjoyed... more than enjoyed your company. You are a very special man. A lovely man. You will ever have a special place in my heart... But..."

She had managed the whole affair wonderfully well, with her woman's skills, but Duncan, if he suspected her tactics, was a very willing victim.

"Don't say it, lass. Don't think of it. Hear me out..."
She had closed her eyes. Turned her head from him and held out the palm of her hand in a silencing gesture.

"No, Duncan. It's home I must go. There is nothing here for me. There is friendship – yes – but kith and kin come surely first."

"Then be my kin, Margaret. Marry me. Be my wife."

She drew her breath.

*   *   *

A curious little incident occurred on the Rock not long after Duncan had made his proposal to Margaret. Lady Fleming, her daughter and their servants, had remained at the castle prior to being escorted to the lands which the Regent had so magnanimously granted. Lady Fleming had, since the raid, seen Duncan and Margaret in each other's company. The nature of their relationship had been obvious. What had also become clear was the fact that it had been Duncan Robertson, one-time member of the garrison, who had guided the attackers to their victory. Lady Fleming remembered the incident of Margaret's whipping. She also remembered the reason for the punishment, or, rather, the alleged reason. No one knew her daughter better than Lady Fleming. Love her though she may, she well knew the girl's capacity for spite and mendacity. At the time she, Lady Fleming, had argued with her husband over the sentence of whipping. Suspecting the truth, she had been appalled that he had taken his daughter's so notoriously unreliable word in the matter, and she had been horrified by the resulting punishment. But, of course, she had been overruled by the Governor. The Governor who was now gone... who had deserted wife and daughter both.

She instructed her daughter to bring her the silver cross, and when this was done – and it was done with a considerable lack of grace – Lady Fleming approached Margaret. There was no question of the spoilt girl making any kind of apology, but Lady Fleming felt that some sort of gesture was in order. She had intended to apologise on her daughter's behalf... on Lord Fleming's behalf, but when the moment came the expression on her face said all that needed to be said. Wordlessly, she handed the silver cross to the Irish girl.

*   *   *

On the twenty-first of September in the Year of Our Lord fifteen hundred and seventy-one, Duncan Robertson and Margaret Lafferty were married at St. Mary's Collegiate Church, Dumbarton, by Brother Andrew.

Historical Notes

Regarding the capture of Dumbarton Castle, Sir Walter Scott gave the opinion – "This exploit of Crawford may compare with anything of the kind which we read of in history."

James the Sixth of Scots and First of England

James did, indeed, go on to unite the thrones of Scotland, England and Ireland with the 1603 Union of the Crowns. He preferred to be known as the "King of Great Britain", and was, indeed, poetically referred to as "Arthur". He was a fascinating man and a remarkable monarch. He came to be known as the "Wisest Fool in Christendom" and the "British Solomon". Thanks to George Buchanan, James was a truly learned scholar and intellectual king. Historians tell us that, in adulthood, he remembered his old tutor without fondness. This was almost certainly because Buchanan had resorted to school-room corporal punishment which was the norm in his day, refusing to exempt young James because of his royal status. Nevertheless, James retained a lasting respect for the old master, and was never slow to boast of the education he had received from him. It is true that

James had Buchanan's books banned, but this was because he profoundly disagreed with their political content. Buchanan had tried to instil in James an understanding that a king was the servant of his people. Buchanan was inclined to democracy. James, on the other hand, grew up to insist on the "Divine Right of Kings", a concept which was to cause great political and religious harm, particularly during subsequent reigns. Had he accepted Buchanan's teaching in this regard he would probably have made an even better king. Even so, most significantly, his reign was characterised by peace – no mean feat in the circumstances of his time.

With regard to the British Empire, Elizabeth the First tends to get the credit for having initiated it by encouraging her sailors in voyages of exploration and by granting a charter to the East India Company. By definition, however, Elizabeth was an English queen and only a British monarch could have founded a British Empire. James was, of course, the first British monarch. The effective British colonisation of North America began during his reign and the long, fascinating and profound relationship between Britain and India was effectively initiated by James. Although the East India Company had been founded by a charter from Elizabeth in 1599, the Company's initial interests lay with the spices of the East Indies. It was King James who sent an emissary, in 1612, to the court of the Mughal emperor to establish the right of British merchants to found a trading post at Surat in India. The subcontinent was, of course, to become the "Jewel in the Crown" of the British Empire, an empire which was to become the largest in human history, with one quarter of the globe eventually under the Union Flag – James's flag. But no... James is most remembered for the "King James Bible".

The King James Authorised Version

Biblical quotations in this book have been taken from the Geneva Bible of 1560, which was the version used by the Scottish reformers at the time of the story.

James first publicly discussed the proposal of a new translation of the Bible at a General Assembly of the Church of Scotland in the year 1601.

Then in January of 1604, at the Hampton Court Conference, at which James presided over a gathering of "bishops and other learned men" to discuss matters of religion, the king declared that the "best-learned men" of the Universities of Oxford and Cambridge would undertake to produce a new English translation of the Bible which would be "…ratified by royal authority… the whole church would be bound to it, and none other." The translation was to be "…as consonant as can be to the original Hebrew and Greek…"

The work of translation was carried out by six teams. Two worked at Westminster, two at Oxford, and two at Cambridge. There were, in total, approximately fifty translators. They laboured for seven years – making no bones about the fact that they were hugely indebted to the work of earlier translators, in particular Tyndale – to produce the finished work which was published by the King's Printer in 1611. King James had intended his Bible to unify the Christians of his United Kingdom. In time it went on to become the Bible of the missionary endeavour of the British Empire, and of most of the churches of the United States of America. Its linguistic, cultural and spiritual influence over a period of four hundred years is simply incalculable. If James truly thought of this translation as his own quest for the Grail, and of his translators as being his knights, then we need look no further for evidence of God having a sense of humour – the head translator was actually called Lancelot.

George Buchanan

George Buchanan was a humanist (a philosophical term which, in his day most certainly not imply atheism, as tends to be the case today), poet, educator and intellectual. He was born at Moss, near Killearn, in 1506. He experienced poverty in childhood and received his early education locally. At the age of fourteen he went to the University of Paris. Ill health brought him home to Scotland and when he was seventeen he experienced some military service with a Scots expedition into England. In 1525 he went to St. Andrews University, graduating in the following year. He then returned to the University of Paris where he first became influenced by Lutheranism. He graduated as a master in 1528 and in the following year became a teacher. He became notably learned in Latin and Greek. On his return to Scotland he became the tutor to the Earl of Cassillis. He wrote a satire criticizing the Franciscans and his arrest was ordered by Cardinal Beaton at a time when persons suspected of Lutheranism were being burned at the stake. Buchanan affected an escape from detention, fleeing first to England and then to Paris. He spent three years at the College of Guyenne in Bordeaux and acquired a considerable reputation as a poet. After a time as Regent at the College du Cardinal Lemoine in Paris, he went to Coimbra University in Portugal.

In 1550 he was arrested by the Jesuits and imprisoned, apparently because of his satire against the Franciscans. He was questioned at length by the Inquisition, spent a year in solitary confinement, and was detained in a monastery during which period he translated the Psalms into Latin verse. 1553 found him back in Paris, then for five years he was friendly with Charles du Cosse, Comte de Brissac, Marshal of France, whose son Buchanan tutored.

Buchanan had been studying the Bible, endeavouring to make a personal choice between the Catholic and Protestant theologies. On his return to Scotland in 1561, at the age of fifty-four, he finally joined the Protestant Church of Scotland. Initially he was inclined to admire Mary Queen of Scots and he was appointed Court Poet, writing Latin masques for important royal occasions. In 1566 he was appointed Principal of St. Leonard's College at the University of St. Andrews. Buchanan favoured Mary's second husband, and when the young King Henry was murdered the poet's attitude toward the queen became hostile in the extreme. He wrote the Detectio, by which he blackened Mary's reputation throughout Europe.

In 1567 he was appointed Moderator of the General Assembly of the Church of Scotland. In the following year he was appointed one of the commissioners who appeared at the Court of Queen Elizabeth with the purpose of proving Mary's guilt regarding her husband's murder.

It was in 1570 that the Scots Privy Council chose Buchanan to be Tutor to the four-year-old King James.

After the events surrounding the capture of Dumbarton Rock, Buchanan continued with his works, De Jure Regni Apud Scotos – advice for King James – and the Rerum Scoticarum Historia, a history of Scotland. He died in 1582 and though widely regarded as having been a great literary genius, he is probably best remembered as the Tutor of James the Sixth.

Thomas Crawfurd of Jordanhill

After his triumph at Dumbarton Castle, Thomas Crawfurd and his men saw further action against the Queen's Party at Leith. This was another successful engagement and it is said that, resulting from it, Crawfurd was allowed to use the motto – God Shaw the Recht – God Show the Right. In September of that same year, 1571, a company of the queen's soldiers from Edinburgh Castle attempted to kidnap King James from Stirling. The Regent, Matthew Earl of Lennox, was captured and fatally shot. However, a force led by Crawfurd put the raiders to flight. In April of 1573 Crawfurd of Jordanhill was yet again in action. On this occasion he and his company assisted in the capture of Edinburgh Castle. When the civil war was ended, Crawfurd was able to retire to his tower-house and estate at Jordanhill. In September of 1575 young King James sent Crawfurd a personal letter of thanks:

"Capten Craufurd, I have heard sic report of your gud service done to me from ye beginning of the weiris against my onfriends, as I sall sum day remember ye same, god willing, to your greit contentment. In ye main quhyle be of gud comfort, and reserve you to that time wt patience, being assurit of my favour. faireweil. Your gud friend. James R."

He received lands, which included Partick Mill, and a pension. In 1577 Crawfurd was made Provost of Glasgow. He died in 1603 – the year of the Union of the Crowns.

* * *

For his not inconsiderable contribution to the raid on Dumbarton Castle, John Cunninghame of Drumquhassil was made Keeper of that fortress. He was granted various lands and revenues, then, in 1577, he was appointed Master of the King's Household and given responsibility for the administration of the revenues of the Earldom of Lennox. He was, however, outlawed for alleged improprieties in that regard, but rehabilitated through the influence of the English ambassador. When King James made his kinsman, Esme Stewart, the new Earl (later Duke) of Lennox and Keeper of Dumbarton Castle, it was only under compulsion that Cunninghame handed over the fortress to its new keeper. In 1585 the Laird of Drumquhassil was falsely accused of plotting to kidnap King James and hanged at Edinburgh Cross.

* * *

When John, Fifth Lord Fleming, escaped from Dumbarton Castle, the little fishing vessel took him to Argyllshire. From there he made his way to France, but was soon back in Scotland. In 1572 he was accidentally hit by a musket-ball when some soldiers were firing a salute in Edinburgh. He was taken to Biggar where he died of the injury.

* * *

After he was hanged and dismembered in Stirling, John Hamilton, Archbishop of St. Andrews, was buried at Paisley Abbey, of which he had been Abbot for many years. His tombstone bears the inscription – Misericordia et Pax – Mercy and Peace.

* * *

After the capture of Dumbarton Rock, Duncan Robertson disappears from the pages of history. Although Margaret Lafferty is not mentioned by name, it is recorded that Duncan and his wife had a daughter.

A Biography

Alexander Tait is a pseudonym. The author is in his fifties. He was born in the Scottish Highlands but has spent his life in the Vale of Leven and Dumbarton area. He was a local government officer for thirty years. His interests are history, religion (he is a Christian), reading and painting. He is an active supporter of Amnesty International. He is married with three children.

THE LONG STAFF – by Clare Wilson
Book 1 of the Staff Wielder Series

A young boy Tom goes to his Grandfather's home in the village of
Cairn Holme to spend his summer holidays. Staying in the small
village deep in the Scottish Highlands his grandfather reveals to him
that he is the bearer of a magical staff. In the wrong place at the
wrong time, Tom finds himself dragged back in time to fight great
evil using the staff he knows little about. Forced to learn the lore
which is his heritage in a matter of weeks, he struggles against dark
forces to help keep he and his family alive. A baptism of fire, the little
boy who is obsessed with magical adventures finds himself in the
middle of a story from which he cannot escape.

(Children's Fiction / Fantasy / Young Adult)
www.olidapublishing.com

THE MAGIC SCALES – by Sam Wilding
Book 1 of the Denthan Series

James's father is missing. With no clue why his dad would run out on him and his mum, he hides out by an ancient stone circle to think. There, James discovers a dead stoat, crushed in an impossibly huge footprint. The mystery of what smashed the little animal leads James into finding Mendel, a wizard from another world called Denthan. Mendel has his own problems though. He's trapped in the body of a goldfish and Denthan's sun is about to die and destroy the planet. James is soon drawn into Mendel's plight and hopes against hope that the goldfish can somehow help him find his dad. Will Denthan be saved? Can Mendel regain his true form? But more importantly, will James ever find his father?

(Children's Fiction / Fantasy / Young Adult)

www.olidapublishing.com

THE SECOND GATEWAY- by Sam Wilding
Book 2 of the Denthan Series

One year on, the zany villagers of Drumfintley are, yet again all that stands between a peaceful world and certain disaster. When a whole new array of monsters and dark magic begin to emerge from the murky waters of Loch Echty all hell breaks loose. Beneath the Scottish loch, Mendel and James discover the submerged village of Fintley, a huge obelisk and a new crystal key. It is soon clear that they face a greater threat than ever before. In this, the second epic struggle to keep the Peck family together, some souls may be lost for good this time... Will James, Craig and Bero still be able to save us all? Will Mendel, the wizard-goldfish, continue to outwit his oldest and greatest adversary? Will the second gateway take the villagers of Drumfintley on a one-way trip to catastrophe?

(Children's Fiction / Fantasy / Young Adult)

www.olidapublishing.com

RETURN TO DENTHAN- by Sam Wilding
Book 3 of the Denthan Series

Another year on, the missing Harrison children return with Mendel, the wizard goldfish. James Peck is yet again at the helm when the people of Drumfintley are thrown into their most dangerous adventure yet. Mendel's plan is to rescue Cathy Peck, but much more besides… His aim is to bring back a world already destroyed by an exploding sun. They are pitched against Dendralon and a host of new creatures in an amazing array of battles that test the resolve and ingenuity of the Scottish villagers and Mendel alike.

Will James reunite his family at last? Will Mendel manage to save the planet, destroyed two years before? Will they all return to Denthan, Drumfintley and normality? What sacrifices must be made?

(Children's Fiction / Fantasy / Young Adult)

www.olidapublishing.com

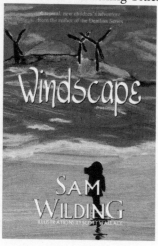

WINDSCAPE – by Sam, Wilding
Book 1 in the Island Adventure Sreies

Set in the Western Isles, Windscape is an exciting children's adventure that explores the dilemma between the usefulness of wind farms and the beautiful scenery they can sometimes destroy. Jenny MacLeod's mother has died and her father is about to lose their farm after mounting debts. The only way for her and her father to keep their home, set on the beautiful Hushwish Bay, is to sign up to a wind turbine project. When protestors invade their beach and her father has a heart attack, the well-to-do Murdochs take Jenny under their wing. She soon finds out, however, that Mr Murdoch has been keeping letters back from her and her father. Letters that could have saved their home without the need to build the wind farms there in the first place. Will Jenny have time to save everything she loves?
(Children's/Adventure/Thriller)
www.olidapublishing.com

Other Olida Publishing Titles

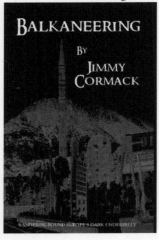

BALKANEERING by Jimmy Cormack

Civil Wars, ethnic cleansing and genocide, mass murderers, liberation movements turned gun-running gangsters and eccentric dictators. And all in recent memory. The Balkans has never had troubles to seek. Jimmy Cormack travels round the parts of Europe the rest of us would prefer to avoid. He examines the history, the geography and the political intrigues that have shaped the region right up to this day. However, he also experiences some lighter moments, meeting a bizarre mixture of misf and dodgy characters and witnesses some wacky, and some near-to-death incidents.

(Literature and Travel / History)

www.olidapublishing.com

Other Olida Publishing Titles

THE EDEN SEED by Damian Peck

Matt Malcolm is a devil-may-care marketing manager who inadvertently discovers an ancient seed that has the ability to extend the normal human lifespan by more than nine hundred years, disease free. Representing a huge pharmaceutical company, he blackmails their competitors who pay up to maintain the status quo. Six months on, however, he loses his job and finds his lover murdered. With the only test crop of The Seed destroyed, a trail of destruction is left over Eastern Europe and North Africa as the rival companies and a religious sect called the Seraphim embroil him in the search for the true source of the wonder drug, known as The Eden Seed.

(Thriller, Fiction, Fantasy)

www.olidapublishing.com

Other Olida Publishing Titles

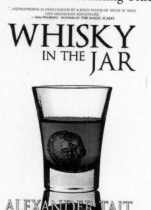

"...AGORAPHOBIA IS CHALLENGED BY A RICH BLEND OF ROCK 'N' ROLL
AND HIGHLAND ADVENTURE."
— SAM WILDING - AUTHOR OF THE MAGIC SCALES

WHISKY IN THE JAR

ALEXANDER TAIT

WHISKY IN THE JAR by Alexander Tait

"Whisky in the Jar' is an historical novel based on the illicit whisky distilling and smuggling activities that occurred around the eighteenth century on Loch Lomondside. Duncan Robertson is an heroic figure who finds himself ensnared in the conflict between the Highland people and the British military a generation after Culloden. It is also the story of the man who writes the novel. A man fighting his own battle against the mental oppression of agoraphobia, alcohol dependency and the threat of job loss. Where Duncan Robertson's weapons are the broadsword and the pistol, the author uses rock 'n' roll and eastern mysticism. These themes are as vibrantly interwoven as any Highland tartan, with richly colourful characters, romance, suspense and dry Scots humour.

(Literature and Fiction / History)
www.olidapublishing.com

THE CUP
by Alexander Tait

In this richly varied collection of a dozen stories, Alexander Tait draws from his rich imagination and historical research to enable his readers to encounter Rock legends of the late sixties, the court of King Arthur and a Roman centurian on the shores of Loch Lomond. Tait's characters are found on Arctic convoys, the beaches of Dunkirk, blitz-torn Birmingham and the surface of the moon. They have been crafted with understanding, warmth and humour. The tales, which range in a time from the crucifixion of Christ to the present day, all deal in their different ways with the eternal battle, within individuals and nations, between good and evil.

(Literature and Fiction / History)

www.olidapublishing.com

Other Olida Publishing Titles

Karen Reid

Hollow Footsteps
A Scottish Historic Novel

HOLLOW FOOTSTEPS
by KAREN ROBERTS

The killing of Robert the Bruce's adversary, John Comyn—a Balloi supporter and rival claimant to the crown, cleared Robert's way to the throne in 1306. But King Robert's family paid a steep price after he took the crown. No mercy was shown to anyone who supported him, even women. Something which Marjorie, his only legitimate child by his first wife, would discover.

Hollow Footsteps is a captivating novel with just the right balance of history and fiction. Roberts keeps her readers on their toes, anxiously turning pages, as she expertly navigates the twisted passageways of time and centuries-old intrigue. Whether you're looking for the thrill of the chase or stolen moments of romance, Roberts is sure to deliver.

(Children's/Adventure/Historical Novel/Romance)
www.olidapublishing.com